D0042345

DEATHWATCH

DEATHWATCH

RAY HARRISON

CHARLES SCRIBNER'S SONS
NEW YORK

First published in the United States by Charles Scribner's Sons 1986

Copyright © 1985 Ray Harrison

Library of Congress Cataloging-in-Publication Data

Harrison, Ray.
Deathwatch.

I. Title.
PR6058.A69424D43   1984   823'.914   85-18415
ISBN 0-684-18425-7

1 3 5 7 9 11 13 15 17 19 F/C 20 18 16 14 12 10 8 6 4 2

Printed in the United States of America.

To Julian and Mandy

DEATHWATCH

1

Constable John Draper strolled in leisurely fashion along Savage Gardens. He felt pleased with his first week of duty in the City of London police. Granted that he'd been a bit green at first, he felt he was getting the hang of it now. It wasn't really so different from soldiering in India. The drunks of London, and the tangle of horsebuses and vans at the Bank, were much the same as the seething mass of natives in Bombay, with their unwieldy bullock carts. The weather was a mite cooler though – and this was an English August! He'd have to try for a transfer from permanent night duty before winter set in . . . but he'd have to be cautious. They seemed to think that a man who couldn't stomach nights wasn't fit to be in the force.

He turned into Trinity Square and glanced across at the grey turrets of the Tower of London. Funny they should call that bit the White Tower. Not a bit the colour of the Taj Mahal. Perhaps it was just that it was less soot-encrusted than the rest of London's buildings. He pulled out his watch; ten minutes before his shift was up, and the police station just round the corner. Three months ago he could well have been on guard duty at the barracks, snatching a quiet fag because the orderly officer never came round before six. He felt a sudden craving for tobacco . . . but they'd dismiss you for smoking on duty in this lot. It would only take a complaint from a passer-by, and you'd be out, whatever you said. Mind you, it was quiet enough this morning. Any other day but Sunday, there'd be a procession of carts along here, going from Billingsgate fish-market to the East End; and not smelling too sweet, either, in this weather.

Now he could see the river at the bottom of Tower Hill. The

first rays of the sun were glittering on its washboard surface, and colouring the orange sails of a barge. It wouldn't last; it was too bright too early. By ten o'clock it would be dull again. But he would be in bed by then, and he'd have seen the best of the day. He turned into Barking Alley – only a couple of minutes now. Odd . . . it looked as if someone had thrown a sack on to the railings of Allhallows church. He'd better mention it at the station; they'd want to get it shifted before service time. From here it looked like a human being, stretched out on top of the spikes, every bit like a fakir . . . Mind you, one row of spikes wouldn't make a very comfortable bed! What was that white blob, through the railings? It was just where the head would be, if . . . Oh Christ! Constable Draper sprinted across, his heart thumping. What was he supposed to do? He tried to remember what they'd told him during his brief training; but they hadn't prepared him for this. He'd have to write a report, of course, but the body would have gone before it was read. He'd better remember how it was – head lolling inside the railing, the tip of a spike protruding from the chest, blood staining the gold . . . blood everywhere, dried on the railings, congealing in a pool on the pavement . . . arms crossed one over the other on the chest; the legs crossed too, the knees bent and splayed outwards, so that the ankles could be wedged between the spikes. It looked like one of those ritual murders he'd heard about in the East . . . He felt a prickle of fear at his neck, and fumbling in his pocket, he found his whistle and began to blow.

Detective-Sergeant Joseph Bragg looked sourly at the stream of people leaving the church. They were chattering brightly to each other, now that the solemnity of the Holy Communion was past. No doubt they were going back to their kidneys and bacon. Well, he'd had to manage with cheese and a lump of bread, while he'd shaved. They'd taken the body away, of course. It was too much to expect them to leave it there long enough for him to see; mustn't bring the cosseted rich into contact with violent reality. That was something which went on in the East End, not the City.

'You say it looked as if it had been laid out for burial,

Constable?' asked Bragg.

'Yes,' replied Draper. 'Or maybe more like them figures you see on tombs inside churches. His arms and feet were sort of crossed, like them.'

'You're quite sure the blood was dry on the railings themselves?'

'Well, I didn't touch it, but it didn't look wet.'

'One thing's for sure,' remarked Bragg. 'He didn't drop on those railings. They're too far away from the church roof. He could hardly have reached them if he'd jumped, and then he wouldn't have landed like that. What time was it you found him?'

'Five minutes to six o'clock, sir.'

'And when was the last time you'd passed through here?'

The constable shifted uncomfortably on his feet. 'I think it would have been about half past four. My beat takes me half an hour, and the previous twice round I'd gone straight down Tower Hill, to check on the warehouses by the river. I did glance along Barking Alley each time, of course, and it seemed all right.'

'But can you see this part of the railings from the street end?' asked Bragg.

'Not in the dark, you can't. There's only this one street lamp, and it's shaded by the trees.'

'It would have been coming light soon after five, surely?'

'Yes, but not light enough to see into the shadows.'

'So all we know is that the body wasn't there at half past four,' mused Bragg. 'Did you notice anything out of the ordinary at any time?'

'No, sir. It was very quiet after one o'clock.'

'You say he was a heavy man, and you should know if you helped to move him. Now, I reckon the top of those railings is at least five foot off the ground. He wasn't carried here and hoisted on to them, that's certain. They'd have needed a cart, then they could have lifted him up and thrown him on to the spikes. Did you hear anything – cart wheels, or a horse neighing?'

'Nothing I took notice of. There's always some traffic hereabouts, but last night it seemed especially light. Mind you, if a cart had been here while I was at the other end of my beat, I wouldn't have heard it anyway.'

'You're new, aren't you, Constable?'

'Yes, sir,' said Draper defensively. 'My first week.'

'You've done well – better than most would have done. If you keep it up, we'll be wanting you in the detective division . . . Ah! It looks as if all our sanctified brethren have at last gone home to Mammon. Let's take a look inside the church, and see if we can find any of those tomb effigies you talked about.'

The main door to the mortuary was locked when Bragg arrived, but he gained entry to the yard through the side door in the alley. He picked his way between wooden crates and empty carboys, and flattened his nose against the window. Inside, he could see the portly figure of the pathologist, bending over a grey slate mortuary slab. Dr Burney was Professor of Pathology at St Bartholomew's hospital, and the top man in his field. Opposing counsel rarely got the better of him in cross-examination, perhaps because of his manner as much as his expertise. He had a round cherubic face and a wide slack mouth, which was apt to compose itself into a grin at the most inopportune moments. Bragg had seen him describe revolting injuries with such a ghoulish smile on his face that defence counsel had turned and run. Even now, with no one near him, he was beaming broadly as he probed the supine body on the slab. Bragg tapped on the glass, and Burney gestured to him to go round to the side door.

'You should be ashamed of yourself, sir,' Bragg greeted him. 'Poking about in people's innards on a Sunday, instead of reading the Good Book.'

'On the same premise,' retaliated Burney, 'why are you breaking into my mortuary on the Lord's Day?'

'I somehow didn't think you'd be able to resist this one.' Bragg gazed down at the white figure on the slab, blood still caking the fair beard. 'It worries me, does this.'

'And so it should, Sergeant. I've never seen anything quite like it before. Our new coroner was down half an hour ago, and he seemed most disturbed.'

4

'What did you tell him?' asked Bragg.

'Oh, very little. I'm not disposed to hold chat with so eminent an official in quite the way I do with you.'

'Thank you for the compliment, sir.'

'He had, of course, been sent a brief report by the ward beadle, and that was evidently enough to cause him concern. I presume you are coroner's officer for the case, have you not spoken to him?'

'Tomorrow will be soon enough,' replied Bragg. 'I've little enough idea what it's all about myself; I'm not exactly seeking an inquisition. Have you come to any conclusions yet?'

'Very tentative ones. As you see, I haven't opened him up yet. But if we presume that the obvious injuries were the cause of death, I can make some pertinent observations.'

Burney screwed up his eyes, as if with pleasure, then picked up a metal probe, and turned to the corpse.

'You can see that he is a large man, well over six feet tall, and I suppose weighing some fifteen stones. I would say that he was aged thirty-two or so, and is reasonably well nourished. The hands are not ingrained with dirt, and the palms are soft, so he wasn't a labourer. On the other hand, his clothes were old and shabby; so there's a possible contradiction there. Perhaps he was an out-of-work clerk, who's been sleeping rough.'

'Was there anything in his pockets to identify him?' asked Bragg.

'That's your department,' replied Burney. 'You can collect his effects from my assistant when you leave. My impression is that he had virtually nothing on him. Now look at this.' He pointed to the left arm. 'You see the abrasions round the wrist, and the same on the other arm? It's clear that he was tied up for a considerable period and, from the extent of the chafing, it would appear that he made prolonged attempts to escape from his bonds. The skin is broken on the knuckles too, and from the bruising one might conclude that a struggle took place, before he was pinioned. I would have thought that several people would be needed, to subdue a man of his physique. Then look at the face: very severe contusions, which were inflicted many hours before his death. You see the bruising and swelling around the eyes?'

'It looks as if he was systematically beaten while he was tied up.'

'And that isn't all,' went on Burney with a loose grin. 'I was just examining his feet. Can you see the weals across the soles?'

'Yes.'

'If you look closely you can see that there is some charring of the flesh, and that blisters had begun to form in some places. In my view these injuries were caused by a hot metal object, say a soldering iron, being drawn across the flesh.' He bent down and sniffed vigorously. 'Yes, there's no doubt about it,' he beamed. 'You can still smell the singeing of the skin.'

'Are you saying he was tortured?'

'Such a conclusion would be consistent with the evidence, certainly.'

'I don't like the sound of that,' muttered Bragg.

'I can't remember the railings of Allhallows,' said Burney. 'Will you describe them to me?'

'I would estimate them to be four-foot-six high,' said Bragg. 'And they are mounted on a six-inch stone kerb. Every six foot or so of length, there is an iron strut on the inside, which acts as a buttress. The uprights themselves are held in two horizontal iron rails at top and bottom. I would think there is a space of about three inches between each upright. A small person could easily get his foot in between.'

'And the top?' prompted Burney.

'Every second upright ends in a spike about ten inches long. In fact it's flat – more like the blade of a spear.'

'How wide is the blade?'

'About two inches, I'd say.'

Burney pondered for some moments, then gave a curiously bashful smile. 'I think we are going to be compelled to draw some exceedingly repellent conclusions,' he said. 'Help me turn him over . . . It's all right, he's just a bit stiff.'

Bragg pushed at the right shoulder, and the corpse rolled over woodenly.

'You see this line of what we might call "entry wounds", parallel to the spine? These are the punctures caused by the railings.' Burney pointed towards the base of the spine with his probe. 'The lowest wound was not significant, because the

6

spike's penetration was arrested by the pelvis. That probably also accounts for the fact that the next one along, in the pit of the stomach, didn't penetrate fully either. In fact the only spear that went right through was at the top of the chest, here. The point entered between the third and fourth rib; now because the breadth of the blade was not between the ribs, but across them, it forced them apart, and the fourth rib was fractured. There is, of course, a corresponding fracture of the ribs by the breast-bone, at the exit wound . . . But it's the one in the middle of the chest that I find most interesting.' Burney looked up with relish. 'I would say that this wound was the immediate cause of death, since the heart was penetrated. Now here, the point was over the eighth rib and, as a result of its entry, that rib was shattered.'

He inserted the tip of his probe into the wound, and poked around vigorously.

'You see?' he asked. 'Not just fractured; the rib has virtually disintegrated at this point. Do you see the inference?'

'I'm sorry, sir,' said Bragg. 'I'm afraid I'm being very dull.'

'It's a question of the force needed to produce that result. I know a rib can easily be cracked, and yet it's a remarkably springy structure.'

'I'd decided they must have brought him along on a cart, and thrown him off on to the railings,' said Bragg.

Burney shook his head. 'I've only seen wounds like this in the case of a man who jumped from an upstairs window to escape a fire, and landed on the area railings. That gives you an idea of the force that would be needed.'

'But there was nothing near enough to give that kind of drop,' protested Bragg.

'Help me roll him back,' Burney said with a flaccid smile . . . 'That's it. Now can you see this contusion down the chest in a more or less straight line?'

'Ye . . . es.'

'And one at right-angles just below the level of the exit wound?'

'I can see that all right.'

'And there are indications of another, parallel to the first, on the other side of the breastbone.' He traced a line with the point

7

of his probe. 'Here, do you see?'

'I still don't understand what you're driving at.'

Burney cocked his head on one side. 'Have you ever seen a carpenter fitting a new frame for a sash window?' he asked.

Bragg shook his head. 'Not of late.'

'Well, he wedges it in the aperture roughly, and when he is getting it to an accurate vertical, he has to tap it with a hammer, sometimes quite smartly . . . And to prevent the window frame itself being damaged, he puts another piece of wood between it and the hammer. Now look at those abrasions again, and imagine them as the edges of a piece of wood laid over the breastbone.'

'Are you saying that they dropped him on to the railings, put a piece of plank on his chest, and hammered it till the spikes came through?' asked Bragg in revulsion.

'It seems the only conclusion that fits all the evidence,' beamed Burney. 'And they would need a fairly heavy sledge-hammer, say of the weight a railwayman uses.'

'And was he alive?'

'Most certainly.'

'Poor bugger! I hope he wasn't conscious.'

'After the battering he'd received, I think we can rest easy on that point.'

'And when do you think he was killed?'

'From the temperature of the body, and the advanced rigor, I'd say shortly after five o'clock this morning.'

Bragg leaned his considerable bulk back in an armchair, by the window of the comfortable rooms occupied by Constable Morton in Alderman's Walk. Below he could hear the rattle of a cab going to Liverpool Street station. Bragg had described the discovering of the body, and Dr Burney's preliminary findings, and now Morton was quietly pondering the implications. Bragg looked across at the handsome face and brown curly hair. It still seemed an enigma that he, the wealthy son of the Lord-Lieutenant of Kent, with a degree from Cambridge, and a social position inferior to none, should want to spend his time as a detective-constable in the police. When Morton had first been attached to him for training, Bragg had objected strenuously, and predicted that he wouldn't last six months. But he'd had to eat his words. He'd found Morton intelligent and quick-witted, and quite prepared to accept the drudgery which formed the biggest part of the job. It was clear that with experience he would develop into a good policeman, and that was the highest praise Bragg could bestow on anyone. What's more, a couple of cases had been solved purely because Morton was out of the top drawer; and it wasn't merely his connections, he had a different way of approaching problems, different thought processes. Which was why Bragg had called on his way back from the mortuary to chew the case over. He didn't really believe the gossip that Morton was being groomed to be the next Commissioner, yet there must be some odd reason why he would spend his young manhood poking about in a stratum of society that his class was barely aware of. Not that there was anything quirky about him. He hadn't a trace of snobbery, and the men clearly liked and admired him. Playing cricket for Kent had something to do with that, no doubt.

Morton frowned in perplexity. 'It's the gratuitous brutality, that I don't understand,' he said. 'The battering around the head, and even burning the feet, make sense if whoever did it was trying to extract information from the man. But I can't see the point of impaling him in such a bestial way.'

'I've been thinking about Dr Burney's view that he was unconscious when he was killed,' said Bragg. 'It's almost like saying that the way he was murdered had nothing to do with him, because he was past caring.'

'You mean it was intended to convey a message to someone else? But to whom?'

Bragg let the question hang in the air, preferring to follow his own train of thought.

'However quiet it was,' he went on, 'and however carefully they watched the constable on the beat, they still took a big risk in choosing somewhere so close to a police station.'

'Perhaps it was important to whoever did it, that it should be Allhallows church,' said Morton.

'I don't know. I went inside to see if there was a stone effigy they'd imitated, but there wasn't one. I did find a brass plate in the corner of the chancel with the figure of a knight on it. His legs were crossed at the ankles, and his arms crossed on his chest, so they may have imitated it. But it was half covered with carpet, so I wouldn't like to say there was any connection.'

'That sort of imitation would point to insanity,' remarked Morton. 'It doesn't really fit a crime that obviously involved several people.'

'Unless the others were well paid. There are plenty of slaughtermen in Whitechapel who wouldn't turn a hair at it.'

'I suppose so.'

'I think that for some reason it was important that he should be seen to have died in that particular fashion. The actual place might not have been as important.'

'You mean any church might have done?'

'I begin to wonder if the church itself is all that significant. Perhaps he just had to be impaled; churches are about the only buildings which have spiked railings around them, nowadays.'

'But why choose one so near to a police station?' asked Morton. 'There are scores of churches in quiet streets, where there would have been no risk of discovery.'

'I don't know of another with such bloody great spears as Allhallows,' said Bragg. 'And the more gruesome the death, the more impact it would have.'

'I suppose the very proximity of Seething Lane station, with the risk of interruption by the police, would reinforce that impact,' suggested Morton.

'Your message theory? And yet there, it was far more likely that the body would be discovered by a constable. They could have been wasting their time.'

'Unless the message was directed at us. They might have been content that the body would have been removed before the public were astir, so long as the circumstances of the killing were known to the police.'

'Telling us to keep off, you mean? Well, the sheer savagery could point to an underworld killing. We shall have a better idea when we've identified the body; not that it will be easy. The clothes are scruffy and cheap – probably bought in a flea market, and there was nothing at all in the pockets . . . except this.' Bragg handed Morton a grubby tie-on label on which had been scrawled in rough capitals:

COFIWCH DIC PENDERYN

'Does that mean anything to you?' he asked.

'I'm afraid not. Is it in code, do you think?'

'It's not a foreign language, then?'

'None that I've ever come across,' replied Morton.

'Ah well, it may have no significance at all. But it's queer it was the only thing in his pockets.'

'It's a funny thing, Bill,' remarked Bragg, 'that to find spikes like a row of Guards' bayonets, you have to go to a temple of peace and tranquillity.'

His conversation with Morton had left him still perplexed, and he had dropped into the Georgian mansion in Old Jewry that served as the police headquarters. Now he was perched on one corner of the duty sergeant's table, tugging at his ragged moustache.

'What I can't sort out is whether the church itself was significant or not,' he said.

'The way the body was arranged seems to show that it was,' suggested the sergeant.

'Yes . . . Then again, they might just be putting one over on us.' He sighed. 'I'll tell you one thing, Bill. I could do without this at the minute. I've got enough on my shovel, with this union business.'

'Just your lucky day, Joe,' said the sergeant, with a grin.

'No gangs of navvies around, are there?' asked Bragg.

'Plenty round the site of the new Surrey Docks, but I've not heard of any coming this side of the river.'

'Young Morton has a notion that it was meant for us. A kind of "keep off the grass" warning.'

'That would be a bit bloody cheeky,' commented the sergeant, then swung round in embarrasssment as a buxom young woman entered. 'Yes, miss? Can I help you?'

'It's my husband,' she said anxiously. 'He's not come home.'

The sergeant gave her a reassuring smile. 'And when did you expect him back?' he asked.

'He didn't say . . . at least, he said he didn't know.'

'When did you last see him?'

'At half past five last night, when he went on duty.'

'You didn't have a row or anything?' asked the sergeant, opening the missing persons book.

'No! That's why I'm so worried. We were going to my mother's this afternoon, for tea.'

The sergeant turned towards Bragg, and lifted an expressive eyebrow.

'All right, my dear, we'll keep a lookout for him. What's his full name?' The sergeant dipped his pen in the inkwell, and looked up expectantly.

The sight of the book, and the formality of the question, seemed to have given substance to her fears, and she just stared woodenly at him.

'His name, please,'

'Er . . . William Foster,' she gulped.

'And where does he work?'

She bobbed her head, then looked up with a dazed expression. 'He usually works at Cloak Lane station, but for this job he was sent up here . . . He wasn't wearing his uniform, though.'

'Are you saying he's a policeman?' asked Bragg.

'Yes, he's a constable. But this was a special job he was on. He wouldn't tell me what it was about, but he was very excited . . . said it might lead to promotion. He said to expect him when I saw him. But he's never been so late before.'

'Constable Foster,' murmured Bragg. 'Yes, I know him. Fair hair, has he? And a seaman's beard?'

'Yes.' She smiled hopefully at Bragg. 'He was in the navy when I met him.'

'I know a bit about the job he's on, Mrs Foster. It could be that he hasn't been able to get back yet. I wouldn't worry. You just go off home, and we'll find him for you. You never know, he might be waiting for his tea.'

She smiled in relief, and hurried out.

'One of your men, Joe?' asked the duty sergeant.

'Constable Foster, from fourth division. Seconded to me for plain-clothes duty on this union job . . . And although I'm not

sure, I think the last time I saw him, he was lying on Dr
Burney's slab.'

2

Catherine Marsden looked round her with a mixture of
excitement and apprehension. The crowd seemed good-
humoured enough but, with so many packed into Smithfield,
she was increasingly being jostled. Early on she had been
hacked across the shin by a man struggling to get past her. She
had smiled graciously at his rough apology, and assured him it
didn't matter, but that had in no way diminished the pain. Now
she'd retreated to an alcove in the wall of the meat market.
Here she was at least safe from being trampled underfoot; but
she was too far from the speaker, and the murmur of the crowd
often drowned his words.

She looked down at her note book. She had written 'Monday
17 August 1891' assertively at the top, but there weren't many
lines of shorthand below it. When the main speaker began she
would just have to try to worm her way closer. She wasn't used
to covering this kind of meeting. When she'd been appointed, a
few months ago, as a probationer reporter on the *City Press,*
she'd been expected to confine herself to charitable and social
occasions – the kind of thing women were supposed to be
interested in. Before long, however, she'd found herself writing
articles critical of the police and of the ethical standards of the
City. Much to her surprise, they'd been published; and as a
result she had been caught up in a murder case, and been lucky
to escape with her life. In fact it had been lucky for her all
round. Even as she was recovering in bed, she had been
approached by the editor of the *Star,* a fairly new radical
newspaper. He had been so impressed with her report for the
City Press that he'd asked her to become their occasional City
correspondent. She hadn't dared tell him that he was mistaken

if he thought she was a radical, and had accepted, subject to her own editor's agreement. Mr Tranter, she recalled, had been transparently delighted. He probably thought that an occasional piece for the *Star* was a small price to pay, if it would allow her to vent her crusading zeal elsewhere. So this evening she was going to do a piece on a political meeting – and for a real national daily!

There was a stir on the platform over by the fountain. This must be the man from the Socialist League. He was in his early thirties, with a straggly beard and pale eyes. Worse still, his voice was weak, and Catherine could catch only an occasional word. Clutching her note pad in one hand, and her bag in the other, she began to wriggle her way forward. Her repeated 'Excuse me, I'm a reporter' didn't seem to be an effective password here. Indeed it produced a reaction bordering on hostility or contempt. She realized how unappealing men were in the mass, particularly working men, in their shapeless shabby clothes. 'Menacing' would be a better word, she thought; then she told herself severely that her reaction was born of the prejudices of her class, and the timidity of her sex.

'Here, young woman! Come and stand in front of me.'

She looked up to see a big, middle-aged man smiling at her.

'Thank you so much,' she said. 'I just need enough room for my pad.'

'You heard the lady,' cried her protector to the men around them. 'Shove over and give her place. She's only doing her job.'

As the pressure on her eased, Catherine was able to concentrate on the speaker. He seemed to have reached the meat of his message, and was emphasizing every other word by battering the air with his clenched fist.

'I tell you, the working man can hope for nothing . . . nothing from the politicians. In the past we've looked to the Liberals to bring change, and they've cheated us. How many working men are there in Parliament? . . . I ask you. How many? . . . After the election of 'eighty-five, the Liberals boasted that they'd put five times as many working men into the House of Commons as there were before. And what did that amount to? . . . I'll tell you . . . Eleven, just eleven . . . And they try to buy our votes with that claptrap. I want you, tonight, to show the Liberals –

and the Tories too – that working men are no longer prepared to be deprived of their rights as human beings.'

There was a general murmur of approval in the crowd, and a ripple of applause.

'We are not prepared to tolerate oppression,' shouted the speaker. 'We are not prepared to endure any longer a system where the rich get richer, and the poor poorer . . . But we are prepared to fight for our rights.'

There was a sustained outburst of cheering from Catherine's right, which for a time swamped the speaker's oratory. She could see the flailing fist, the impassioned mouthing, but could hear never a word. He looked rather like a puppet, she thought, cupping her ear. When the cheering subsided there seemed to have been little improvement in the content of his discourse.

'We will fight the capitalists, whether Tory or Liberal, whether manufacturer or landowner . . . We will demand a democracy where the power lies where it belongs . . . in the hands of the working men of this country. And we will show the politicians we're not prepared to wait for it . . . we want it in our time, not theirs.'

Catherine glanced up at the big man shielding her.

'It's all hot air, miss,' he said with a wink.

But even as he spoke, a commotion broke out on the right, and she could hear rhythmical clapping, and shouts of 'Now! Now! Now!'

The noise seemed to excite the speaker even more. 'And if they're not willing to give it to us,' he squeaked, 'we'll take it.'

There was fighting in the audience now, and a tide of struggling men was surging towards the platform.

'This lot's not for me,' growled the big man. 'I'm off. And you'd better do the same, if you know what's good for you.'

Catherine disregarded him, her pencil blunted by her efforts to record her impressions.

'We'll destroy this rotten society, comrades, and the gutters will run with blood . . . ' The inflamed torrent of words ceased abruptly, as the fighting men crashed into the platform and overturned it. Catherine was aware of a sudden feeling of space, as the less combative in the audience melted away. She jotted down enough rapid notes to jog her memory when she got home, and was about to put her pad in her bag when she noticed a group of men advancing on her. They looked angry and threatening.

'Wot you been writin' dahn?' demanded one, his fists clenched.

'I've just been making notes for my paper,' replied Catherine, shrinking back.

'We don't want no papers 'ere,' shouted another.

She felt that at any moment they would charge her, and wondered desperately which way to run. Then suddenly she felt her arm seized from behind, and thrust up her back with such force that she was doubled up. She screamed in pain and fright.

'Stinking capitalist cow,' shouted a rough country voice behind her, and she felt the note pad torn from her fingers. 'Here you are, lads.' The pad was thrown on the ground in front of the men. 'Tear 'em up, so's nobody can stick 'em together again. An' as for you, missus, I'll make you sorry you ever showed your rotten face here.' Catherine was spun round, and pushed roughly towards the market buildings. When she resisted, her arm was forced further up her back till she cried out. She realized that she was being hustled into one of the aisles of the meat market, which she knew would be deserted at this time in the evening. She had done a column on Smithfield the previous week, and she had a vivid image of herself, hung like a side of beef, with a hook through her throat.

Then her arm was released, and her assailant took her hand.

'Come on,' he said in a normal voice, 'you've got to run like a gazelle,' and began to drag her down the echoing hall.

'Stop!' she shouted. 'You're pulling my arm out.'

'We can't. If we do, we're dead. Keep going as far as Charterhouse Square . . . We'll get a cab there.'

'Oh! . . . Oh! I've lost my shoe,' cried Catherine.

'Leave it.'

'But I can't run like this!'

'Then get rid of the other.'

They bolted out of the market building, just as an empty hansom rattled by. 'Cabby!' shouted her companion in a stentorian voice. The driver checked his horse and looked back dubiously, then stopped as they chased after him.

17

'Ninety-five Park Lane – quickly! And keep away from Smithfield.'

At the peremptory note in the man's voice, the cabby flicked his horse, so that they were flung back against the cushions. All the way down Charterhouse Street, the man was peering back round the edge of the cab, and it was only when they had negotiated Holborn Circus that he relaxed.

'I wouldn't like to go through that very often,' he said with a sudden grin.

Catherine took a sidelong look at him. He was a young man under the grime, his hair a tangled greasy mop. His clothes were indistinguishable from those of any other workman at the meeting. But at least he wasn't hurting her now. He wasn't even pressing against her . . . she shrank into her corner as he suddenly jerked upwards – but he was only opening the trapdoor in the roof.

'You can go gently now, cabby,' he called. In response the horse dropped into an easy ambling trot, and with her diminishing fear, Catherine's sense of outrage grew.

'What right have you to drag me away like this?' she protested.

The man grinned. 'The same right as any law-abiding citizen, pursuing his favourite hobby.'

'How do you know where I live, anyway?'

'You told me yourself, not two months ago.'

'I did?' Catherine looked at him again. The white teeth, regular features, and the teasing cultured voice. 'Oh!' she cried. 'I suppose it had to be you!'

'Constable James Morton saves the heroine yet again, just as the curtain falls,' he said mockingly.

'I wish you'd mind your own business,' she exclaimed.

'Such ingratitude! Would you like me to return you to that mob?'

'They would have done me no harm,' she said peevishly.

'I really think you ought to be locked up for your own good.'

'It was a perfectly ordinary political meeting. Now, thanks to you, I haven't even got my notes to work on.'

'It wasn't an ordinary political meeting and, if you print one word about it, I'll leave you to your fate next time.'

18

'Why wasn't it?'

'I'm sorry. I can't tell you that.'

'You're not concerned with me,' cried Catherine angrily. 'You're just trying to muzzle the press.'

'Have you forgotten what happened when we last met?' he asked coldly.

'I'm sorry, I shouldn't have said that. I ought to be thanking you. I feel very guilty that I didn't seek you out.'

'All part of the service,' he replied, flippant again.

'But you must understand that I won't drop a story, just because you say I should.'

'And you must understand that I can't tell you why there isn't a story for you,' he exclaimed irritably, 'because if I did, you'd rush straight off and print it.'

They relapsed into angry silence as the cab trotted along Oxford Street, and they had turned down Park Lane before Morton broke it.

'Very well,' he said. 'But if I tell you what's behind it all, will you promise not to print a word until we say you can?'

'Who do you mean by "we"?' asked Catherine.

'For this purpose, Sergeant Bragg and myself.'

'And the information would be given to no other journalist?'

'Not if it's in my power to prevent it.'

Catherine smiled sweetly. 'Then of course I give you my word. You'd better come in for a while . . . Goodness, I've lost my hat and shoes, and my skirt is torn. I only hope no one sees us.'

Morton paid off the cab, and they hurried up the steps. But just as Catherine stretched out her hand, the door was opened, and a tall woman emerged, dressed in a floating yellow gown and a large hat with a bird on it.

'Hello, darling,' she said in surprise. 'I'd been wondering where you'd got to. It's cook's night off, but there's sure to be something cold in the larder. I'm off to Daddy's exhibition at Agnews. Do I know your friend?'

'This is Constable Morton, Mamma.'

'Good,' she said vaguely. 'Then you'd better take him to the kitchen and give him a cup of tea. I'll be back by ten.' She sailed down the steps, and away.

'That was Mother,' said Catherine, pulling a face. 'Nevertheless, tea is a good idea.'

'What is the exhibition she mentioned?' asked Morton, as she searched for the tea caddy, and set cups upon the table.

'Oh, Daddy is a painter. He does portraits most of the time, but occasionally he paints pictures to sell through the galleries . . . Mother describes them as mournful Scotch cattle, and rutting deer!'

'William Marsden RA?' asked Morton.

'The same. Now we haven't come to chatter, so you'd better begin.'

'This house seems so normal and secure,' said Morton, 'I find it difficult to believe that what just happened can be real.'

'I only have to move my arm, and I can believe it,' said Catherine ruefully.

'I'm sorry. Believe me, it was necessary.'

'I'm prepared to believe that you thought it was necessary,' she reposted.

'Very well. I'll not try to spare you. In the early hours of Sunday morning, a man was murdered near Tower Hill . . . in a particularly barbaric fashion. He was laid unconscious on the railings of Allhallows church, and battered down till he was impaled on the spikes.'

Catherine gave a grimace of revulsion.

'That man was a police constable,' went on Morton. 'And he had been doing the same job that I was doing this evening.'

'What job was that?' asked Catherine.

'We've been ordered to keep a covert watch on public meetings involving the industrious classes. Over the past weeks, such meetings have become increasingly violent. Now, the radical politicians have begun to join in the fun.'

'But millions of people really do live in the most appalling conditions,' Catherine objected.

'Well, let's not argue that one at the moment. I'm quite prepared to accept that now almost all working men have the vote, there must be a fundamental shift in politics. But bloody revolution isn't English.'

'Put like that, it sounds as if the entrenched interests are preparing to fob the working class off with the illusion of democracy, and deny them its substance . . . I suppose the working man is fortunate; they don't feel the need to extend even that to women.'

'It's impossible to explain anything to you,' exclaimed Morton. 'You're . . . '

'I'm a stinking capitalist cow! Remember?'

'That should prove to you what an emergency it was!'

'Well,' said Catherine, mollified, 'the men around me seemed peaceable enough. The trouble started over to my right.'

'I know. I was there. And you are totally wrong, if you think it was a spontaneous disturbance. It was well organized; first the clapping and chanting, and then the fighting . . . But the group that made for you hadn't been involved in the fighting. Those men were looking around the crowd as it dispersed, and as soon as they saw you were making notes, they set off at a run.'

'But if, as you say, it was an organized affray, you would think they'd want it reported,' said Catherine.

'Look, I don't pretend to understand it,' exclaimed Morton irritably. 'All I know is that if I hadn't managed to get over, you'd be dead now, or maimed. And if you don't believe that, I'll arrange for you to see Constable Foster's body in the mortuary.'

Catherine shuddered. 'All right. You've bludgeoned me into submission. What do you want me to do?'

'Just nothing. They've got your note book, and if no article appears, they're unlikely to pursue you further.'

'But I was doing it for the *Star,* not for my paper.'

'It makes no difference. Do nothing, and take care.'

'It sounds as if I should be saying the same to you.'

Morton grinned. 'Ah, but then I'm paid to take risks,' he said.

'You've brought it on your own head, Bragg. If you hadn't been so assiduous in exposing the failings of my predecessor, you wouldn't be stuck with me.'

Bragg was sitting in an uncomfortable chair in the Temple

chambers of Sir Rufus Stone QC, the new coroner for the City of London. Sir Rufus was standing with his back to the empty fireplace, as if he were addressing a jury. His large head, with its mane of grey hair, was thrust forward; one hand played with a heavy gold albert draped across his ample stomach, while the other was waved dramatically to emphasize a point. This oratorical style, thought Bragg, was somewhat old-fashioned. He declaimed rather than persuaded, aiming to compel concurrence with his views by the strength of his personality.

'I asked for you as my officer for this homicide, because I feel that I can trust you. And until I have a better acquaintance with the personnel of the City police force, I have no intention of trusting anyone else.'

'It's just that I'm heavily involved in a tricky surveillance operation that could go on for some time . . . '

'Can't help that,' interrupted the coroner. 'You'll just have to put up with it. I want it to be perfectly clear to everyone at Old Jewry that in matters affecting my jurisdiction, I do not intend to be a cypher. I have been brought in to cleanse the Augean stables, and cleanse them I will . . . I've never had much time for coroners, myself – an antiquated office, occupied for the most part by a rag-bag of ancient practitioners of medicine. But, by God, it's going to work effectively within the boundaries of the City of London. Are we agreed?'

'Yes, sir,' muttered Bragg.

'I went down to see the body, and authorize the post-mortem examination. Have you seen it yet?'

'I saw Dr Burney shortly after you left.'

'But have you seen the body?'

'Of course.'

Sir Rufus glared at Bragg as if he were a hostile witness, then strode over to his desk and sat down.

'There's only one possible verdict,' he pronounced, 'if the account of the constable who found the body can be relied on. We can rule out natural causes, accidental death and suicide; and in this case the misadventure amounts to plain murder.' He smiled at his own pleasantry. 'Can it?' he asked.

'Can what, sir?'

'Can it be relied on?'

'I visited the scene of the crime with him. Unfortunately the body had been removed by then.'

'You didn't expect them to leave it there, for a peepshow, while you hauled yourself from your bed did you, Bragg?'

'Since it took almost two hours before I was informed I'd been appointed coroner's officer, no, I didn't.'

'Two hours, eh? That's two hours too long. The present procedure is intolerably cumbersome. Perhaps it would be an improvement if I went to the scene of the crime myself.'

'I don't think that's necessary,' said Bragg hurriedly. 'But the detective on the case must see the body before it's moved.'

'I don't know, Bragg . . . I qualified in medicine at St Thomas's, before I took to the law. I expect I still remember a fair bit.' He glanced towards his bookcase, and Bragg recognized the spine of a well-used copy of *Gray's Anatomy* there.

'Anyway,' he said, 'it can.'

'What can?' asked Sir Rufus, roused from his reverie.

'The account of the constable can be relied on. Although he was new to the force, I formed the view that he has a very methodical mind, and a good memory. And he wasn't panicked by the grisly state of the body. I expect that's because he did some soldiering in India.'

'Will he make a good witness?' asked Sir Rufus.

'No doubt of it.'

'We've no other statements at the moment, I take it?'

'No. We're going round the stables, to find out if any carriers were in the vicinity around five o'clock. And next Sunday morning at that time, I'll have several men questioning everyone in the area.'

'It seems a rather hit-and-miss proceeding.'

'When you haven't got a lead, it's the only way to start.'

'I wonder why he was put to such a barbarous death,' mused the coroner.

'If we knew that, we'd be a long way to solving the murder.'

'We've got to catch them, Bragg,' he warned. 'I'm not having a "person or persons unknown" verdict at my first inquest.'

3

Bragg and Morton tramped up the narrow wooden stairs, and reached a landing covered with brown linoleum. There was a door opposite, with a large glass panel, on which was etched 'Amalgamated Society of Engineers'. A bit like a gin palace, thought Bragg, though with their temperance leanings they wouldn't welcome the comparison. He hammered on the door, and after a considerable pause it was opened by a short, thick-set man, in a black frock coat and a crumpled white collar.

'I want to see the secretary of the union,' said Bragg.

'That's me,' said the man, making no move.

'We're police officers.' Bragg showed him his warrant card.

'Oh. Will it take long? Only I'm going out in ten minutes.'

'That will depend on you, sir.'

'Better come in then.' He led the way through the small outer office into a rather larger room beyond, with a view of the river. The man motioned them to chairs, and sat down behind a shabby desk. 'What is it you want of me?' he asked.

Bragg took out his note book. 'Perhaps we should start with your name.'

'Why?' asked the man truculently.

'It's just easier if we don't have to refer to you as "Mr A",' replied Bragg with a smile.

The man looked suspiciously at them for a long moment. 'Daniel Crisp,' he said.

Bragg wrote the name deliberately across the top of a new page in his note book, and underlined it twice. Then he looked up. 'I understand,' he said, 'that your union held a meeting on Tower Hill last Saturday, the fifteenth of August. Is that correct?'

'Yes . . . Saturday evening.'

'We are making enquiries into a disturbance which occurred during and after the meeting, and I wondered if you could help us.'

'I didn't go, myself. It wasn't ordinary union business, you see.'

'But you've heard about the fighting that occurred?'

'I wouldn't say "fighting",' Crisp demurred. 'There may have been a bit of a scuffle – some men get worked up about things, but there wasn't a breach of the peace, nowhere near. Can't see why you're bothered about it.'

'There has been a fair amount of disturbance at union meetings, of late, and we're beginning to wonder why.'

'It's not surprising, is it? With the sort of unions you have around nowadays.'

'How do you mean, sir?'

'Well, the old craft unions, like ours, know how to behave. They don't go rabble-rousing.'

'Isn't John Burns a member of your union?' asked Morton. 'Surely he was sent to prison some years ago, for inciting a riot?'

'That bloody man,' said Crisp bitterly. 'He's nothing but a politician. It's his kind that are going to bring ruination on us.'

'So you are worried?' remarked Bragg.

'Worried? No. But we don't want to be dragged down by that lot.'

'Why should that happen?'

'Because these new unions have no bottom to them. Look at the Gasworkers' Union. All unskilled men. They formed their union four years ago, and their first move was to threaten to go on strike for an eight-hour day. I grant you they got it, but only because they caught the employers off balance. And what happens then? Two years later they try the same tactic. Only this time the employers were ready for them, and they were glad to go back on any terms. The trouble is, I've got members working alongside them at the gasworks. We've put in a lot of time, building a proper relationship with the owners, and it's all gone for nothing.'

'You wouldn't go on strike, then?' asked Bragg.

'I'm not saying that; but in a proper, well-conducted union, there should be no need for it. Our members are highly skilled, and the owners know their profits depend on them. Both sides acknowledge that we could go on strike; and everybody realizes that if we did, both sides would suffer. The employers can't replace us with an army of spud-eating Irish. So we negotiate. We ask for what we think the trade can stand – or maybe a bit more; and the owners allow themselves to be pushed to a bit less than we're asking for, and we settle.'

'Presumably the unskilled men can't bring the same pressures to bear,' remarked Morton.

'No, they can't. And by trying to, they overreach themselves. But they're doing all right if only they'd be content.'

'You surprise me,' said Morton. 'Ever since I can remember, people have been talking about a depression in trade.'

'That's because the press represents the capitalists,' said Crisp. 'No doubt it's true enough for them. Trade has been slack, and the profits left for the middle classes have fallen. But the working man is better off, because his wages have fallen less than prices.'

'Not a working man faced with losing his job to somebody even hungrier than he is,' growled Bragg.

'My concern is with my members' interests,' retorted Crisp defiantly.

'Then why does your union hold inflammatory meetings that result in civil disturbance?'

'That's totally uncalled for! Our attitude is to take a responsible lead in the workers' movement; to show that there's a middle way between slavery and bloody revolution.'

'And in the process to keep the lid on, and preserve the comfortable relationship you have with the bosses,' said Bragg.

Crisp's face flushed darkly. 'I've not got time to bandy politics with a policeman,' he said. 'And I should think you have better things to do . . . Here, Jim!' He beckoned to a man who had poked his head through the door. 'Come and talk to these . . . gentlemen from the police about the meeting on Saturday.'

Jim proved to be a slim, balding man, with an appealingly ingenuous face. He perched himself on the edge of the desk, and smiled at Bragg and Morton.

'Do I take it that you were at the meeting on Saturday evening, sir?' asked Bragg.

'That's right. I was the chairman.'

'Was it supposed to be just for union members?'

'Not really. That was the reason it was held in the open air, so that anyone could join in.'

'Then what were you trying to achieve?'

'I don't suppose you know a lot about the labour movement, being a policeman,' Jim observed pleasantly. 'But as a union, we feel that it is being manipulated by people outside the movement, for their own ends.'

'Mr Crisp has told us about John Burns.'

'Has he, now?' Jim looked quizzically at Crisp, who avoided his gaze. 'Yes. Well, I suppose the worker has always been manipulated. If you ask me, the worst of all has been the Church, assuring you of treasures in heaven, if only you'll work for nothing on earth. That doesn't go down any more, of course, though there are still a few loonies like Ruskin and William Morris, who want to take us all back to the Middle Ages. But the people who worry us are the middle-class intellectuals. Half of them are do-gooding ninnies, that left to themselves wouldn't amount to a row of beans; but the others are would-be politicians who've got nowhere in the existing parties, and intend to ride to power on the backs of the workers.'

'And you say your meeting on Saturday was intended to counteract this kind of influence?' asked Bragg.

'Yes. We're not alone in that. Most of the old craft unions are taking similar action.'

'Can you tell me why it ended in uproar?'

'Frankly, no.' Jim smiled disarmingly. 'There was a fair turnout of our members, and about as many outsiders. We had the chairman of our Birmingham branch as the main speaker. He's a well-known radical, and we thought he ought to strike the right note. And so he did. It was when he was explaining our commitment to reform through the ballot box that the trouble started. There was some shouting, and a skirmish developed at the back. There seemed to be an attempt by a number of people to push towards the platform, but our members stood firm, and it all fizzled out.'

'Did you recognize any of the men who started the trouble?' asked Bragg.

'No. They were too far away.'

'Did you hear what they were shouting?'

Jim looked embarrassed. 'Yes, I did . . . They were chanting "Blood not votes".'

'Shall I tell you what I think?' asked Crisp irritably. 'I reckon it's the capitalists, trying to discredit us by making people think we're tarred with the same brush as the unskilled. It'll bring ruination on the lot of us!'

Bragg spent part of the next morning at Smithfield, examining the place of Monday's meeting. It was cluttered with meat wholesalers' vans, and traps from the local butchers, but by three o'clock it would be virtually deserted. The focal point had been the fountain, where they'd erected the platform, and the crowd had fanned out to the west. The ground was level and unobstructed. If the objective had been to capture the platform and end the meeting, a determined assault from the east or south would have easily succeeded. It hadn't, after all, been a union meeting, but a political rally aimed at the working classes in general. As such the crowd would lack cohesion, and might be less able to repel a sudden foray. Bragg realized that his thoughts ran in military images. He must guard against falling into the easy assumption that all these outbreaks were connected. Mind you, Jim had implied that there was nothing spontaneous in Saturday's disturbance . . . He seemed bright, that one. Cleverer than Crisp. Bragg wondered if he too were aiming to manipulate the workers for his own ends . . . According to Morton, the Smithfield crowd had been well behaved, and good-tempered. The clapping and chanting had begun as if on a signal, and the fighting had erupted only on the south flank. Again the military metaphor. Well, if the two disturbances had been planned by the same people, they'd organized themselves a deal better at Smithfield. Bragg observed wryly that they would have started their push just about opposite the Second Division police station. They didn't mind taking risks, these people; though compared with Allhallows, the risk was negligible. There'd only been a desk sergeant and two constables in the station; and by the time they'd wakened up, it was all over.

He wandered back to Old Jewry, irritable and frustrated, the ashen face of Constable Foster's widow etched on his brain.

'Joe,' called the duty sergeant, as he made for the stairs, 'Sir William wants to see you straight away.'

Lieutenant-Colonel Sir William Sumner was the Commissioner of the City of London police force. He was still new to the job, and ran the force in much the same way as a regiment. Not that it was inappropriate; most of the men under him were ex-army. Perhaps they found it easier to accept than Bragg, who'd rebelled against unreasoning discipline when he was twelve, and been big enough to have his way. Sir William boasted that he knew every man in his force, and his attempts to demonstrate a paternal interest often undermined the authority of the senior officers. It was generally known that his assistant commissioners had been reduced to mere office boys by his constant interference in work which he had theoretically delegated. Even so, it was unusual for him to summon a detective-sergeant to see him.

'What's it about, Bill?' asked Bragg.

'Dunno. A Major somebody went up to see him ten minutes ago, and he sent for you straight after.'

Bragg went up the elegant staircase, through the anteroom with its row of bentwood chairs, and, rapping on the Commissioner's door, went inside.

'Ah, Bragg. Sit down, will you?'

Sir William, short and stiff, with a goatee beard, was sitting behind his desk, his face dark with indignation. To Bragg he looked just like a magazine drawing he'd seen of the Prince of Wales giving evidence in the Tranby Croft card-sharping case. Sitting opposite him was a bulky man of about fifty. He had a square jaw and heavy face, florid from either sun or whisky. His hair was cropped very short, and he wore a carefully tended moustache.

'This is Major Redman, Bragg. He's in charge of the Metropolitan Police's Special Branch.' The Commissioner's voice held a note of distaste which was evidently lost on his visitor. 'The major has come to see me about disturbances at political meetings, and, since you are in charge of our operation on the ground, I thought you should listen to what he has to say.'

Redman shifted his flint-grey eyes briefly to Bragg, then turned again to Sir William.

'You will be aware from the papers,' he began in an incisive tone, 'of the increase in political activity amongst the lower classes in recent years. We needn't go into the underlying reasons for our present purposes, though no doubt it has a lot to do with teaching them all to read and write. Suffice it to say that a large part of the present electorate is so ill-educated, that they are likely to accept every lunatic bit of propaganda as gospel truth. And we have our share of political agitators. You'll remember, Mr Commissioner, that fifteen years ago there was a sizeable republican movement in this country. It was one of the reasons for my branch's being formed – to keep an eye on the situation. Since then Britain has collected a sprinkling of anarchists and socialists from Europe, to say nothing of the Fenians from Ireland. They've let off a bomb from time to time, but my people have usually had an idea of what was going on, and no great harm has been done. But now we detect a new situation developing. The dock strike showed the lower classes that they can hold the country to ransom, if they choose. On top of that, some socialist leaders are openly declaring that they will use the power of the workers to destroy society as it is. What happened in Smithfield the other night, could soon be happening all over the country.'

'How do you know what happened in Smithfield?' asked Sir William icily.

'I had one of my men there.'

'What? In my area . . . without even consulting me?' Sir William was suddenly beside himself with anger.

'I'm sure you realize that it isn't practicable to work through the ordinary liaison channels in this kind of surveillance work.'

'I expect to be consulted!'

'Very well, sir,' said Redman composedly, 'I will arrange for the Home Office to send you a general notification that my officers may operate in the City of London police area.'

'My men are perfectly capable of keeping an eye on these meetings,' exclaimed the Commissioner petulantly. 'Bragg, there, is even now co-ordinating the operation. I see no need for your people to be involved.'

'The Special Branch was created purely to monitor political activities,' said Redman firmly. 'My officers are specialists – trained for the job. They're aware of the political currents in this country and abroad, and we aim to be one step ahead of the agitators. Without in any way criticizing the City force, Mr Commissioner, it isn't a job for amateurs.'

Bragg could see Sir William's face taking on a brooding look; usually the prelude to giving way ungraciously.

'If it's any comfort to you, sir,' went on Redman, 'my branch operates throughout the country without liaising with local police forces.'

'I don't want comfort,' exclaimed the commissioner irritably, 'I want a good reason why part of the Metropolitan Police is operating within my area, independently of my force.'

'It's partly a question of having the necessary expertise, and partly the need for confidentiality and speed.'

Sir William began to bridle again.

'I'm sure the Home Office will confirm,' went on Redman, 'that our remit extends over the whole of Britain, at our total discretion.'

'Then what is it that you want?' asked Sir William grumpily.

'I want you to withdraw your men from this surveillance. It's no disrespect to them to say that they are obviously policemen. The government's instructions to us are not to bottle up the emerging political forces by repression, but to penetrate them. In that way, appropriate action can be taken without alienating the liberal-minded majority of the electorate.'

'What do you say, Bragg?' asked the commissioner.

'Well, sir, I confess the major has a point. It's difficult for us to relate what's happening in the City to the broader trends in the country.'

'Very well,' said Sir William sententiously. 'In the circumstances, I am prepared to agree that your officers shall take over the surveillance of political and associated meetings within

31

the City police area.'

'Excellent,' smiled Redman, rising to go.

'There's just one thing,' said Bragg. 'I'm investigating the murder of one of my men. He was killed after one of those meetings.'

'Drop it,' said Redman curtly.

'Drop it? . . . I bloody won't!'

'In the context, it's not significant.'

'I don't think you understand,' said Bragg, trembling with anger. 'I sent one of my men to report on a meeting, and the next morning we find him impaled on some churchyard railings. If you think I'm going to drop that, you can bloody well think again.'

'Then, Mr Commissioner,' said Redman contemptuously, 'perhaps you will direct the sergeant to abandon his enquiries.'

'It's not possible,' said Sir William uncomfortably. 'The investigation, as you should know, is under the control of the coroner for the City. Sergeant Bragg is his officer, and I have no control over it.'

Redman looked at the commissioner incredulously. Then he picked up his hat from the side table. 'We'll see about that,' he said, and strode from the room.

4

The next day was sunny, with little or no breeze, and by lunchtime the pavements of the City were thronged with people glad to escape from their stuffy offices. Women shop assistants and typewriters, daring in their thin blouses, gazed longingly into jewellers' windows. Groups of men lounged outside the pubs, a glass of beer in one hand and a sausage in the other. A general torpor seemed to have descended on the City, an aimlessness that suggested little work would be done that afternoon.

Morton, walking along Cheapside, found his progress impeded by a bunch of silk-hatted stockbrokers, strolling towards the Bank. He stepped into the gutter to overtake them, and, as he did so, glimpsed a man who was evidently going in the other direction, and had drawn into a doorway to let them pass. The face struck a chord of recognition; and what's more, Morton had an impression that even though he had hurried on, the man had looked twice in his direction. Morton stepped out into the street, and gazed after the retreating figure. Of course! 'Karl! Karl!' he shouted, as he ran after him.

The man seemed to quicken his pace, then, as Morton came up with him, looked round in disbelief.

'Great heavens! James! What are you doing in London?'

'My dear Karl!' exclaimed Morton, seizing his hand, 'I'm sorry I didn't recognize you immediately. I thought you were in Germany.'

'I was, until a few weeks ago. I was going to write to you. I expected you to be running the estates in the country.'

'Have you time for a drink?'

'Why, yes. I have done my bit for the Fatherland today.'

Morton led the way into a tavern, and they ordered wine. As Morton put his hand in his pocket, Karl intervened.

'Please to let me pay. You look as if you have struck some bad luck.'

'Not at all,' said Morton with a laugh. 'These are only my working clothes.'

'Thank God! There is nothing so contagious as ill-fortune.'

'Whatever are you doing in England?' asked Morton excitedly.

'If you remember, James, my father had been moved from London to Paris, before I came down from Cambridge.'

'Of course. You stayed with us at the Priory for a time.'

'Well, I went back to Prussia for a few weeks, but it was so boring!' Karl made a grimace. 'So I went to stay at the embassy in Paris, with my parents . . . and there I met a most charming girl; you know, really warm-hearted.' He gave a salacious grin. 'She kept me on a string for two whole years – and then decided to marry a banker!'

'You haven't changed!'

'It was not time entirely lost. I found myself a studio in Montmartre and did a little painting. It improved my French, even if I was not a success as an artist; and there were always the girls . . . I painted nudes exclusively.'

'Naturally!'

'Ah, your wit is still as sharp.'

'And your command of English is as idiomatic as ever. But why are you here in London, looking more like a diplomat than an artist?'

'Alas! James, I protest I deserve a better fate. My poor father, on whom I had unashamedly sponged, was recalled and compelled to retire. He was a protégé of Bismarck, and when our gracious Emperor took over the reins of his government last year, my father was one of the casualties.'

'I'm sorry to hear that. What is he doing now?'

'He has not begun a decline, or anything like that. Indeed, I rather think he is enjoying, er . . . pottering about – that's right, isn't it? – pottering about at home. No, James, I am the real casualty, because after that I perforce had really to work for my living. My father's influence was still strong enough to get me a post in the Trade Ministry, so I gave away my palette, said goodbye to Lulu and Fifi, and became a very stuffy German functionary.'

'I can't imagine anything making you stuffy, Karl. Are you here for long?'

'As long as I can contrive. I persuade myself that the further I am from Berlin, the less likely they are to er . . . find me out. By some benign stroke of fortune, my name was pulled out of the hat to come to England, to prepare for the state visit of our lord and master to London last month. In fact I have just come from a thank-you reception to the City officials . . . But the best of it is, that I have persuaded Berlin to let me study British agricultural methods while I am here. So long as I send an occasional turgid report back, I should be able to make it last till autumn.'

'Then you must certainly study the agriculture of Kent. I'm sure my parents would be delighted to have you stay with them again.'

'How are they? Well, I hope.'

'Yes. Father is very involved with his official duties, but Mother and Emily are going to visit the American side of the family next month.'

'So you all are prospering?'

'Why, yes – with all too little effort, I'm afraid.'

'Then why this exceedingly démodé ensemble?'

'I've told you. It's my working clothes. I'm a policeman.'

'You are being whimsical, of course.'

'Not at all! I joined the police force as a constable, and by dint of two years' plodding on the beat, I was accepted into the detective division.'

'My dear James, how very earnest of you. You would make a better German than I . . . And what precisely do you detect?'

'Anything that comes along, theft, fraud, murder. I'm still learning my trade, of course. I've been attached to a great bear of a man, called Sergeant Bragg.'

'A curious name,' remarked Karl. 'It means to boast, does it not?'

'I'm very fortunate. He's absolutely brilliant. He's the kind of man that refuses to take things just at their face value. He worries away at a problem until he's discovered the real truth. It does not always endear him to the authorities, but he doesn't seem to mind.'

'Now he would never make a German.'

'We've been keeping a covert watch on disturbances at union and political meetings. It was quite amusing till we found one of our men murdered.'

'Murdered?'

'Impaled on a spiked railing, in fact. I've never seen Bragg so angry. He swore he would find the culprits, if it took him a year – but it won't, more like a fortnight if his record is anything to go by.'

'Perhaps he has a Teutonic streak after all. Enough of your revolting career, if that is what you call it. When can I come down to Kent? I imagine Emily is quite grown up by now.'

'Yes, very sophisticated and very bored. She'd love to see you again. Why don't you come down for this weekend? With any luck I shall be there. I'm playing cricket at Maidstone on Saturday, and I hope to stay till Sunday evening.'

'I'd be delighted to,' said Karl. 'Unfortunately I have almost committed myself already. My cousin Helga Speidel is in London. You may remember her as Helga Kitz; she came to a May Ball at Cambridge in 'eighty-five. Her husband has just been killed in Africa, and I persuaded her to visit me in England for a while, away from grieving relatives. I had promised to take her into the country.'

'For goodness sake! Bring her too. I'll send a telegram to my mother to expect us all.'

'This is very good of you, James. You will find Helga still as beautiful and full of fun . . . Well, this is splendid! I cannot think of anything I would rather do – always assuming we do not have to watch you play your cricket!'

'I tell you, Bragg, in all my years in public life, I've never come across such a blatant attempt to pervert the course of justice.'

Sir Rufus Stone was striding up and down his chambers, spluttering with indignation.

'This Tory administration has no respect whatever for the

rule of law.'

He paused, and thrust a minatory finger towards Bragg and Morton. 'I will not have some jack-in-office telling me to suspend the investigation into Foster's death, and waive an inquest. I am Her Majesty's coroner, holding office direct from the Crown, not some tuppeny-ha'penny civil servant who can be dismissed if he doesn't acquiesce!'

'What reason did he give, sir?' asked Bragg.

'Public policy, he said. Public policy! In heaven's name, what does a shiny-elbowed clerk know about public policy?'

'What department was he from?' asked Morton.

'The Home Office. I have his card somewhere.' Sir Rufus strode over to a side table, and began to rummage through a litter of papers.

'It seems to tie in with a visit we had yesterday, from the head of the Special Branch.'

'The political coppers?' Sir Rufus looked up sharply.

'Yes. He saw the commissioner, and put pressure on him to withdraw our men from the surveillance of public meetings in the City.'

'I hope Sir William sent him about his business,' exclaimed Sir Rufus.

'I'm afraid that he finally agreed to do what was asked.'

The coroner's lip curled in scorn.

'What's more,' went on Bragg, 'when I mentioned the Foster investigation, I was told to drop it.'

'Damnation, Bragg! These petty pen-pushers don't even know the legal structure of the kingdom they're supposed to administer. Sir William put him right, I trust?'

'Yes, sir. He said the investigation was under your control, and that I acted solely under your direction.'

'That's something, at least. I hope he remembers that, when he comes to complain, as no doubt he will, about my use of police manpower.'

'May I ask, sir, what answer you gave to the Home Office?' said Morton.

'You may.' Sir Rufus resumed his theatrical pose before the fireplace. 'I told him to go back to his political masters, and remind them that they persuaded me to accept this office – at considerable financial sacrifice – to minimize the no doubt political repercussions arising from the aura of corruption surrounding my predecessor. I said that I took the gravest exception to their attempt to interfere with the judiciary, and that while I held this office, I would carry out my duties without deviating from the course dictated by my conscience.'

'What did he have to say to that?' asked Bragg with a smile.

Sir Rufus laughed. 'Why, the pompous upstart had the temerity to remind me that all High Court judges are sovereign coroners *ex officio,* and he threatened to remove the inquest from my jurisdiction to the Old Bailey. He even told me that they would see it was held *in camera,* so that there would be no publicity. That's what they mean by public policy, Bragg – no publicity! Well I told him that if there was any such chicanery, I would resign my office, and publish my reasons for doing so in *The Times.* So there we are. The inquest goes ahead tomorrow as planned. Unfortunately, Dr Burney has a prior lecture engagement, so he won't be able to give evidence as to the cause of death; but we'll go ahead anyway.'

'Might I suggest,' ventured Bragg, 'that you merely take evidence of identification tomorrow. That might satisfy the Home Office that you are co-operating with them.'

'Satisfy? Don't like the word "satisfy", Bragg. I don't mind deluding them, or lulling them into a false sense of their own importance, but "satisfy" them? – never! . . . Very well. I would have to adjourn it anyway.' Sir Rufus wagged his finger again. 'But I don't want you, or anyone else in the police force, to get the idea that I can be manipulated.'

Catherine Marsden threw *The Times* on to the table crossly. At least Constable Morton had kept his word, and there was no mention in the papers of the fracas at Smithfield, or indeed of the murder he had talked of. 'Preached about' was more like it. She felt a spasm of irritation at the way she had been bamboozled into withholding her story. Typical male arrogance, to think that he knew best. And having obtained her promise of silence, he hadn't really told her anything. True, it had been a dreadful murder, but there wasn't any evidence to connect it with the meeting the victim had been observing.

She formed a sudden resolve to write the column anyway – perhaps just to see how it looked – and picked up her pencil. But if she did, she would only present herself with the moral dilemma of whether she should send it for publication or not. It really was intolerable that he should be able to put her in such a position. Of course, the lever he had used had been the circumstances of their last meeting. But obligation had its limits, and he'd no right, in return, to assume a proprietorial air with her . . . Not that he'd really done so. To give him his due, he hadn't attempted even to seek her out after saving her life. Indeed, she was herself grievously at fault there. Far from inviting him to tea, once she'd recovered, in order to thank him, she hadn't even shown him the courtesy of a letter. But it was hardly surprising. After all, she had regained consciousness to find him staring at her bare bosom. It was difficult to embark on social niceties after that. Anyway, he probably didn't expect to be thanked. 'All in the service,' he'd said on Monday . . . The arrogance of the man, to drag her half across London, and claim that saving her life was his hobby. Was he going to continue interfering?

Men were insufferably conceited. She found it almost impossible to respond courteously to the Guards' subaltern, who had of late been seeking her out. She despised his conviction that whatever he was doing was supremely important, that his wishes should be complied with, and the arrogance of the underlying assumption that force was justified to obtain acquiescence. And yet her friends fought over such absurd popinjays. At least it was unfair to equate James Morton with such as him. On the other hand, on Monday evening he had been distinctly coarse. But why should she expect anything else? It was probably the cultivated voice he affected . . . yet what was wrong with that? Speaking properly wasn't the exclusive preserve of the well-to-do.

She looked at herself critically in the mirror. Why did she have to have such an unfashionable face? – the prominent chin, the high forehead, and above all the long high-bridged nose. She snorted with irritation. She remembered on her fourteenth birthday, overhearing her aunt commiserating with her mother.

'I'm sure,' she had said, 'that Catherine will be beautiful when she is old.' . . . Well she was glad that she wasn't just a pretty nincompoop. At least she could make her own way in the world.

'You're very restless this evening, darling.' Her mother put down her embroidery. 'Is there anything troubling you?'

Catherine sighed. 'I suppose I was just thinking how unsettling it is, when people come in and out of one's life, without ever becoming part of the pattern.'

Her mother looked up quizzically. 'That was a very handsome young man who brought you home the other night, dear.'

Catherine laughed in exasperation. 'Mamma, you really are incorrigible!'

'I think I was very clever to notice it, considering his attire. I thought you were going to a fancy-dress party as a sweep and a begger-maid.'

'Really, Mamma! You're not in the least concerned that I was alone in the house with him for an hour; until now you haven't commented on the fact that I'd lost my hat and my shoes, and my dress was torn. All you can say is that he was good-looking.'

Mrs Marsden held up her hands in mock self-defence. 'I assure you, my dear, that I have no intention of asking if your friend is an eligible bachelor.'

'Well, I'll tell you, to set your mind at rest. He wouldn't be on even the most desperate mother's list. He's just an ordinary policeman, who has a disconcerting propensity for getting me out of scrapes.'

'Oh, that one?' said her mother. 'Well. I'm glad someone's looking after you. I gave up trying when you were twelve.'

5

'I got this note, asking me to see Constable Goff.' The duty sergeant at Whitechapel Metropolitan Police station took the letter from Bragg, and perused it.

'City Police, eh? Well, you've just about caught him. Half a minute.'

Goff proved to be a fresh-faced young man, brisk and alert. 'It was about the circular on the Allhallows murder,' he said. 'I think I might have seen them. I was on duty that night, and around half past four Sunday morning, I saw this cart going along Royal Mint Street, towards the City.'

'What made you notice it?' asked Bragg.

'Several things, really. It was a big flat hay lorry, and you don't generally see them around at that time on a Sunday. Then again, it was empty.'

'You mean, since it was going towards the City you'd have expected it to be loaded?'

'That's right. And with a cart of that size you'd normally have two horses in tandem, but here it was only being pulled with one. That suggested they weren't going to take on a full load, wherever they were headed for; and yet there were four or five men on it. It made me curious, that's all.'

'Did you get a good look at the men?'

'Not really. I was just coming out of Cartwright Street, when they went across the top. There aren't many gas lights there. What bit of time I could see them head-on, I was more struck with the horse than anything else. I don't go much for greys myself, but he was a beauty. A big shire stallion, all of eighteen hands. He had a big white star on his forehead, and a white stocking on all but the off-side hind leg.'

'Unusual markings,' remarked Bragg. 'Should be easy enough to find. What impression did you get of the men?'

'Big labouring chaps, I would guess. Most of them were lying on the cart, on what looked like sacking. I only got what I'd call a fair idea of the driver. He was a big man, big as you, I reckon.'

'Did you see his features?'

'Not well enough to describe them. He had a bushy beard, and his hat was pulled well down. You couldn't hardly see his face.'

'Hmn. Do you think it's possible that our murder was a distraction, while the rest of the gang tried to break into the Mint?'

'Not from anything I've heard,' said the sergeant, reaching for the incident book. 'When was it, now? Sunday August sixteenth?' He ran his finger up the entries. 'Nothing here.'

'It was a long shot,' said Bragg. 'Only we are about as near to the Mint at Seething Lane as you are here.'

'Well nobody tried to divert our attention from anything, that night,' said the sergeant. 'As you can see, there were only a couple of drunks, and an old man's pocket picked in Aldgate High Street. There isn't an entry after half past one.'

'What does a hay cart suggest to you?' asked Bragg.

'Shouldn't think it belongs to anyone round here,' said Goff. 'They use them to bring in hay from the country, and most times they go back empty.'

'Who owns them?'

'Mainly carriers in the small towns like Ilford and Barking,' said the sergeant. 'From further out, it comes up the river by barge.'

'And where do the carts unload?'

'There are a couple of merchants in Whitechapel.'

'Can I ask you to keep an eye on the carts coming in, for a couple of weeks? I don't want to approach the merchants direct, in case one of them is involved. If you spot the horse and cart, we've got the first real lead on this business.'

'Yes, 'course,' said the sergeant. 'We can't keep a permanent watch, naturally, but I'll pass the word.'

Bragg hurried back to Old Jewry, and left a note about the horse and cart for the stop-and-question team. Then, at a loss for anything constructive to do, he headed back towards the Royal Mint. It was an area of narrow streets and verminous courts. Even in the bright sunlight the rows of houses were mean and dejected, their grimy windows looking out in blank hostility on the world. It was probable that Foster had been held in one of these buildings. Bragg gave a wry smile at the thought of knocking on these doors. 'Excuse me, sir, but did you hear any screams in the early hours of Sunday morning?' Fat lot of good it would do, in an area like this. There'd be plenty of screams hereabouts, no doubt, but not often those of a man.

Bragg turned into Royal Mint Street, following the route of the cart. If you were coming from the East End, it was the obvious way to take; in narrow streets for most of the way, then along the deserted north face of the Tower, and across Tower Hill to the churchyard. They would have needed to watch for a time, to make sure the constable was well away on his beat. After that, it would have only taken a few minutes. Odd, that he'd always envisaged them coming the other way, from the west. He looked around for a likely place to conceal the cart, while they'd waited for the all clear. They wouldn't have crossed over Tower Hill at that stage, and they'd have been exposed on the Tower boundary; so that left the east side of Trinity Square. He must get someone to make house-to-house enquiries on Monday . . . There was nothing further he could do now. In a few hours' time the police would be stopping whatever traffic was around at four o'clock on a Sunday morning. In the meantime, he felt justified in making the best of what was left of Saturday. He wandered down towards the river. A steam launch was tied up at Tower pier, and a laughing crowd of people in holiday clothes was boarding her. For a while he watched the boatmen steadying the squealing women as they stepped on to the side of the launch and jumped down. Where were they going? He looked across at the kiosk . . . to Greenwich. On a sudden impulse he dashed across for a ticket, and jumped aboard.

It was a relief to be out on the river, away from the heat, and the all-pervading smell of horse dung; though the river itself smelled like a sewer on a hot day, when the tide was out. He got a glass of beer from the bar, and went on deck, where there was a little breeze. There was plenty of traffic on the river. Pleasure steamers were weaving confidently between strings of lighters moored in the stream, while sailing barges toiled fitfully up-river in the faint wind. On either bank were tall warehouses, like castles behind the battlements of their piled wharves, a fringe of small craft moored to each.

All too soon, thought Bragg, the fogs of autumn would descend, heralding the long winter. It was small wonder that the working people were deserting their cramped and dingy surroundings to spend a brilliant day like this in the country. He sometimes wondered what they made of it – about as much as he had of London, when he'd first arrived. A curious mixture of fascination and antagonism, that made you as quick to attack what made you uneasy, as to enjoy what was attractive. He remembered, as a lad of eighteen, being enthralled by the great buildings of London, and exhilarated by the constant swirl of traffic, the streams of people bustling by, knocking into you, exchanging a pleasantry – people you'd never seen before and likely would never see again. It was the sheer exuberance of life that was attractive to a lad fresh from the country. Even without friends, you had only to get out on the streets, and you couldn't feel lonely . . . Except at night. Then the other side of London took over, the furtive shadows, the menacing alleys, the sudden unidentified noises. During the two years he'd worked as a shipping clerk in the City, he'd never been out after eleven o'clock at night – at least, not alone. Then, one winter night, he'd been passing under a railway arch, when he'd felt his arm grabbed from behind. He'd twisted sideways, and lashed out in fierce panic. The man he'd hit had slumped to the ground, and he'd turned to face the others – but there was none. It had only been an old man, wanting the price of a cup of tea. It must have been that moment, Bragg thought, that disposed him to look below the surface of life; to discover what happened to the brilliant butterflies, when their wings became too tattered to bear them. That concern about individuals struggling in this metropolitan maelstrom had hampered his career in the police force; it sent him down-river on this brilliant August day to forget the look of dull incomprehension on a woman's face.

As soon as they tied up at Greenwich pier, the passengers streamed off into the town. Bragg paused to light his pipe, then strolled after them. Once away from the riverside, the breeze vanished, and the sun's heat radiated back from the pavement and buildings. He took off his hat and mopped the back of his neck, vowing once again that he would buy a jacket of lighter weight. He pushed into the bar of the Grapes, and ordered a pie and a pint. There was a curious mixture of people around him. Mainly, they were volatile East-Enders determined to enjoy themselves; but there was a fair sprinkling of Kentish country-men, and here and there a seaman listening to the hubbub in dark resentment – probably from the naval hospital. Bragg ordered another pint, and almost immediately regretted it. The atmosphere in the pub was smoky and sweltering, the smell of sweaty bodies and soiled clothes distasteful. He took his beer outside and swilled it down, then set off up the hill towards the park. There was some respite from the sun under the trees which bordered the grounds of the hospital. But Bragg noticed that even their neat lawns had been scorched by the summer heat.

Then he was in the park, surrounded by a mêlée of screeching children, running after hoops, splashing in the pool, fighting over balls. Their parents, having gained a foothold some fifty yards into the countryside, were sitting serenely amid the babble, eating sandwiches and drinking beer. Some of the men had taken off their coats and collars, and even rolled up the legs of their trousers. Perhaps they, too, had been paddling. The very idea made Bragg feel parched – but he'd have to wait till he'd climbed to the top of the hill. At least there'd be a breath of air there; in the meantime he might as well be as cool as he could. He took off his coat, conscious that he had lost a button on the back of his trousers, and that one loop of his braces was dangling free. He dragged himself up the path to the Royal Observatory, wondering again why there should be a statue to General Wolfe in this place. Perhaps it was appropriate, though; he felt as if he'd just scaled the Heights of Abraham himself.

In this part of the park he was amongst the intelligentsia; middle-class fathers pointing out to their sons the brass rail let into the ground to mark the Greenwich meridian, while their proud and hopeful mothers looked on from the shelter of their parasols. Well, there was no harm in it, thought Bragg. For all their selfish, entrenched attitudes, there was no harm in it. He strolled over to the astronomical clock, and pulling out his watch, set it right to the second – though he knew full well that it would be a good minute slow next morning. Up here was a faint stirring, as much up-currents of hot air as real breeze. Bragg wondered whether to take off his collar and tie . . . but such conduct didn't become a sergeant of the City police. Going about with flapping braces was bad enough. Instead, he would make for the refreshment kiosk, and have a beer. Back home in Dorset, they'd be in their shirt sleeves, open at the neck, with at most a light smock as evening approached. Here everyone was dressed formally, as for the office, in frock coat, or morning suit. There was an occasional young man in lounge suit or blazer, a silk-clad girl on his arm; but those apart, there was little to choose between the nobs and the workers. Go anywhere in the park, and look around you, and you'd swear you'd seen everybody before. Of course, the clothes of the lower classes were poor quality, and a bit scruffy, but they were of the same kind as their betters. That was on the credit side. Bragg recalled his grandfather's tales of bewigged, powdered men in coloured silk coats, arriving in their carriages for a dance at the local manor house. The very thought made him shudder in disgust. He took his beer to a small table under a tree, and sat contentedly watching a small boy throwing a stick for a dog to retrieve. Even here, surrounded by millions of people, give a boy a dog and a stick, and the world could go hang. The thought began to grow in him that he was being sentimental, that his own childhood had been far from idyllic; but he resisted it. He was having a day off, forgetting his problems, renewing himself.

He got to his feet, and bestowing an unwanted pat on the boy's head, made his way towards the bandstand. A concert was in progress, and Bragg paid for a deckchair and programme. It was the band of the Royal Artillery from Woolwich – and splendid they looked, too, in their scarlet and blue. He didn't recognize the music and, as there was no number displayed, he couldn't find out which item it was. No matter, it was fine stirring music. Bragg wondered how many young men would be disposed by it to take the Queen's shilling. He settled back in his chair, and let the music wash over him, his eyelids heavy. It was really a very fine bandstand, the elaborate cast-iron railings around the plinth picked out in gold leaf, the roof on its slender pillars pinched up in the middle like a pagoda. In a way, the wrought-iron spike that surmounted it was too elaborate, too fussy . . . What was the term for it?. . . He was sure he knew . . . 'Finial', was that it? . . . No, that was masonry . . . it was more like . . .

When Bragg awoke, the bandstand was empty, the shadows of the trees long across the grass. He got stiffly to his feet, and saw that the last of the audience was drifting away. The onset of evening had not brought any appreciable lessening of the heat, and his heavy slumber had left him dull and irritable. He decided he was hungry. After all, he had breakfasted at six, and his lunch had consisted of one very small meat pie. He'd have a snack now, and get his landlady, Mrs Jenks, to make him some supper when he got back. He settled for a beef sandwich, and a pint of beer. Then, his good humour restored, he sauntered slowly down the hill towards the park gate. The sun was sinking behind the tall elms, and the grassy area by the gate was deserted. All the children, and their hoops and balls, had been gathered up and carted off by impatient parents, back to the safety of their mean dwellings. A solitary park attendant was methodically spearing pieces of newspaper, that flapped like seagulls in a breath of air, and putting discarded beer bottles into a sack over his shoulder.

The streets were virtually empty now, as Bragg made his way back to the river. There wasn't a boat at the pier, and a sizeable queue had formed there. At a guess, it would fill one steamer, with a few left over for the next. He stood in line for a while, but there was no sign of a boat coming to fetch them. The temperature must still be in the high seventies. Over the road a publican had placed tables on the pavement. A few men were sitting there drinking, and exchanging banter with people in the queue. Bragg shifted his weight from one tired foot to the other, then glanced back. Only five other people had joined the line behind him. He'd easily get the next boat but one.

Abruptly he left the queue, and was soon relaxing with a glass of beer in his hand. The trouble with the steamers was that they'd get several of them down here for five o'clock, and when the rush home began, they'd all leave at once. So if you missed that lot, you had to take your chance. The blue was leaching out of the sky now, leaving it ash-grey. In an hour it would be dusk, and there was still no sign of a steamer. While he didn't have to account to Mrs Jenks as he would to a wife, there were limits, nevertheless. And since his work often kept him out to all hours, he made a point of being regular when he could. He would have enjoyed the trip back up the river, but it would have to be the train. At least, he'd be able to keep the windows open, to create some draught. He got to his feet, and walked through the shadowed streets to the railway station.

When he got there, the platform was empty. He felt an irrational fear that he had come to the wrong one; and equally irrationally, he was reassured when a group of men followed him shortly afterwards. He strolled up and down the platform, reviewing the events of the day in mellow contentment. It wasn't real countryside. Nothing that was deliberately set aside for people to tramp over could be . . . at least not the intensively farmed countryside he'd been brought up in. But it gave them a glimmer of how England had been in the time of their forebears. But he was sentimentalizing again. Most of the people he'd seen today would be glad to get back to their dingy streets. People were always glad to get home. He heard the clatter of the signal arm dropping, and looked down the line at the squat bulk of the engine as it coasted towards them. He walked to the end of the platform, so that he would have less far to walk when he got off at London Bridge. Indeed, he walked so far that the engine came to a stop at his shoulder, and he had to go back some yards to find an empty compartment.

He dropped the window at each end, to allow the maximum of draught to develop, then sat in a corner facing the engine. The porter was just blowing his whistle, when the door to his compartment was flung open, and a crowd of men scrambled in. They sat down in an orderly way, and though they seemed to know one another, they exchanged only the scantest of conversation. One or two of them glanced at Bragg cursorily, and then disregarded him. Nevertheless, he felt irritated by their presence. He had looked forward to a journey back on his own, to prolonging the mood of fulfilment. Now it had been shattered. He gazed disconsolately out of the window, at the soot-encrusted houses as they slipped past. When the train stopped at Deptford he glanced across, but they showed no sign of leaving. One of the men had poked his head out of the window, and was looking back down the platform. Probably watching the guard wave his flag. Then he made some remark over his shoulder, and suddenly all the men got to their feet and trooped out of the compartment. The last of them was about to close the door, when he hesitated, then opened it again and handed up a young woman. She settled herself, panting, diagonally opposite Bragg.

'You only just caught it,' he remarked, as the train moved off.

'Yes,' she gasped. 'I really shouldn't run like this, it's bad for me.' She began to fumble at the waist band of her skirt, and he averted his eyes. Suddenly she let out a moan, and as Bragg swung round, began to scream. She was clutching her chest, her face twisted in pain. Bragg started to his feet.

'No! No!' she cried, tearing at her blouse, and writhing on her seat in agony. 'Oh, please . . . please stop it!'

Bragg strode across, and perching on the seat by her, put his arm on her shoulders to comfort her. 'Where does it hurt?' he asked.

She appeared not to know he was there, and now began wrenching at her shift, a frenzied 'ah . . . h' rising to a screech. In exasperation Bragg could hear people knocking on the wall from the next compartment. A fat lot of good that would do! It seemed to Bragg that the girl was having some sort of turn; her face was ashen and her eyes wild. He leaned forward to speak to her, and she suddenly lunged at him, scratching his face, shouting 'Stop! Stop! Leave me alone!' He jumped to his feet and grabbed both her wrists, lest she do herself an injury. However demented she became, there was no point in trying to stop the train. It would be far better to let it go on to London Bridge, and get her to a doctor . . . She had stopped struggling now, though her screams continued unabated. He held her still, and was thankful to feel the train slowing for the station. Then, just as it stopped, she slid her body forward off the edge of the seat, and wrapped her legs around his thighs, at the same time renewing her struggles to break his grip.

Bragg was aware of the door being flung open. 'Get a doctor!' he cried. 'She's ill.'

'Help! Help!' shouted the girl, in a distraught voice. 'He's been interfering with me.'

Bragg started back incredulously, and stared down at the girl half lying on the seat, her skirts pushed up round her thighs, one stockinged knee on either side of his legs.

'He's been trying to rape her,' cried an angry voice from outside.

'Get hold of him!' shouted another.

Bragg hastily dropped her wrists. 'I tell you she's been having a mad fit,' he shouted. 'Get a doctor!'

There was a crowd now, at the open door, clearly intent on seizing him; and Bragg saw with relief a policeman forcing his way through the press.

'Constable!' he called. 'This young woman needs a doctor.'

At this the girl burst into hysterical sobs. 'He tried to rape me,' she cried.

Bragg realized the absurd tableau they presented, and stepped backwards out of her encircling legs. This brought a howl from the crowd.

'He's going to get away!'

'I'm not,' cried Bragg. 'I'm a police officer, and this young woman's wrong in the head.'

'Then you just stay there,' said the constable firmly, 'while we get her out.' He entered the compartment and put a hand under her shoulder. 'Come on, miss, try to get to your feet.'

She rose unsteadily, and was helped down to the platform, where she was enveloped in the embrace of a stout red-faced woman.

The constable turned to Bragg. 'You say she was having a fit?' he remarked. 'She seems to have scratched your face.'

'Yes, she did,' said Bragg.

'And your wrists?'

Bragg involuntarily raised his hands, there was a crisp click, and he found himself staring dumbfounded at the handcuffs pinioning him.

'Get down on the platform, so the train can go,' ordered the constable. 'And don't try to get away.'

'You've got it wrong,' cried Bragg wildly.

'Maybe, but I prefer to have you safe, while I sort it out.' The constable gestured to the red-faced woman. 'Will you take the young lady into the waiting-room, madam?'

'Indeed I will!' she asserted, and the girl hobbled painfully away with her.

The constable turned to the crowd. 'Now you people, if you saw anything of the incident, please wait here a moment longer; if you didn't, go home. There's nothing more to see.'

There was a desultory cheer from the crowd, and it began to disperse.

'Come on, we might as well put you in the waiting-room, too,' said the constable, giving Bragg a shove. 'Now you sit in that corner and don't move. I'll be back when I've got the witnesses' particulars.'

Bragg sat dumbly in the corner, staring at the still sobbing girl, while the woman glared at him belligerently. He couldn't comprehend . . . it had all happened so quickly. How could she make such an accusation, when she knew full well it wasn't true? She didn't seem in pain now, nor deranged. So why didn't she tell them what had really happened?

The constable re-entered, and crossed to the girl, who was dabbing at her tear-streaked face with a handkerchief. 'I'm going to send you to hospital,' he said. 'And you can tell me what happened tomorrow morning, when you're feeling better.'

'I . . . can't,' sobbed the girl. 'My mother won't know where I am.'

'Don't worry,' said the constable soothingly. 'We'll get word to her. What's your name?'

'Mary Jessop.'

'And where do you live?'

'Twelve, St Mark's Road, Kennington.'

'Right you are,' said the constable, writing carefully in his note book. 'Madam, I wonder if I can ask you to accompany the young lady to Guy's hospital. I'm afraid there don't seem to be any cabs, but it's only just down the road.'

'I'll be glad to,' said the red-faced woman emphatically.

'Tell the sister on duty what's happened, and ask her to examine Miss Jessop. Tell her I'll be round first thing tomorrow to take a statement.'

The woman put her arm around the girl's waist, and escorted her, limping, to the door.

'Well now, sir,' said the constable, turning to Bragg.

'Don't bloody "sir" me,' said Bragg savagely. 'I'm a policeman too.'

'That's as may be, sir. But for the moment, we're just going to take a walk.' He unlocked the handcuff from one of Bragg's wrists, and snapped it on his own. 'Come on,' he said.

They pushed through the curious crowds into the main hall of the station, its gas lamps glowing, then out into the darkened streets. They walked in silence, with the measured tread of a policeman on his beat, but Bragg could feel the tension in the constable, alert for any attempt to escape. The lights of the Dover Castle were garish in the gloom. It looked a fine new pub, and he'd promised himself a drink in it, some time. He'd probably never feel like it now. Then they were in Borough High Street, and crossing to the Metropolitan Police station. To Bragg it had all the quality of a nightmare. Even feeling the unrelenting pull of the handcuff, it was unreal. He knew he must wake up soon, but somehow he couldn't bring it about. The dream was destined to work itself out.

'Constable Fitch, of the railway police,' announced his captor.

'Oh, yes?' said the duty sergeant laconically.

'I want to charge this man.'

'Petty offence?' asked the sergeant.

'No, felony.'

The sergeant stooped down, and produced a charge book from under his desk.

'Name?' he asked.

'Joseph Bragg.'

'Address?'

'Eleven, Tan House Lane, London EC.' As he said it, Bragg knew that he was even then asleep in the back room on the second floor.

'Occupation?'

'Sergeant of police, City of London force,' said Bragg.

The duty sergeant cocked an eyebrow at the constable, then stolidly wrote it down.

'What's he charged with, then?' he asked.

'Attempted rape will do for now.'

'Indeed!'

'When will he come up?' asked the constable.

'It can't be before Monday morning, now.'

'Right. I'll be along. What time?'

'Say ten o'clock – the magistrates' court, over the road.'

'I know it.' The constable scribbled his signature at the foot of the page, unlocked the handcuffs, and strode out.

'Fred!' called the sergeant. 'Lock this one up, will you?'

Bragg tried to struggle against his dream. This was beyond reason, beyond even unreason. He simply had to wake up . . . A hand was under his elbow, he was propelled gently down a gloomy corridor, there was a rattle of keys, he felt a push in the small of his back, and a door clanged shut behind him.

6

'We'd better push it out of the stable, before we start the engine,' said Morton. 'It's a bit erratic till the ignition tube gets really hot, and I prefer to have plenty of space around.'

'Are you certain it is safe?' asked Helga.

'Of course it is,' said Emily briskly. 'Daddy drives it all the time.'

'I have never been so close to a horseless carriage before,' said Karl excitedly. 'Might I be allowed to drive it?'

'If you still want to, after the picnic,' said Morton with a smile. 'Will you turn that wheel by your left hand, Karl? It releases the brakes on the back wheels.'

The men pushed the vehicle on to the gravelled drive.

'Right, Parker,' said Morton. 'You can strap the basket on the back.'

'A Cannstatt Daimler, eh?' remarked Karl, peering at the medallion by the front wheel. 'Do you mean to say that you had to go to Germany for it?'

'At the moment there's not much alternative. Just a second, while I switch on the petroleum.'

'I know what it is like!' exclaimed Helga in delight. 'It is just like a travelling four-poster bed!'

'It's got the same body as a victoria,' Emily countered.

'Ah yes, but the canopy held up by four pillars, and the valance around it, and the curtains to pull. It is the first motorized bed!' Helga laughed merrily.

'If you ladies will sit facing the back,' said Morton, 'and you, Karl, on my left, we'll be off.'

'I hope you do not have to draw the curtains at the back,' said Helga, 'or we will not even see where we have been!'

'Are you all settled?' asked Morton.

'Yes,' shouted Karl. 'Ah, this is the horn, I see. I shall blow it on all our journey.' He pressed the bulb experimentally, and Helga threw up her hands in pretended apprehension.

Morton cranked the engine round, till it fired, then climbed into the driver's seat. 'I'm not as adept as my father at driving this contraption,' he said with a smile. 'So if it jerks a little as we move off, you won't have to mind. Helga, I shall have to push this lever towards you to engage the drive belt. Would you hold your legs to one side? Otherwise I shall be in danger of catching them.'

Helga gave him a conspiratorial smile and gathered her skirts together. 'Is that good?' she asked.

'Fine. Right, Karl, an appropriate fanfare on the horn, please!'

With a lurch to right and to left, they began to move down the drive, the engine throbbing evenly.

'This is magnificent!' shouted Karl. 'How quickly will it go?'

'They say it will reach sixteen miles an hour, but we are only allowed to drive it at four miles an hour in the country, and two in towns.'

'Ah, the absurdity of the English.'

'It's the short-sightedness of officials and politicians every-where. My father is creating a devil of a fuss to get it altered. He's even written to the War Office, recommending that the army should develop them for transport.'

'Militarism against eccentricity,' exclaimed Karl. 'I wonder which will win? The generals, I suppose. It is usually so with the British.'

'Karl!' chided Helga. 'You forget that Sir Henry is a general also.'

'My dear cousin,' replied Karl blandly, 'you also forget that I was on the same staircase as James for three years, when we were at Trinity. Such intimacy confers privileges. And as for Emily, I love her as a sister.'

They swept off the gravel and on to the rutted country road.

'To where are we going?' called Helga. 'I have difficulty in keeping my hat and my seat also on so rough a road.'

'About a mile down the lane,' replied Emily. 'Just behind

those trees. There's a lovely meadow by the river, where we used to swim when we were children.'

'Ah, yes . . . Karl told me you were half American.'

'Can't you swim?' demanded Emily scornfully.

'Good heavens, no! My mother would never have allowed anything so unladylike. In any case, there has always been someone to carry me.' Helga darted a mischievous glance at Morton.

'I see the turning,' shouted Karl, and honked vigorously on the horn.

In a moment they were bumping over the short grass, and coming to an abrupt halt by the river bank. Karl unstrapped the picnic basket, and Emily began to lay out the food on a white tablecloth.

'Ah, lobster!' cried Karl, and seizing a claw, waltzed around with it. 'The apogee of my ambition – to sit on the bank of an English river, with my greatest friend, and two ladies whose beauty ravishes the senses . . . and to eat lobster!'

'That is far from *galant*,' Helga reproved him.

'On the contrary, it is the highest compliment a man can pay – to the lobster, for the ladies need no compliments.'

'Go away, Karl,' said Helga with a smile. 'You are a foolish man.'

'If you will pass me that last morsel, cousin, instead of concealing it for yourself, I will tell you about the picnics we used to have on the Backs at Cambridge.'

'No, no! Please don't. You have told me so many times already.'

'Have I? Ah, well. Can you blame me for being an anglophile, on such a perfect occasion? Often I wish that I had been born British . . . Indeed I seem to have a closer affinity with almost any nation of Europe than the pompous, stuffy Germans; and yet I have the misfortune to be one.' He intercepted a startled look from Emily. 'Do not concern yourself about Helga,' he said with a smile. 'She was born in Vienna. It is in the highest degree unlikely that the Viennese are Austrian at all. They are certainly not German.' He rose to his feet. 'Emily, my dear, your hospitality seduces me from my duty. I promised my masters in Berlin an account of farming in

Kent, and I must send them something. Now, if we were to cross the river by the stepping-stones, and walk along that path, I surely could truthfully claim first-hand acquaintance with harvesting cereals, and pasturing cattle. Are you coming, you two?'

'No!' protested Helga, as Emily rose to her feet. 'It is much too hot. We will stay here. And Emily . . . make sure he carries you across the river.'

'He'd probably drop me,' retorted Emily with a perfunctory smile, taking Karl's arm.

'Karl is very fond of Emily, is he not?' said Helga. 'He seems very happy here.'

'When we were at Cambridge, he was almost one of the family. Mother was delighted to see him again. She won't mind, however long you want to stay.'

'But you must return to London, tonight?'

'I'm afraid so.'

A momentary look of disappointment flitted across her face, then she smiled impishly at him. 'For what reason did you choose so eccentric a vehicle as the travelling bed?' she asked.

'It was entirely my father's choice, though no doubt you would think the canopy somewhat feminine.'

'I thought it was the influence of your *amoureuse*.'

'I'm not encumbered in that way,' said Morton with a smile. 'In fact, it was largely for my brother's benefit. I suppose you weren't aware that I have an elder brother?'

'No. That I had not realized.'

'He was with the army in the Sudan, and was badly wounded. He is paralysed from the waist down, and his wound has never really healed.'

'James, I am sorry.' She reached out her hand to touch him briefly.

'Mother and father foster the idea that he is in charge of the farming,' went on Morton. 'He isn't, of course. He sits in his room with maps of the fields painstakingly hatched in, to show where the various crops are; and the bailiff comes up every day to take instructions, then goes off and does what he thinks best. It's a situation where no one is really in charge. Anyway, from time to time, when the weather is good, they wrap Edwin in

57

blankets and prop him in the corner of the Daimler, and father drives him round the estate.'

'And the canopy, and curtains?' asked Helga.

'To keep off the wind and rain. If he caught a cold, it might develop into pneumonia, and he could die.'

Helga looked at him speculatively. 'And in the meantime, you play at policemen?'

'Something like that.'

'Life can seem very cruel, James, but I think our destiny is worked out for us in advance, and it is without point to struggle against it.'

'Do you believe in predestination?' asked Morton, curious.

'Not precisely. I suppose I believe that good must triumph over evil – that is my convent education influencing me . . . No, it is not even so simple. I think that in any situation you can fight against your fate, and become embroiled deeper and deeper. Or you can accept it, and look for the good in it, as you have done.'

'I gather you have had your share of personal tragedy.'

Helga smiled reflectively. 'Yes. And yet at this moment, I wonder if what has happened to me is the ultimate tragedy it seemed. You should not believe what you hear about the gay, abandoned life of Vienna. I was brought up in a strict Catholic household, and grew to hate it. Not for me, dancing till dawn. You may not believe it, but I reached the summit of my social experience when I visited the von Friedeburgs in London, and Karl invited me to your May Ball. It was so exciting! I've treasured the memory ever since.'

'Trinity would be flattered at being preferred to Vienna,' smiled Morton.

'But it was meant to be, it was part of my destiny,' went on Helga. 'On my return home, I found the environment even more stifling than before. So when Herr Speidel asked for my hand in marriage, I made myself so agreeable, that my father assented.'

'I thought your husband was an officer in the German army,' said Morton.

'No, he was a clerk at their embassy in Vienna. Perhaps that is unfair to him. He was a very senior and distinguished official, or my father would never have entertained his suit. But I was twenty, and he was forty-six . . . For a time I felt emancipated, then, a mere six months after our marriage, my husband was posted back to Berlin. I went with him of course. It seemed to me that my particular fate was dealing with me most cruelly, for society in Berlin is unbelievably rigid, and there was no one of my age in my husband's family. I can tell you, I longed to be back in Vienna. Then suddenly my husband was posted overseas – to Africa.'

'What part?'

'Windhoek, in South West Africa. He was the administrator of the protectorate. I am sure that he was very clever, and very brave; but he was not in a position to overrule the military, and he trusted their judgement too readily. When the Herero natives rose against us two years ago, he felt that he could negotiate with them about their grievances. The army guaranteed his safety, so he went with a detachment of soldiers to meet their chiefs – and they were all massacred.'

'It wouldn't be the first time, in a colony, that soldiers misread the situation,' said Morton.

'The government at home proclaimed him to be a hero, who had sacrificed his life for the Fatherland – but he wasn't . . . And even if it were true, what use is a dead hero to a woman?'

'And what happened to you?' asked Morton sympathetically.

'I was shipped back to Berlin, and received into the bosom of my late husband's family. That meant the start of a lifetime of decorous widowhood – at the age of twenty-three. It seemed to me the final malignity of fate. And then I heard that the von Friedeburgs were back in Germany. Even the Speidels' social code couldn't prevent me from visiting my own aunt and uncle. It was like dawn breaking, a new beginning . . . And here I am sitting by this beautiful river, talking to you.'

Morton pulled a blade of grass, and chewed on the white stalk. 'I wish I had a clearer memory of that May Ball,' he said.

'After all the champagne I'm not surprised it is blurred,' she laughed.

'The following year, another of Karl's cousins came. Let me see . . . Magda someone . . . Whatever is her name?'

Helga looked puzzled.

'Magda Brun, James.' Karl came from behind, and threw himself to the ground. 'She's my cousin on my father's side: a worthy German *hausfrau* nowadays. I doubt if Helga even knows of her existence. Well now, James, Emily and I have concluded – without too much reluctance on my part – that my knowledge of English farming is scanty in the extreme. I would therefore wish to inflict myself on the hospitality of your family for, we think, a week.'

'Excellent! I'm sure my parents will be delighted.'

'And you persist in this stupidity of going back to London, to look under stones for murderers?'

'I'm afraid so.'

'Then, James, you are a traitor to your class!' Karl suddenly sprang at Morton, knocking him on to his back, and seizing his wrists. 'I can understand a man being a traitor to his country,' he grunted, 'but never to his class.'

Morton squirmed and struggled, but the suddenness of the attack had taken him by surprise; his arms were at once too far apart and too near the ground for him to exert any leverage. He raised one shoulder from the ground and felt Karl's steely strength, as he countered with still more pressure.

'Am I right?' Karl panted. 'Do you admit you are a traitor?'

Morton glanced around, trying to keep the half-smile on his face. The way to break Karl's hold would be a sudden arching of the body. But that might catapult him into Helga; and anyway, the juvenile tussle might develop into something more serious.

'Very well,' he said. 'I admit it.'

Karl regained his feet with an agile spring, and brushed the grass from Morton's coat.

'I am sorry, my friend. I should not make amusement out of your work. How is your murder progressing?'

'There haven't been any new ones, if that's what you mean. But equally we haven't caught anyone.'

'You mean to say that your magnifying glass has not detected a single clue?'

'It's early days, yet . . . I'll tell you what, though, there's something you might be able to help us with. In the pocket of the murdered man was a luggage label with some letters on it.

Here, I'll write them on this bit of paper.' Morton carefully printed the words COFIWCH DIC PENDERYN, as close to the original form as he could remember, and handed it to Karl. 'I thought it might be in some Balkan dialect or other.'

'None that I recognize, though I would not claim to be an authority. Is it in cypher, do you think?'

'We don't know.'

'But why the label? Do you think the writer meant to tie it on to something?'

'You're forgetting that it was found in the pocket of one of our constables.'

'Oh, it's all beyond me,' Karl said with a shrug, and handed the paper back to Morton; then he checked. 'You are certain the letters were in those three groups?' he asked.

'Yes, I'm sure of that.'

'It is just that the middle group strikes a chord. It seems absurd, but when we lived in London we had a housemaid; I forget her name, Bronwen I think. She came from Cardiff, and her brother's name was Dic.'

'Welsh?' cried Morton in surprise. 'Good heavens! . . . I wonder . . . '

7

Bragg was slumped despondently against the cell wall. For two nights he had slept very little, apprehensive that his nightmare might take another diabolical twist. Throughout the whole of Sunday he had tried to recall every detail of the happenings of the previous evening; but in his jaded condition he could hardly distinguish between remembered fact and speculation. By nightfall, the antics of the young woman had assumed secondary importance, and he had become obsessed with the phalanx of silent men jumping into and out of his compartment.

Once or twice he had thought of escaping from the whole hideous predicament. The police station was built much like an ordinary house; his cell was at the back, on the ground floor, with vertical bars covering the window. He'd come across stronger ones in an upstairs nursery. But what was the good? It would be seen as clear proof of his guilt – and reasonably enough. He'd have taken the same view himself. Anyway, he wouldn't be able to take up his former life again; and if he went home to Turner's Puddle, the Dorset police would be on the lookout for him. He might as well go through with it . . . Blast it! He was innocent, after all.

Soon they would be coming for him, to take him to the magistrates' court. He scratched at his two-day growth of beard. A fine sight he would look. He stood up, and slapped ineffectually at his crumpled clothes. He'd asked for a razor that morning, and the constable had laughed and told him he should know better . . . At least they seemed to accept that he was a policeman. There was a kind of cautious sympathy about them, a mixture of compassion and apprehension, that a copper should be charged with such a crime. Yet it went further than that. In their eyes he was already guilty. That was what they desired. Just as soon wish that the villain in a melodrama would turn out a saint, as want him acquitted. There'd be no excitement in that . . . And yet they treated him well. They'd even sent out for some boiled haddock for his breakfast. Bragg had heard that the more spectacular murderers, such as Dr Palmer, were treated with respect by the prison warders, even with awe . . . till they were topped. Well, at least it couldn't come to that. But prison was bad enough . . . His mind shied away from the implications, and he began to go through the facts again. The trouble was that if you tried to put them – force them, rather – into a pattern, it was so fantastic that no one would believe it. Yet if there was no pattern, he had become the victim of a mischance against which the odds were incalculably high . . . Then again, accepting the girl was going to have a crazy turn, somebody was likely to be around, so why not him? The girl was the key figure; he must concentrate on her. She'd accused him of attempting to rape her, and she was lying. That was another crucial fact. But what had she gained by it? She hadn't demanded money from him, so what had she achieved? . . . unless her object had been to get him arrested. But that was absurd, he'd never clapped eyes on her before . . . But was it?

There was a rattle at the door, and Bragg glimpsed an eye at the peep-hole; then the key turned in the lock, and a watchful constable entered.

'Right, we're off to court,' he announced. 'Sorry, but I'll have to put the darbies on you.' He produced a pair of handcuffs from his pocket, and closed one on his own wrist.

'Oh, God!' exclaimed Bragg, in disgust. 'I'm not going to try to escape, lad.'

'Now you know it's got to be done,' the constable said roughly. 'With what you're charged with, we can't take chances.'

Bragg held out his wrist with a sigh, and heard the handcuff snap shut.

'It's only over the road,' said the constable.

'I know. I've given evidence there more than once.'

'Have you? Well, it'll be a bit different this time.'

Bragg let the jibe go over his head. He was more affected by the curious stares of the passers-by. It would add a little spice to their morning's shopping. They'd whisper excitedly to their neighbours how they'd seen a man handcuffed to a policeman, crossing Borough Road.

It was only when Bragg was standing by the door leading to the back of the dock, that the constable removed the handcuff. He could hear a half-articulated gabble from inside the court, followed by the noise of people sitting down. So the court was now in session. He glanced to his right, and saw a flight of stone steps leading down to a strong iron grille. He wondered if he would find himself in those cells at the end of the proceedings . . . He must remember to ask for bail.

Then an aged usher poked his head through the door. 'Is that Joseph Bragg you have there?' he asked the constable.

'Yes, sir,'

'You can bring him in, now.'

Bragg stumbled up a short flight of stairs, and emerged at the back of the dock. There, a uniformed constable motioned him to the bench at the front, where he sat down. The bewigged magistrate was leaning over his desk, conversing with the clerk below him. At the back of the court Bragg could see the constable who had arrested him. On the barristers' benches in the well of the court was a solitary figure dressed in an immaculate frock coat. Probably the prosecuting solicitor retained by the police, thought Bragg.

The clerk turned from the magistrate with a smile, then adjusted his gown and the white tabs at his throat.

'Joseph Bragg?' he asked.

'Stand up,' hissed the constable behind him.

Bragg rose hastily. 'Yes,' he said.

'You have been charged,' went on the clerk in a conversational tone, 'that on Saturday the twenty-second of August eighteen ninety-one, you did feloniously attempt to rape a female person, to whit Mary Jessop. Now this is an indictable offence, which cannot be tried in this court. Our function is therefore ministerial only, and any trial must take place in a higher court. Do you understand?'

'Yes, sir.'

The clerk sat down, inexplicably it seemed to Bragg, for his homily had not even dealt with the court's function properly. It proved, however, to be the cue for the magistrate himself to begin.

'Mr Bragg,' he said in a high-pitched voice, 'I am told that you are a sergeant of police.'

'Yes, your worship.'

The look of distaste on the magistrate's face suggested that he found it difficult to believe. 'In that case,' he went on, 'I will make my remarks as brief as possible. If there is anything you do not understand, you should ask me.'

'Yes, sir.'

'Now these are merely preliminary proceedings, and if the case runs its full course, we shall be sending depositions to the assize court, which will contain the statements made by the complainant, the witnesses and yourself. These will form the documents on which your trial proper will be based. As a police officer yourself, you will realize that in the short space of time since the alleged offence, the police have not been able to interview all their witnesses, or to complete their investigations. Accordingly I shall limit the proceedings this morning to considering the information that has been laid, and then I shall adjourn the court for a few days – do you understand?'

'Yes, your worship.'

'Very well, you may sit down . . . Yes, Mr Philpot?'

The frock-coated man rose to his feet. 'Your worship, I am appearing for the prosecution in this case,' he announced in a deep vibrant voice. He was a handsome man, in his mid-forties, with an easy manner. Bragg surmised that he had been too poor, or too ill-connected to make a career at the bar, and had settled for police prosecutions as the next best thing. Certainly he seemed to regard this court as his stage, looking about him at the empty benches for a non-existent audience.

'This charge is based on an information laid by the complainant, Miss Mary Jessop,' he went on. 'I have it here for the court.' He passed to the clerk a sheet of paper, closely covered with handwriting. The clerk glanced at it briefly, then turned and handed it up to the magistrate. The latter picked up his spectacles from the desk, perched them on his nose, and having taken a preliminary stare at Bragg, commenced to read. The prosecuting solicitor seemed to be experiencing the unease of a mediocre actor, in mid-stage for a spell, with nothing to say. He shifted from one foot to the other, put one hand in his trouser pocket, fiddled with the documents in front of him, even looked round at Bragg with a half-smile.

Eventually the magistrate looked up. 'My first concern,' he said, 'is as to whether these proceedings have been brought in the correct court.'

'Your worship?' rumbled the solicitor.

'It would be inconsiderate in the extreme, if we were to aggregate to ourselves in this court cases which properly belong elsewhere.' The magistrate allowed himself a thin smile, which was no doubt meant as a signal for the court officials to appreciate his sally. 'It appears from this document,' he fluted, 'that the offence is alleged to have occurred on a railway train travelling from Deptford to London Bridge station. Now Deptford is within the jurisdiction of the Greenwich division, and since the assault is alleged to have begun immediately after the train left Deptford station, I would have thought that the offence was committed within the jurisdiction of the Greenwich court.'

The clerk reached for one of the volumes laid, spine uppermost, in a row along the edge of his desk.

'Your worship,' said Philpot, 'I would submit that the offence was taking place all the time during the journey from Deptford to London Bridge, and therefore it must equally have been taking place within the jurisdiction of this court.'

'In fact, of course,' replied the magistrate, 'the *locus* of the offence was throughout a particular railway compartment, which just happened to be travelling along a particular line at the time . . . Are you saying, Mr Philpot, that, if we accept for a moment that an attempt was made to rape the complainant, then the attempt colours the whole of the journey, wherever the physical interference may have occurred?'

'Yes, your worship.'

'This is hardly satisfactory. Let us suppose that a man attempted to rape a woman while within the boundary of the Greenwich division, and succeeded after the train had crossed into the Southwark division. Now there are theoretically two separate charges, the attempt, and the rape itself; and one could argue that the attempt would be triable in Greenwich, and the rape in Southwark.'

'In practice, your worship, the lesser charge would be subsumed into the greater,' said Philpot.

'Perhaps. But it is equally possible that the prosecution might want to prefer them as alternative charges . . . Let me put another possibility to you. A man might press his attentions on a woman as soon as the train left Deptford, and desist before it crossed the boundary. Would it be right for him to be brought to trial anywhere but Greenwich?'

'Your worship,' Philpot said diffidently, 'I was prosecuting here in a recent case, where a man who had been travelling first-class on a train, while only in possession of a second-class ticket, was apprehended at London Bridge station. Mr Wyndor, who was trying that case, did not seem to share your worship's concern about jurisdiction.'

'This case,' the magistrate observed drily, 'is not about railway tickets.'

The clerk rose to his feet. 'There is a note in *Wigram* which appears to be relevant, your worship,' he said.

'Read it.'

' "Where any indictable offence has been committed upon any person or property in or upon any waggon, cart or other carriage, employed on any journey, whether by road or rail, or on board of any vessel upon inland waters, the offender may be required to answer for his offence in any county through which the carriage or vessel may have passed in the course of that journey or voyage." '

'Ah, yes. I see,' said the magistrate thoughtfully. 'And *a fortiori* any division of any county through which it might have passed . . . Very well, Mr Philpot, I accept that the case is within the jurisdiction of this court. Now then, we must set a date for the committal proceedings. When will you be ready?'

'Your worship, there is a great number of witnesses to interview. Perhaps I could arrange with your clerk for a suitable date.'

'Nonsense, Mr Philpot. The essence of the information is that these two people were alone in a railway compartment. I trust the police are not going to waste the time of this court with a procession of people who can say no more than that they heard cries coming from the next compartment.'

'If your worship pleases.'

'Very well. The committal proceedings will take place on Friday the twenty-eighth. That should give both sides plenty of time . . . Mr Bragg,' he turned to the dock, 'I see that you are not represented today.'

'No, your worship.'

'I would strongly advise you to retain someone to look after your interests. Have you anything you want to say now?'

Bragg's mind seemed drugged, remote from the play-acting that had been taking place. There was something he'd intended to say, something important . . .

'No, your worship . . . except that I'd like bail,' he blurted out.

'You would?' The magistrate looked at him as if he were some strange microbe wriggling in the lens of a microscope. 'The court would not normally consider bailing an alleged rapist. The overwhelming responsibility of the court must be the protection of the public.'

'Your worship,' said Bragg in as steady a voice as he could command, 'I have been a police officer for over twenty years, and there has never been the slightest suggestion of any impropriety on my part in all that time. As to the present charge, I am innocent of the offence, and shall so plead at the proper time. I am convinced that the incident was manufactured by criminals who wanted me immobilized. To remand me in custody would be to play into their hands. Finally, let me assure the court that I have no intention of absconding, and that I will provide appropriate sureties for my appearance in court.'

The magistrate looked down at the information on his desk, his brow furrowed. Then he looked up. 'Mr Philpot, what have you to say to this?'

Philpot rose smoothly to his feet. 'I am instructed not to oppose bail,' he said unctuously. 'Indeed, the police have made certain enquiries concerning the defendant, and I am instructed to place this letter before the court.' He extracted a paper from his bundle, and passed it up.

The magistrate perused it carefully, then cleared his throat. 'This is a letter from an Inspector Cotton of the City of London police. He confirms that the defendant is a police sergeant under his control, and that he has hitherto been of exemplary character. I do not know whether the implication is that Inspector Cotton is able to entertain the possibility that the present charge could be justified, or not. However, in view of the recent strictures of the Lord Chief Justice on giving bail in every possible case, I am prepared to give the defendant the benefit of the doubt. Very well, Mr Bragg, you are remanded on bail to answer the charge on the twenty-eighth day of August, on your own recognizance of twenty-five pounds.'

Bragg felt a young scapegrace again, rushing from the dame school to look for birds' nests, or sticklebacks in the brook. Of course, it was only an interruption of the proceedings, but it would give him time to find out what was behind the incident on the train. Above all, he was free, able to feel the sun on his face, not cooped up in a basement cell. The sooner he got home for a bath and a shave, the better. He'd gladly put up with Mrs Jenks's scolding over his crumpled clothes . . . But could he afford the time? He had only four days to get at the truth. It would take an hour to heat up the water in the copper, and that would be half a day gone. On impulse he stopped at a barber's shop in Cornhill. The window was decorated with sponges, shaving soap, badger-hair brushes, macassar oil. It was probably expensive. He looked above the window, where a sign proclaimed 'Toni's Hair Emporium for Gentlemen'. It sounded as if they could even sell him a wig if he needed one. He went in and took a seat by the wall. There were three barbers working there, all Italian by the look of them. They chattered brightly to their customers and to each other, as if entertainment were included in the price of the haircut. Between attacks on their customers' locks, they would snip frenetically at the empty air, as if fascinated by the crisp sound of their scissors. The man in the chair by the window was nearly finished, now. He was peering into the mirror, bestowing his approval of the barber's handiwork. Like as not, it would be the owner of the shop working in the window and by the till. Well, he should know his business. With a deft twirl, the barber swept the white cotton cover from the customer's shoulders, and brushed a few hairs from his coat collar. The man took a handful of change from his pocket, and passed over two silver coins. That was a damned generous tip! Bragg could get his hair cut for half that, at his usual place. He looked around for a price list, but there was none. The barber was now proffering the customer's tall silk hat; a stockbroker, no doubt. Oh well, he couldn't get out now, whatever it cost. Dear God! He had to find twenty-five pounds for the court. He must be mad!

'Pliz, Capitano.' Bragg removed his dusty bowler and hung it on the hat stand, then lowered himself into the barber's chair.

'And what for you zees morning, Capitano?' He had black hair parted in the middle, then plastered down in long waves across his temples, and a long drooping moustache. Bragg had seen him caricatured at the music hall, scores of times.

'Shave, please,' grunted Bragg.

'Of course, Capitano.' The barber took a clean white cover from the cupboard, and draped it over Bragg's shoulders, tucking it in carefully at the neck.

'You 'ave left ze sheep in ze dock, eh Capitano? You run to ze Eenglish wife eh? . . But first ze shave. Ees good!' He began to strop a razor, leaning into the stroke, so that the strop bowed like a hammock. He was talking to another customer now, looking anywhere but at what he was doing. One slip, and he'd slice his hand off, with that pressure. Then the barber laid the razor tenderly on a marble shelf, and rapidly worked up a lather in a cup. He moistened Bragg's face with a sponge, and began to plaster the lather over Bragg's whiskers with a brush. There was far too much of it, thought Bragg. He, himself, would work up the lather on his face; a dab of the shaving brush on the soap, and a brisk scrub around the stubble, and there was plenty of lather for a shave. He squinted down his nose at his reflection in the mirror. The barber must have been apprenticed in an ice-cream parlour. He looked more like a vanilla cornet. Then his head was pulled gently backwards till the nape of his neck rested on the chair.

'You weesh to kip ze moostache?' asked the barber.

'Yes', replied Bragg tersely.

'Eet ees not good for you. Eet maka you look old. You no lika look young for ze Eenglish wife?'

'Leave it,' growled Bragg.

'Aye aye, Capitano,' said the barber with a smile. 'Ze wife in Stockholm, or Copenhagen, or Riga, she lika ze moostache . . . Poor leetle Eenglish wife.'

He was paring away the rind of lather with long sweeps of the razor, occasionally scraping the accumulation on to the index finger of the other hand. Bragg could hardly feel the feather touch of the razor; perhaps this was what people paid for, to be smoothed and caressed and cosseted. The barber's fingers, as he moved Bragg's head from side to side, were infinitely gentle. Bragg closed his eyes, and drifted into a hedonistic languor. He could hear the barber in the distance, now chattering in Italian. Why did he think he was a seaman? Perhaps it was the growth of beard. Obviously he wasn't in uniform, but they didn't bother in some of the coasters. In his present dishevelled state, he could well have just finished a quick trip from the Baltic. Bragg heard a metallic scraping sound to the left of him. Perhaps the shave was finished . . . He hoped not; he wanted to linger below the surface of life for a little longer.

'Eet ees a leetle warm,' murmured the barber at his elbow, then suddenly Bragg's face was enveloped in scalding stifling folds, being pressed around his nose and chin. He struggled to free himself, thrashing about under the suffocating cover, fighting for breath. He lurched to his feet, tripped over the foot-rest, and went sprawling amongst the hair clippings.

'Eet ees too 'ot?' The barber looked dolefully down at him, the gently steaming towel in his hand.

Bragg scrambled to his feet in chagrin. Bloody silly exhibition he was making of himself. 'I was asleep,' he muttered.

'So sorree! So sorree!' The barber was beside himself with anguish, darting across with his brush, and scrubbing at Bragg's coat.

'Enough,' Bragg said roughly.

The barber dropped his brush, and stood beseechingly by his chair.

'Pliz,' he said.

Bragg allowed himself to be tucked up in the cotton sheet again, while the barber sponged the remaining lather from his face and dabbed it dry. Then he took a pair of scissors from the shelf and trimmed Bragg's ragged moustache.

'Ees good?' he asked, holding out a hand mirror.

'Yes,' grunted Bragg. 'How much?'

'No charge, no charge!' beamed the barber. 'Have good time wiz ze Eenglish wife . . . and come again.'

Bragg smiled, put a shilling by the till, and went out into the sunshine. He stroked his fingers over his smooth cheeks. He seemed to be experiencing the worst and the best today. When all this was over, he'd go to Toni's and have the lot – shave, shampoo, haircut, maybe even a manicure . . . well, perhaps he'd draw the line at that. But first he'd work to do. He hurried through the courtyard at Old Jewry, and went up the stairs at a run.

There was nothing on his desk. He'd expected at least a brief note on the results of the operation early Sunday morning. He wanted to follow that up, before he turned his attention to the girl. Perhaps Morton might know. He turned towards the door, just as it was opened by an apologetic desk sergeant.

'Sorry, Joe . . . '

Bragg remembered the startled look on his face as he'd entered. 'What is it, Ted?'

'Inspector Cotton said you was to go and see him, if you came in.'

'Right. Is he in now, d'you know?'

'He was a minute ago. I saw him come out of the commissioner's room.'

'Fine.' At least it would give him the chance to thank Cotton for his letter. He'd still be in a cell, but for that. He went along the landing and tapped on Cotton's door.

'Sit down, Bragg.' Cotton clasped his hands behind his head, and leaned back in his chair. He contemplated Bragg in silence for some moments.

'Well now,' he said. 'What's all this about?'

'I gather you heard about the incident from the railway police.'

'I did, indeed. I was dragged into the office at eight o'clock on a fine Sunday morning for a long telephonic conversation with one of their inspectors.' He didn't sound particularly mad about it, thought Bragg. Indeed his tone bordered on the genial. Well, let them have their quiet chuckle, as long as he could get it sorted out.

'I've thought about it a good bit, you can imagine,' Bragg went on. 'It's too long a shot for it to be an accident. Someone had me set, I'm sure of that.'

'Hmn.' Cotton looked at the ceiling for a moment, then sat up straight. 'The question is, what happens now?' he said briskly.

'I'm going to investigate the girl's background. She's got to be a fraud.'

'That's not possible.'

'But she must be,' protested Bragg. 'Every word she said was a lie. She must be the weak link. I'd like to pull Thompson off the Foster murder for a couple of days to do the leg-work.'

'You don't understand me, Bragg.' There was a hint of amusement in the set of Cotton's mouth. 'It's not possible, because you're suspended.'

'Suspended?' echoed Bragg in disbelief.

'That's what I said. The commissioner decided to suspend you on full pay, pending the outcome of your trial. Even you must realize, Bragg, that we can't have an officer who's on remand for rape, going about investigating other crimes. It would undermine people's respect for the police.'

'But . . . what about your letter to the court?' stammered Bragg in dismay.

'You don't think we'd let a tuppeny-ha'penny force like the railway police hold one of our men, do you?'

'But I didn't bloody do it!' cried Bragg in exasperation. 'Can't you see? It must be tied up with some case I'm on here.'

'We shan't overlook the possibility,' said Cotton smoothly. 'All your cases will be kept going. Your rape charge is in the hands of the railway police, of course.' There was now a distinct gleam of triumph in his eyes.

'Fat lot of liaison there'll be between the two forces,' said Bragg bitterly.

73

'Arrangements exist, Bragg. You'd be surprised.'

'And if I'm found guilty?'

'That would be up to the judge, of course. But he'd hardly be more lenient to a policeman than anyone else . . . often it's the reverse.' Cotton clearly contemplated the possibility with equanimity. 'Almost certainly you would lose your pension as well – but then, you haven't got any dependents, have you?'

Bragg tiptoed up the steps from the street to the front door of the terraced house where he lodged. Normally he would have gone down the area steps to Mrs Jenks in the kitchen, but now he wanted to be alone and think. He put his latchkey carefully in the lock, and eased open the door. It was surprising how much more noise you seemed to make when you were trying to be quiet. Stepping inside, he gently closed the door, and turned to find Mrs Jenks emerging from her sitting-room, a duster in her hand.

'Wherever have you been, Mr Bragg?' she admonished him in her high-pitched plaintive voice. 'I've not set eyes on you since Saturday morning, and you said you wasn't working.'

'I'm sorry, Mrs Jenks,' said Bragg dejectedly.

'That's two dinners I've cooked, and had to throw away.'

'I'm sorry. I was detained.'

'Well, you could have let me know. How is a body supposed to look after you, if you never say whether you're coming home or not?'

'I shall be at home for the rest of today, at any rate. If anybody wants me, I'm in bed.' She made way reluctantly for him, indignation quivering in every line of her plump body, as he pushed past her, and, running up the flight of stairs to the floor above, gained his bedroom.

He considered stripping off and donning his nightshirt, but his weary body didn't feel up to it; so, closing the curtains, he went to bed in his shirt. He'd expected to drop off to sleep immediately, but two nights on the plank bed in the cell had left his body sore and aching, and he couldn't get comfortable. His mind, too, was flitting about restlessly, flirting with trivialities, avoiding the overwhelming reality that his life had been shattered. In the half-light he watched a spider lower itself from the curtain rail on a thread of gossamer. It wouldn't last long; Mrs Jenks was a terror for cobwebs. He remembered being told by an old lag how they kept spiders as pets in prison, how they would catch flies, pull off their wings, pop them living into the spider's web, and watch . . . Strange, really, that a convict should gain pleasure from watching the fly being bundled up in silk, and imprisoned in a corner of the web – a kind of death cell – till the spider was hungry.

He turned over, towards the wall. There was a photograph of his wife there, taken not long before she'd died. When he first took lodgings here, he'd hung it on the wall, so that it seemed she was looking down at him. He scarcely looked at it nowadays. He studied it briefly. The face was tense from the effort of keeping still, and fuzzy because it had been enlarged so much. It wasn't really like her at all . . . She'd been so proud and pleased when he'd joined the police. It was as well she was dead. Cotton was right, he didn't have any dependents, it didn't really matter. He put his head under the bedclothes, and drifted into sleep.

He was awakened by a loud knocking on the door, and Mrs Jenks came into the room.

'Mr Bragg, you have a visitor,' she said. 'He's waiting downstairs.'

'Who is it?'

'A policeman.'

A sudden panic gripped him. 'What's his name?'

'I forget. That nice young man you've brought here before.' She crossed to the window and jerked back the curtains. 'It's time you got up anyway, you'll never sleep tonight.' She caught sight of his coat and trousers lying in a heap on the floor. 'Really!' she exclaimed. 'What a sight these will be! It's like running after a child, trying to keep you decent. Now you put on some other clothes, and I'll give these a good brush.'

Bragg found Morton perched uncomfortably on the horsehair sofa in his sitting-room. As Bragg entered he sprang to his feet, and squeezed his hand warmly. 'I wanted to say how sorry I am at what's happened,' he blurted out boyishly.

'Thanks, lad.' Bragg sank into his chair by the empty grate.

'It isn't the rape charge itself, so much as that bastard Cotton. He's out to get me this time, and no mistake. It stands to reason the key to this business is in my other cases, yet I've been suspended. "Your cases will be kept going," ' he mimicked. ' "We shan't overlook the possibility," and all the time he could hardly stop himself laughing.'

'I suppose he's been given the opportunity that he's been waiting for,' said Morton.

'Bloody swine. He took delight in telling me I'd lose my pension, as well as get a stretch. I'd like to strangle the bugger. You can see what will happen. He'll pass my cases to some bloody nincompoop, who'll never bother to compare notes with the railway police.'

'Actually,' said Morton diffidently, 'they've passed your cases over to me.'

'You?' Bragg's jaw dropped. 'Christ Almighty! All of them?'

'Yes.'

'What about the Foster case?'

'I gather they're putting forward my name to the coroner for his approval.'

'But you've not been in the detective division more than nine months! What bloody good are you?'

'I know.' Morton looked down at the toe of his boot. 'Inspector Cotton said he thought I was ready for greater responsibility.'

'Responsibility!' snorted Bragg. 'They're all out to get me put away. Christ, lad!' he cried, his voice shrill. 'Do you know what the penalty is for attempted rape? It's penal servitude for life! And no bugger is lifting a finger to help me. That sodding railway constable is going round taking statements, as if it was just a case of a lecherous old fumbler putting his hand up a young girl's skirt.'

'Well, that's why I've come,' said Morton self-consciously. 'I don't suppose you are . . . well, flush with money, and I'd like to see you are properly defended . . . It would be no hardship to me,' he added lamely.

'Thank you, lad,' said Bragg grimly. 'I'm sure it was well meant; but I'm innocent, and I have this naïve idea that if you're innocent, you shouldn't be found guilty.'

'You know perfectly well it doesn't work like that,' said Morton.

'Thank you all the same, lad, but I'll manage.'

Morton looked crestfallen for a moment, then he looked up. 'If I'm appointed coroner's officer for the Foster case in your place, then I can try to do what you would have been doing. I certainly wouldn't make much progress on my own, I shall need your advice.'

Bragg summoned up the ghost of a smile. 'Well, now, I spoke to a Constable Goff at Whitechapel police station. He says he saw a flat hay cart drawn by a big grey shire, going along Royal Mint Street at about the right time. I left a note about it for the stop-and-question team.'

'I know, I've heard about it.'

'I was thinking that if it's the one we are looking for, they must have concealed it while one of them scouted round to see that the beat constable was out of the way. Somewhere like King Street, or the bottom of Minories would do. I reckon that house-to-house enquiries there might produce some useful leads.'

'Right, I'll do that.'

'Oh, and I asked the sergeant at Whitechapel to keep a lookout for the cart in the High Street, for a week or so. You'd better make contact . . . You know, I have it in my bones that the Jessop girl is connected with that killing.' He glanced at the clock on the mantelpiece. 'Blast it! I'm in court again Friday, and I've slept the best part of today away . . . I shall have time enough to sleep, unless we get this sorted out.'

8

Next morning Bragg received a note from Sir Rufus Stone, asking him to call at his chambers. Bragg was glad of the excuse to get out of the house, away from an increasingly suspicious Mrs Jenks. The sky was overcast, and a gusty wind blew swirls of dust and paper along the pavements. He walked quickly, and as a result had to sit in the ecclesiastical gloom of the clerk's room for ten minutes. Precisely on the stroke of ten, the clerk beckoned Bragg to follow him up a flight of stone steps, where he tapped reverentially on Sir Rufus's door.

The coroner was seated at his desk, perusing some papers, and, without looking up, he waved Bragg to a chair. For a few minutes he read intently, then grunting his approval, he signed his name with a flourish.

'I wanted to get that opinion out of the way,' he said. 'After all, I still have to earn my living . . . well, now, in view of what happened to you on Saturday, I felt it would be useful to have a chat.'

'You've heard about it?' asked Bragg cautiously.

'I was told about it at great length and with considerable relish, by your immediate superior.'

'That would be Inspector Cotton. He's been gunning for me for years.'

'It's clear enough who engineered it all,' declared Sir Rufus. 'What we have to do is decide on our response.'

'I can make a fair guess myself.'

'Guess nothing, man! It stinks of the Special Branch. A law unto themselves, they are. Once their lackeys in the Home Office had failed in their attempt to suborn me, it's natural that they would try to eliminate my officer. We should have

78

expected it . . . You won't get any support from the police, you know that.'

'I know.'

Sir Rufus peered at Bragg for a space, his head cocked on one side. Then he rose, and took his favourite pose in front on the fireplace.

'I've accepted the police's recommendation concerning your replacement,' he announced. 'But only because it suited me. Let no one think,' he frowned, 'that my acquiescence is a precedent for the future. I recognised Constable Morton's name from our last meeting. I hope I am correct in surmising that he is someone with whom you have a congenial working relationship.'

'Why, yes,' replied Bragg in surprise.

'Excellent – since that is exactly what you will be doing.'

'I don't follow.'

'Come, come, Bragg,' said Sir Rufus testily. 'It's as plain as a pikestaff. Since when have the police been prepared to entrust the case of a policeman's murder to an inexperienced detective officer?'

'He did call on me, last night, to ask for my help. Though how I can give it without landing him in trouble, I'm not sure.'

'I'll tell you, if you can abide in patience awhile,' exclaimed Sir Rufus. 'As I was saying, the appointment of young Morton demonstrates that your miserable commissioner has given in completely to Home Office pressure. I have a suspicion I shall be told that resources are too scarce to spare any other men for the Foster investigation. No doubt they hope that I shall find myself hamstrung; but they'll be wrong. It's only a convention that the coroner should look to the police to provide his investigating officer, and a recent convention at that. There would be nothing to prevent my appointing someone outside the police – provided I was prepared to remunerate him out of my own minuscule stipend. I therefore propose to appoint you as assistant coroner's officer for this case. The course has two aspects to commend it. Firstly, I shall retain the services of someone in whose acumen and integrity I can trust. Secondly,' Sir Rufus pursed his lips, 'it will cost me nothing, since I understand that they are continuing to pay your salary.'

Bragg laughed ruefully. 'It won't be of much avail, if I'm inside.'

Sir Rufus jerked round in astonishment. 'But we shall fight, man. We shall fight!'

'It takes money,' said Bragg flatly.

'Nonsense! There are plenty of lawyers who would pay you for the privilege of having a crack at this administration. I'd like to do it myself, but I'd probably make a mess of it. Still, there's young Charlton Marshall, just taken silk; he used to be a pupil of mine before he forsook the chancery for the criminal bar. He'll do it for me . . . I shall have to find a solicitor to instruct him; must observe the professional niceties. But don't you worry about that.'

'I can't let you . . . ' began Bragg.

'Say no more! It's me they're after. You are nothing more than a pawn . . . But they'll find out that I protect my pawns. That's all for now, I think.'

'Thank you, sir,' said Bragg, rising to leave.

Sir Rufus looked up. 'I suppose I am correct in assuming you didn't do it?' he said.

'Hello there.' Inspector Davis rose from his chair, and shook Morton's hand warmly. 'How's the detective division?'

'I'm beginning to get the first glimmer of what it's all about,' said Morton with a smile.

'What's this rumour about Sergeant Bragg? I heard he was caught raping a woman in a train.' Davis smoothed down his luxuriant whiskers with the back of his fingers, lest the slightest irregularity should let in the devil to him also.

'At least I know that's not true, but he has been charged with attempted rape.'

Davis drew in his breath with a hiss. 'Bad business,' he said. 'Just his word against hers, is it?'

'It would appear so.'

Davis shook his head in perturbation. 'He was a good man, was Joe Bragg. Would knock spots off his bosses, though I say it as shouldn't.'

'It's as a result of his suspension, that I've come to see you, sir,' said Morton.

'How do you mean?'

'I've been appointed coroner's officer on the Foster case, in his stead.'

'You?' Davis thoughtfully groomed his moustache with a thumbnail. 'What is it you want, then?' he asked warily.

'The only thing in Foster's clothes, when he was found, was this.' Morton placed the luggage label on the desk before him. 'There is a suggestion that it's written in Welsh. I wondered if you could confirm that.'

Davis looked at it briefly. 'Sorry boyo,' he said with a smile of relief. 'I come from Pembroke. It's as much as I can do to say "good health" in Welsh. I'll tell you who would know, though; Sergeant Griffith, from fifth division. He's from Cardigan, and he's great on that sort of thing – belongs to the London Welsh Society. He'll be sure to know.'

It was with some reluctance that Morton walked down to Seething Lane police station. Sergeant Griffith had been an unwitting participant, barely a month ago, in a practical joke perpetrated by Bragg at the expense of Inspector Cotton. Morton knew he would not get any co-operation if he mentioned Bragg's name.

Sergeant Griffith received him with cold formality.

'It's a point that has arisen on the Foster murder,' began Morton.

'Oh yes?'

'There was a label in his pocket, with some words written on it which we think may be Welsh. Inspector Davis said you speak the language like a native, and would be sure to recognize it.'

'I am a native, Constable,' said Griffith softly, 'and every day I thank God for it.' Nevertheless, his manner seemed to be thawing a little.

'Here it is.'

Griffith examined the label. '*Cofiwch Dic Penderyn,*' he pronounced sonorously, relishing every syllable. 'Oh yes, it's Welsh all right.'

'What does it mean?' asked Morton.

'Now I'm not as fluent as Inspector Davis makes out, but "*Dic Penderyn*" is obviously a man's name. So the whole

81

message should read, "Remember Dic Penderyn".'

'Who was he?'

'I haven't the slighest idea.'

'He would have been a Welshman?'

'With a name like that, there's no doubt of it.'

'I wonder who could tell me.'

'If I were you,' said Griffith, 'I'd get on to the Cardiff police. If they don't know themselves, they'll be able to find out.'

Catherine Marsden walked up Bishopsgate, peering anxiously about her. 'Between St Botolph's and the White Hart,' that's what the desk sergeant at Old Jewry had told her. She'd been so embarrassed by his obvious assumption that it was an assignation, she hadn't even asked which side of the road it was on . . . Yet another church. How on earth could one square mile have ever supported a hundred churches? It proved to be St Ethelburga's. Oh well . . . 'Just gone off duty,' the sergeant had said, with the kind of knowing grin that always raised her hackles. Stupid ignorant men! Did they think that fawning on them was a woman's only function? . . . Another church, on the opposite side. Catherine crossed, and peered at the faded lettering on the notice board by the door. St Botolph's. Good! And there was the White Hart, on the corner – but between them was a gentlemen's outfitters. She halted in disappointment, then noticed a narrow alley running between the church and the shop. So this was Alderman's Walk? She took a few paces down it, and discovered a black-painted door with the number one screwed into the lintel above it. She banged the gleaming brass knocker, and waited. After a moment she heard steps descending the stairs, and the door was opened by a motherly figure in a black dress and white apron. Evidently a servant . . . Interesting.

'Yes, madam?'

'I would like to speak to Constable Morton, if I may?'

'Please come in.' The woman led the way up the lino-covered stairs to a landing, and opened a heavy mahogany door. She ushered Catherine into a hallway, and thence into a large sitting-room with chintz armchairs and rich curtains.

'If you would wait here, madam, I will find him. Who shall I say has called?'

'Catherine Marsden.'

The woman smiled, and was gone. At least she didn't leer and wink. Come to think of it, she didn't seem at all surprised that a young woman should come calling on him, unaccompanied. Perhaps it was the kind of lodging-house where people of both sexes lived. Behaviour would be bound to be more free and easy in such a place . . . It was a very comfortable lodging, nevertheless. The furniture was solid, and well-used, the carpet soft. Catherine crossed over to the window and took hold of a curtain. It was a heavy brocade, in what she guessed was a William Morris design – rich deep colours, with a hint of medieval mystery. One thing was certain: they had cost a pretty penny. She could almost hear her father's voice, chiding at her evaluation of art in terms of mere money. But one had to be practical. Anyway, he was ready enough to accept his thousand guineas for a portrait.

'Excuse me, madam.' Catherine jumped back, and dropped the curtain guiltily. A middle-aged man in black morning-coat and striped trousers was standing inside the door.

'I'm afraid that Master James has gone out for a moment. If you would care to wait, my wife will bring you some tea.'

'Thank you, thank you,' she babbled, and scurried back to her chair. So it was 'Master James'? Not a lodging-house at all, but the home of a well-to-do family. Well, that would account for the lack of surprise at her calling, if there were other members of the family about. Thank goodness it hadn't been his mother who had come in, to find her fingering her curtains like a draper's assistant . . . But at least the room made more sense now. Anyone who could afford furnishings like these wouldn't need to take in lodgers.

There was a rap at the door, and the woman came in with the tea. Silver tray, silver teapot and sugar basin, fine china; 'opulent' seemed to be the only word to describe it. And she couldn't say that it reflected any particular value placed on her visit, for she had called unexpectedly. No doubt anyone would be entertained thus . . . or any young woman . . .

'Miss Marsden! How delightful! I see you have been looked

after.' Morton stood in the doorway, with a broad smile on his face.

'Thank you, your servants have been very courteous.' Catherine put down her cup on the table. 'And in return I must have afforded them some amusement, for when the butler came in, he found me examining the curtain material like a pawnbroker assessing a pledge.'

'We've not quite come to that, yet,' said Morton.

'Nevertheless, you have put me in an acutely embarrassing position. Why on earth did you allow me to take you down to the kitchen last Monday, and give you a cup of tea like any common bobby?'

'But that's exactly what I am, and anyway, you did it most charmingly. No doubt you take after your mother.'

'You mean the automatic connection between a policeman and tea with the cook?'

'Perhaps,' said Morton slyly, 'but rather what I suspect is your mother's ability to rise triumphantly above any problem.'

'Huh! She doesn't recognize that they are there,' exclaimed Catherine.

'Just so.'

'Well, I didn't call on you to wrangle about my family,' said Catherine crossly.

'You would hardly expect me to be so impolite as to enquire the reason for your visit,' Morton said lightly. 'Indeed I would wish to postpone that *dénouement* for as long as is possible. These rooms are seldom graced by the presence of a beautiful lady.'

'Your mother would not be pleased to hear you say that.'

'My parents' house is in Kent. I live here alone – except, of course, for Mr and Mrs Chambers, who look after me.'

Catherine was gripped by sudden panic. 'We can't spend time discussing your domestic arrangements,' she said harshly. 'I came to see you, because the crime reporter of the *Star* told me about Sergeant Bragg's arrest. So stop rallying me, and tell me what I can do to help.'

Morton studied her seriously. 'You would really wish to?' he asked.

'Of course. He was just as instrumental in saving my life as you were.'

Morton looked nettled for a moment, then smiled. 'One thing is certain; this is not an occasion for doing good in secret. It would be pointless to try to help him without his knowing. If you are prepared to risk a rebuff, we can take a cab now, and go to see him.'

'Very well.' Catherine rose to her feet, settled her hat on her head, and swept haughtily out of the room.

It was an anxious Mrs Jenks who opened the door to them.

'You don't know how glad I am to see you, Mr Morton,' she said. 'He's been out all day; and he had his supper in his own room, with never a word to me. He's not done that for five years and more.'

'He's under some strain, Mrs Jenks,' said Morton. 'He will be all right.'

Mrs Jenks lowered her voice to a shrill whisper. 'Mrs Parsons, from next door, said she heard at the shop that he's been interfering with young girls . . . Well, he's never brought any of them here,' she added self-righteously.

'None of it is true, you may be sure,' said Morton firmly. 'Some allegations have been made against him, and we shall be able to prove that they are merely malicious. That's why we have come here this evening.'

'I do hope you're right, sir.' Mrs Jenks seemed on the verge of tears. 'He's a proud man, is Mr Bragg. He couldn't bear to have people saying that about him.'

It was a surprisingly buoyant Bragg that they found, when they entered his sitting-room. The windows were flung open, and a fire roared in the small grate. Bragg fussed over Catherine, and evidently saw no need to question her presence.

'Tell me if you are too hot in here,' he said, as she settled into her chair. 'Mrs Jenks must think I need cheering up, but if I let the fire out, she'll be offended. So we shall just have to sweat it out.'

'You seem very cheerful, Sergeant,' remarked Morton. 'After last night, I expected to find you hanging from the doorknob.'

'A good night's sleep can work wonders. Added to which, I've had a very interesting day.' Bragg pushed a spill into the coals, and laid it across the bowl of his pipe.

'In the first place,' he went on when it was drawing nicely, 'I had a meeting with our new coroner. Now there, miss, is a man who would fight the whole world, rather than compromise himself; and you brought that about.'

Morton noted that Catherine blushed with pleasure.

'Anyway, he is firmly of the view that Saturday's incident was arranged by Special Branch, to get at him. I'm a mere pawn, he says. That being so, he insists on arranging for my defence – not for my sake, mark you, but for his own. However, since he's getting one of his cronies to do it for nothing, I could hardly refuse.' He smiled apologetically at Morton. 'Indeed, had I not agreed, I think he would have gone ahead, none the less.'

'Well, that's a relief, anyway,' Morton remarked.

'When is the hearing?' asked Catherine.

'On Friday. So I've got a couple of days to sniff around.'

'I would like to help in any way I can,' said Catherine.

'Thank you, miss . . . Now let me tell you what I've been doing this afternoon.' He knocked the loose ash from his pipe, and propped it alongside a vase on the mantelpiece. 'While I was in that cell, last weekend, I tried to think through everything that happened on the Saturday. I knew that there was a pattern there, that I couldn't quite force to the surface. So today, I went over the ground again.'

'In Greenwich park?' asked Morton.

'Yes. It was different, of course, because there weren't any crowds today. But I followed every step I'd taken, and tried to remember who I'd seen, and what they'd been doing. Naturally, you don't take much notice of what's going on around you, when you're off duty; but enough sinks in for you to be able to stir it to the surface, if you try. All that afternoon I'd been half-aware of something odd. There had always been people around, wherever I'd gone. I remember thinking how nowadays everybody dresses alike. Now I realize that everywhere I went, I was followed. I can't prove it, because I never went anywhere isolated; but in my mind's eye, I can see that the same group of men was close by, every step I took. What makes me so sure, is that they were only men, and young men at that. It just isn't natural for a dozen men to hang around together all afternoon, and neither women nor booze in sight.'

Catherine darted an exultant glance at Morton, but he was absorbed in Bragg's story.

'When did you first become aware of them?' he asked.

'Just as I was crossing the High Street, to go up to the park. They were standing on the corner, doing nothing in particular, just looking wooden.'

'Could they have travelled from London with you, on the same boat?'

'They could have. The boat didn't leave for some minutes after I boarded it. I headed straight for the bar, so they could easily have followed me on. They'd hardly have been waiting at Greenwich on the off chance I'd go there.'

'And are you saying that they are connected with the Jessop girl?'

'I'm sure of it. I'd swear it was the same group of men that got into my compartment at the last minute.'

'And out of it again at Deptford,' added Morton.

'That's right. I don't know if I'm imagining it or not, but as I think back, I seem to hear a train door bang, a few seconds before the girl entered my compartment.'

'She would have had to be on the train, wouldn't she? However good these people are at improvising, she would need to be on hand. I wonder what they would have done had you returned by boat.'

'She might have fallen overboard, and claimed I tried to drown her. The men could have screened it from the other passengers . . . Does it all seem wildly far-fetched to you, Miss Marsden?'

'Well, I can't pretend to be totally objective,' Catherine replied. 'But you are arguing that there was a Machiavellian plot against you. Most people would find it easier to believe the girl.'

'And that would include a jury?' asked Bragg, his face grim.

'I'm afraid so.'

'You are right, of course. So I may only have two days of liberty left; I shall be lucky to get bail if I'm committed for trial.

We've got to use them well.'

'The girl is the only point of attack,' Morton said thoughtfully. 'I take it you would be able neither to identify nor trace any of the men.'

'True,' said Bragg. 'I thought I would go down to Kennington tomorrow, and see what I can find out.'

'I might be able to help,' said Catherine. 'Whatever the outcome of the trial, Miss Jessop has lost her reputation. To me, it means that if she would lend herself to such a stratagem, she hadn't got any reputation to lose. I'll browse through the newspapers for the last few years to see if I can find anything similar. And if you like, I'll have a word with the *Star*'s crime reporter.'

'If you do,' said Morton with a worried frown, 'you must be discreet. I wouldn't want to alert the papers to what is going on.'

'I'm hardly likely to spoil my own scoop, am I?' Catherine said sharply. 'You do remember that I'm to be given a head start over the other journalists, don't you?'

'You know,' remarked Bragg, 'I can't get over how realistic it all was. I'd have sworn she was having a brainstorm, till they opened that bloody door . . . sorry, miss.'

'Perhaps she's an actress,' Morton mused. 'It sounds almost like something out of a melodrama. I've a few acquaintances in the profession, I'll ask around.'

'Discreetly, I hope,' said Catherine acidly.

'But of course.' Morton gave her a slow smile, then turned to Bragg. 'Is there anything I can do?' he asked.

'I'm still convinced that all this is somehow linked to the Foster murder. I don't know how, but the sooner that is solved, the sooner this mess will be untangled.'

'Now that I've been confirmed as coroner's officer,' said Morton, 'I've seen the report of the operation on Sunday morning. They found a man who saw that horse and cart on the morning of the murder. He was going along Cooper's Row with his van about twenty past five, when a flat lorry, drawn by a grey shire answering the description in your note, came into the street from Trinity Square. He says the cart was empty, and there were three men on it, plus the driver. They must have been in a hurry, because the horse was trotting. As you know, there isn't room for two big vehicles to pass in Cooper's Row, so the cart had to give way – and very ungracious they were, according to our witness.'

'Did he get a good look at the men?' demanded Bragg.

'At the driver, yes. The others turned away, which is significant in itself. The driver, of course, had to get down so that he could back the horse. Our man describes him as a right bludger, with bulging brown eyes, and a full beard. All in all, our witness was glad to get away unscathed . . . Oh, and he mentioned that while he was backing the horse, the driver called him Jewel.'

'That's a queer name for a carthorse.'

'Yes, but the man is adamant about it. He used to have a pony named Jewel, when he was a child.'

'Good! good! It's beginning to come together,' exclaimed Bragg. 'If only we had more time . . . Did you have any luck with your enquiries in the Minories area?'

'I didn't get confirmation to act in the case till late this afternoon,' said Morton. 'I'll go round there, first thing tomorrow.'

9

Morton had begun to feel that he had spent the whole of his life kocking on doors. The houses of the well-to-do, in Vine Street and the Crescent, had been fairly straightforward. In no case had members of the family been up at five o'clock on a Sunday morning. Indeed, at only three houses had servants been astir, and then only kitchen maids lighting the fire, and making tea for the other servants. The workers' dwellings in King Street and Queen Street were more difficult. In a good dozen there had been no reply at all; and in almost as many the door had been opened by children, the parents presumably being at work. Where an adult was at home, he had been met with hostility or indifference. No one had heard or seen anything. What was even more dispiriting: he would have to come back again for the houses he'd not eliminated. He wondered how many visits that would mean. It would certainly take longer than two days to cover them all, and if the neighbours were anything to go by, he wouldn't get any information from them.

He had then decided that before he had his lunch, he would visit the other streets in the area Bragg had indicated. And here he was, with only two more houses to go, and nothing to show for it. He knocked on the door of a modest house in Paternoster Row. He could hear children calling within, but no one came. He was about to go next door, and be done with it, when the door was opened by a rosy-cheeked young woman, in a bright checked apron and carefully tidied hair. She looked as if she had been a maid in some large household, and had the assurance that came from it.

'Can I help you?' she asked in a Kentish burr that lifted Morton's spirits.

'I am a police officer, and I am making enquiries in connection with an accident that happened at five o'clock on Sunday morning the sixteenth of August, near Trinity Square. I wonder if anyone in your household was about at that time, and might have seen anything.'

'Five o'clock!' she laughed. 'I like my bed too much to be about at that hour. What date did you say it was?'

'The Sunday before last, the sixteenth.'

She looked thoughtful. 'Just a minute.' She took a few steps down the hallway. 'Jim!' she called. 'When did Bonny foal?'

Morton heard an indistinct shout in reply.

'Come 'ere then,' called the woman. 'There's a man wants to see you.' She stood in the doorway, smiling amicably at Morton till her husband appeared. ''Tis a policeman,' she said. 'He's on about an accident, five o'clock last Sunday morning but one. I thought that was when Bonny foaled.'

Her husband was tall, lean and smelled strongly of horses.

'I wondered,' Morton repeated for the umpteenth time, 'if you had happened to be about, and whether you had noticed anything.'

'Well now, let's think.' The man seemed neither so intelligent nor so chirpy as his wife. 'Bonny had her foal about half past four. I know that, 'cause I had to put it in the book. O' course I had to stay on after that, till I knew they were both all right. What time did I come in for my breakfast, Annie?'

'I'd say near enough half past six, love. Alexina had just woken up for her feed. I remember thinking you'd get no sleep, coming in at that time.'

'Where were you at five o'clock, sir?' asked Morton.

'Round the corner in the stables, in Trinity Mews.'

'But you didn't go out, so you couldn't have seen anything,' Morton said, anxious to bring the interview to an end.

'That's right,' said the man slowly. 'But it's like I say, the vet was with me through the foaling; once it was over, though, he went home. I reckon that would have been near enough five o'clock.'

'Splendid!' Morton felt a surge of relief and excitement. 'Where can I get hold of him?'

The man drew a watch from his waistcoat pocket and studied

it. 'I expect he'll be at home now, having his dinner. He lives in Goulston Square, number eight; opposite Whitechapel Baths. 'Tis only ten minutes' walk.'

Morton's opinion of the ostler rose considerably, for it took him almost precisely ten minutes to reach Goulston Square. The veterinary surgeon was obviously a man of some eminence in his profession, for he occupied an imposing house, with a burnished brass plate and bell-pull. Morton stated his business to a smartly dressed maid, then turned on his heel and studied the ornate brick and stone façade of the public bath house opposite. The value of this house must have plummeted when that monstrous temple to Hygeia had been erected along the opposite side of the square.

'Come in, Constable. I'm just having a bite. If you don't mind talking while I eat, we'll get it over now. I have to be off again in half an hour.'

'That's very good of you, sir. It shouldn't take so long.'

'Pull up a chair, and have some of that pie. I warrant you haven't had any lunch.'

He was a ruddy-faced countryman, with a shock of untidy brown hair. Despite the warm day, he was dressed in a lounging suit of light tweed, and his brown boots gleamed.

'I gather, sir, that in the early hours of Sunday the sixteenth of August you attended a mare in Trinity Mews.'

'Just a minute. I'll have to get my book . . . You'll find a bottle of beer in the sideboard.'

He was soon back, turning the pages of a large diary. 'Here we are . . . sixteenth. Yes, a mare called Bonny was foaling.'

'I don't suppose you noticed what time you left the premises?' asked Morton.

'I'd be a poor man, if I didn't. We charge on time spent. I've put five o'clock, and as I charge to the nearest quarter-hour, it could have been seven minutes either side.'

'The reason I'm asking, is that there was an accident about that time on the other side of Trinity Square, and a man was killed. I wondered if you'd seen anything.'

'No.' The man's brow furrowed. 'No, I didn't go through the square, I cut through George Street, and up Minories. All I saw was a cart pulled up in George Street.'

'What was it like?' Morton asked, trying to keep his voice level.

'Oh, it was a big flat lorry. Nothing special about it. It was the horse that took my eye. I'm on the committee of the Shire Horse Society, and I do a lot of judging at shows. Not that he was a show horse, because the markings weren't right, but I've never seen a finer animal.'

Morton consulted his note book. 'A stallion of about eighteen hands, grey with a white star on the forehead, with white stockings on all but the off-side hind leg.'

The vet looked up in surprise. 'That's exactly it. Are you saying this is the vehicle involved in the accident?'

'It would appear so. There weren't any actual witnesses, but we now have three people who saw that cart in the area at the time. I don't suppose you know who owns the horse?'

'No, I've never come across him.'

'If you do, will you let us know?'

'Certainly.'

'Did you see anything of the men on the cart?' asked Morton.

'There were . . . Let me think; I'd better get this right, hadn't I? I'd say there was one man sitting on the side near the pavement, and one on the other. And there was another lying asleep on the cart.'

'And the driver?' prompted Morton.

'A big man, with a bushy beard . . . and bald. As bald as a hen's egg. He was just putting on his hat, as I turned the corner. Hardly a hair on his head, and I wouldn't have put him at more than forty.'

St Mark's Road was a quiet tree-lined cul-de-sac, on the other side of Kennington Road from the church. It must have been a very desirable area, fifty years ago, thought Bragg. The villas were large, and set in spacious gardens. But now the paint was peeling from the windows, and the semi-circular carriage drives were choked with weeds. They had been swamped by the inexorable tide of artisans' dwellings that had spread out from London and engulfed Clapham, Brixton, even as far as Streatham. Now the villas were dismal and desolate, their once proud owners fled to Blackheath or Sutton.

Bragg leaned against a plane tree outside the open gate of number twelve. Indeed it would never close again, for the wood had rotted around the bottom hinge, and the bolts had pulled through. It drooped from its imposing stone pier like a broken wing. Behind it rubbish had accumulated: leaves, paper, broken twigs. No one who lived in the house took any pride in it. Its severe Georgian outline struck him as gaunt and stark, as if one could expect life to exist within only at a low ebb. The curtains at the windows were of different materials and colours, but all were faded. No attempt had been made to furnish the house harmoniously, because it wasn't lived in as one unit. It was the kind of place where the owner lived in the back, on the ground floor, and let all the decent rooms to people who were, themselves, little better off. And they all mouldered away quietly together, house and people; and nobody cared. They never complained to anyone, for that would not have been genteel. So they sat with their gas fire and their cat until they faded into nothing, and their place was taken by someone else . . . someone like Mary Jessop, who was ruthless and cunning, and bent on his destruction.

He tried to remember what she looked like. In the train, of course, her face had been distorted with simulated pain; and afterwards she'd been looking distraught and hysterical. If she walked past him now, with a smile on her face, he'd like as not fail to recognize her. She'd had a cap of brown hair, pulled into a bun at the neck; that much, at least, he remembered. Perhaps if he watched long enough, he might see her. On the other hand, he might be seen himself. That would be folly. What if they sent for the police? A man who'd tried to rape her, seen lurking outside her house. They'd have him in clink, as soon as spit. Bragg watched for a few moments longer, then slowly retraced his steps.

Around the corner, in Kennington Road, was a little general store. It looked sparkling and prosperous, its shelves well-stocked with great round cheeses, blocks of butter, boxes of biscuits. As luck would have it, there was no other customer at that moment.

'Some twist, please love,' said Bragg.

The woman opened a drawer under the counter, and pulled out a rope of tobacco, which hung in her fingers like a dead eel.

'Who lives at number twelve, St Mark's Road now?' asked Bragg.

'It's still owned by Miss Percy.' She took a knife and sawed through the tobacco, then flung the severed piece on to a scale. 'That'll be tuppence-farthing,' she said briskly.

Bragg made something of a business of searching his pockets for a coin. 'I used to live there when I was young,' he said. 'Of course it was a grand house in those days.'

'Did you?' the woman asked with interest. 'What's your name, then?'

'Johnson, Arthur Johnson. My mother was the housekeeper there for a bit, after my father died . . . I loved it. I always come back to have a look at it, when I'm in this part of the country.'

'It's funny,' said the woman, with a puzzled frown. 'I'd have thought I'd remember you. We only lived in Ashmole Street.'

'I'm sure I remember you,' said Bragg. 'As soon as I looked through the window, I was certain of it.'

'I was Ada Colley then,' said the woman wistfully.

'That's right! I remember you in a blue dress, with a sailor collar, playing with a hoop in the street.'

'Do you?' she smiled. 'It's a long time ago, but d'you know, I can still remember that dress . . . '

'You were a good bit younger than me, of course. But you were a good-looking girl, even then.'

Her face lit up with pleasure. She'd probably not been told she was pretty, thought Bragg, since her boyfriend was fumbling her under the stands of the Oval cricket ground.

'I suppose Miss Percy lets rooms?' he asked.

'Oh, yes,' she said eagerly. 'In fact, there's one vacant at the moment. I could put in a word for you, if you like?'

'No, thanks,' said Bragg hastily. 'I live in Exeter now. I travel in hairdressers' sundries, and once in a while I get round here.'

'We sell combs and hairnets and suchlike,' said the woman hopefully. 'I could put a bit of business in your way.'

Bragg laughed. 'Well, if you could take five hundred dozen, I'd be delighted.'

'Oh!' she said, crestfallen.

'No, love. I just sell from the manufacturers to the big wholesalers. I only get to this area twice a year, and I thought I'd pop over to look at the old place. I must say, it's beginning to look a bit dilapidated.'

'Well, they all are. Sooner the better they knock them down, and build some houses that people want.'

'Better for trade, anyway,' said Bragg with a sly grin, and she smiled happily back.

'I thought I recognized a woman and her daughter,' said Bragg. 'They were going up the steps to the front door, so I didn't get a proper look at the mother – she'd be a good bit older than you, I expect. The daughter was slightly built with brown hair in a bun. She'd be around twenty-five.'

'Oh, that's the Jessops. You wouldn't know them, they've not been here more than a few weeks. She's the widow of a vicar, they say; always in at church meetings, and visiting round the parish. Poor as a crow, I'd say. They hardly spend a penny in here.'

'It's a funny world, isn't it? Ah well, I suppose I must be on my way.' Bragg put a sixpence on the counter.

'I shall be finished in an hour, Arthur,' she said, pressing his palm with her fingers as she gave him the change. 'If you like, I could show you round . . . '

As soon as he got back to the City, Bragg made for the Guildhall library. He took down the Crockford's clerical directory for 1888. That ought to be about right, he thought: an up-to-date one probably wouldn't show the Revd Jessop, if he'd been dead some time. He carried the massive tome to a table, and sat down. To his dismay there were almost two pages of Jessops. It hadn't seemed the sort of name for a parson, somehow. They were all over the country, too; Durham, Stow-on-the-Wold, Birmingham . . . He began to make laborious notes of the essential details, then threw down his pencil in disgust. He was kidding himself, if he thought he could get round this lot. It would take him months – and then he'd find nothing. Whoever had set this lot up wasn't stupid. He would have looked at Crockford's too; the details would fit. He got up, and walked home disconsolately. In honest truth, he wasn't used to working in this way; he was used to going in openly, using the power of the police, getting rough if he had to, but getting results – and quick. Now he was reduced to wheedling crumbs of information from palm-stroking doxies. He kicked angrily at a stone, and watched it bounce along the pavement till it came to rest in the gutter. That's where he'd end up, if he didn't get a move on; a broken old lag in a doss house.

In his preoccupation, he went down the area steps when he arrived home, and into the kitchen. Mrs Jenks looked up with a blend of relief and pleasure. 'Why, Mr Bragg, I didn't expect you. The kettle's on, I'll make a cup of tea.'

He hung his hat on the back of the door, and sat in his usual chair, on the left of the kitchen range.

'Oh, I forgot,' said Mrs Jenks excitedly. 'There's an important-looking letter for you. I took it upstairs, as you've not been coming down . . . I'll go and get it for you.'

'Don't worry, Mrs Jenks. It can't be all that important.'

'It's no trouble . . . ' and she was gone.

Odd, thought Bragg, how even after living fifteen years in the same house, they still addressed each other by surname and title. It seemed stilted and unnecessary, since they were rubbing shoulders all day. It was more the way those old biddies in Kennington would behave, to preserve the illusion of their superior social status. Well, he and Mrs Jenks hadn't got a social status, real or fancied. But they had to preserve the proprieties – or if they didn't have to, it was clearly what she wanted. And the formal mode of address was probably her way of keeping him at a distance. Well and good. She wasn't all that special; a nice armful perhaps, but shrewish with it. She provided him with a very comfortable home, and it wasn't worth upsetting that by trying anything on . . . But in a month he might be spending the rest of his life in prison. A bit of hard labour of a pleasanter kind might not come amiss, just in case . . .

'There you are.' Mrs Jenks appeared, her eyes bright, her bosom heaving from her exertions. She thrust a stiff envelope into his hands, and watched expectantly while he opened his knife and slit along the top. He took the letter to the window to see better.

Dear Sir,

This is to inform you that a conference has been arranged at the chambers of Mr Charlton Marshall QC, 3 Pump Court, Inner Temple, at the hour of eleven in the morning of Thursday 27th inst. Our Mr Ingledew will have the honour to wait upon you there.

Mr Marshall has requested that you should furnish him directly with a particularization of the incident not later than the evening of the day before the conference.

Yours faithfully,
Lickerish Crump & Merriman

'Is it good news?' asked Mrs Jenks anxiously.

'Yes . . . I think you can say that,' replied Bragg, folding the letter and putting it in his pocket. 'At least, things are beginning to move.'

'When I said I would come to this meeting, I did not expect a route march,' said Karl plaintively. 'You must remember, James, that I am an aesthete, not an athlete.'

'The Artillery Ground is only round the corner,' Morton replied with a smile.

'For why does a trade union have a meeting on artillery premises? Is this British militarism at work again?'

Morton laughed. 'It's one of the few large open spaces in the City. During the summer public meetings are often held there. It saves the cost of hiring a hall.'

'From the look of the sky, we would have been better inside. Do you know, there were two inches of rain on our last night in Kent. Our train back was an hour late. I think the weather is coming from that direction . . . I tell you, James,' Karl added gloomily, 'the idea of thunderstorms coming from Europe, gives me apprehensions.'

'It was your idea to come to one of these meetings. I won't let you back out now.'

'Ah, but I was speaking figuratively, James. You said it was possible that this meeting might break up in disorder.'

'I thought that was what intrigued you.'

'So it did, in the security of my armchair. But now I recollect that on the Continent, when people riot, they turn on the nearest foreigner and hang him from a lamp post.'

'Don't worry! With me, you are under the protection of the law. Anyway, there aren't any lamp posts in the Artillery Ground.'

'My mouth shall remain firmly closed, nevertheless,' said Karl.

There was a sizeable crowd at the meeting, and only the head and shoulders of the speaker were visible above the audience. He sounded as if he was faithfully reading a prepared speech, seldom lifting his head to look at the audience.

'Forty years ago, we made more steel than France, Germany and America put together,' he declaimed in a thick expressionless voice. 'And now America alone makes seven hundred thousand tons more than we do. And why is that? Because all the nations we trade with have put up tariff barriers – Russia, Germany, France, Austria, and now America . . . '

'He must have swallowed an encyclopaedia to spew out these streams of facts,' whispered Karl.

'What interests me is the crowd,' replied Morton. 'You'd think they would be bored stiff, but they aren't. You'd go a long way to find a less inspiring speaker, and yet one can feel an air of expectancy in the audience.'

'Perhaps they have come for the fight,' said Karl uneasily. 'Where are your men?'

'Our men are not here.'

'They aren't!' exclaimed Karl in consternation.

'After Foster was killed, they decided our men were too conspicuous. The job is being done by Special Branch men now. They are trained for this kind of thing – and they have the advantage of looking just like everyone else.'

'But how can we be sure they are here?' Karl asked in some agitation.

'Well, let's try to pick one out, shall we? Disregard what he looks like, that won't be any guide. Watch what he does. He won't be interested in the speaker, but in the crowd's reaction. He'll be listening to what is going on around him, and looking at faces in the audience. It's not easy to spot them when things are quiet; but when the crowd gets agitated it's not difficult, you can see they're not part of it . . . There! You see that man to the right of speaker – with whiskers, and a light-brown bowler?'

'Ye . . . es.'

'Watch how he keeps half turning his head. Now! Did you see him turn round with a smile, to the person behind him? He's probably getting a good look at someone further back in the crowd.'

'The people appear to be angry,' said Karl. 'I tell you, James, it is not good for a foreigner to be at such a meeting.'

The speaker's voice seemed to be getting huskier by the minute. 'Is this the time, brethren, to destroy our engineering industry? . . . The life blood of our country? . . . When it is the only part of our economy able to compete with foreigners on equal terms. I tell you that quality is the only way we can sell to the tariff countries . . . We must make the goods they can't make . . . We must make the goods they make, to a higher standard of quality. Then we will survive.'

Husky or not, he was awakening a response in the crowd.

'The Americans would like it if we went under, the Germans would like it. Oh yes, they'd all like it. Once our standards have been allowed to drop, they know we'll never be able to compete with them again. We'll be finished. Brethren, this union says to the employers, "We will not allow you to destroy this industry by diluting the skilled workers with unskilled." ' Sporadic cheering was breaking out in the crowd now. ' "We will not allow you to destroy this nation, to line your own pockets . . . And if you try, we will fight you with every means in our power." '

The speaker gathered up his notes, and stood back blinking as the cheering was replaced by rhythmical clapping, and a chant of 'Strike! Strike! Strike!' This time there seemed to be no fighting. No one was moving away. A young apprentice lad looked round with a grin; he was clapping and shouting with the rest, and he couldn't have been much above fourteen. Now there was a swoop on the platform; the speaker, to his evident astonishment, was hoisted shoulder-high, and the crowd began to march in an orderly procession from the field.

'You British!' said Karl, with a theatrical sign of relief. 'I shall never understand you.'

'I'm not sure that I understand us, myself,' replied Morton. 'At least, not this evening.'

10

When Bragg reached Marshall's chambers, he was greeted by a pimply youth in an ill-fitting morning coat. His collar was a couple of sizes too large, and his head stuck out of it on his long neck, like that of a pink tortoise from its carapace.

'Mr Bragg?' he enquired. 'I'm from Lickerish Crump & Merriman.' He obviously had a careful mother, who had fitted him out for his new career in clothes that would last for some years.

'You're one of the partners, I suppose,' said Bragg.

'Indeed no!' The lad looked startled, then detected the amusement in Bragg's glance. 'In truth, I am under articles to Mr Oddie. He instructed me to meet you here for the conference.' He hesitated. 'I hope you know what it's all about, for I don't.'

'If I knew what it was about, I wouldn't be here,' Bragg observed cryptically.

'Mr Oddie said you would have sent instructions to counsel yourself,' said the boy mournfully. 'I'm sure it's all very irregular.'

'In time, lad,' said Bragg in a fatherly tone, 'you'll learn that it's only the irregular that makes the regular worth putting up with.'

'Are we all here?' asked Marshall's clerk brightly. 'Then follow me.'

He took them down a short corridor, tapped on a white-painted door, and ushered them inside. Charlton Marshall rose from behind his desk, nodded perfunctorily to the solicitor's clerk, and held out his hand to Bragg.

'You are my client, I take it?' He had a musical voice of

middle pitch, his face was clean-shaven, showing a strong chin, and he had a long nose with flaring nostrils. Bragg had an immediate impression of controlled energy and purpose.

'I'm sorry to say that I am,' he replied.

'I had dinner with Sir Rufus last night,' Marshall said, gesturing them to chairs, 'so I know about the other factors underlying this case; the substrata as we might say. Of course we shan't be able to dig down to them, but it is as well to know that they are there.' He glanced at the solicitor's clerk, amused at his look of wooden incomprehension.

'Thank you for the summary of events,' he went on. 'It was very clear and concise, as one would expect from a policeman. Have any further facts emerged since you compiled it?'

'No, sir.'

'And are any more likely to emerge?'

'If I'm honest, no. The railway police are not going to break their necks to discredit their main witness, and our lot refuse to entertain that there could be a connection between what happened to me and the cases I was investigating.'

'Then I think it would be prudent of us to acknowledge that, on the present state of our knowledge, we shall have an uphill task with a jury.'

'You mean, they'll regard touching up a vicar's daughter as equivalent to violating the Virgin Mary?'

'I wouldn't have expressed it quite so picturesquely,' said Marshall with a smile.

'But if our client is innocent . . . ' the pimply youth interrupted.

'Mr ah . . . ' Marshall glanced down at a note on his desk. 'Mr Ingledew, as you progress in your profession, you will learn that matters of guilt or innocence are for the jury and the judge to wrangle over. We merely provide the raw materials for that contest. Our function is to present our client's case to its fullest advantage, and frankly, I prefer not to know whether he is innocent or guilty.'

'No sir,' mumbled the youth.

'If you wished to rationalize it,' Marshall went on, 'you could say that we proceed upon the hypothesis that our client, assuming he so pleads, is innocent until incontrovertible evidence of his guilt is thrust upon us.'

'Yes, Mr Marshall, sir.'

'All of which is scarcely calculated to allay your anxieties,' Marshall said, turning to Bragg with a smile. 'However, we have the great advantage that you have been charged with a very serious offence. Which means that tomorrow's hearing is merely a preliminary skirmish. The trial proper will not take place for some weeks . . . That reminds me, I must get my clerk to see if it can be transferred to the Central Criminal Court. I would be much happier with an Old Bailey jury, than one at the Surrey Assizes.' He scribbled a note on his pad.

'Thinking it over last night,' said Bragg, 'I'm fairly certain that some of the men who had followed me around that day were in the crowd on London Bridge station.'

'I'd be surprised if they weren't,' replied Marshall breezily. 'Our officious friends, if I may use that expression,' he shot a warning glance at Bragg, 'had to be ready for any eventuality. Their paramount concern was that whatever action they took had to be totally effective. It's easy enough to see how it was done. It must always have been intended to use the girl, if they could – so much more effective for the destruction of a policeman than, say, assault.'

'I suppose so,' muttered Bragg.

'They must all have followed you from London, with the girl kept well out of sight. It's odd, isn't it, that we are much more likely to take note of a member of the opposite sex, than of our own . . . On Greenwich station, they would have had to screen the girl from you; which meant that the men couldn't board the train until both you, and then she, had got in. It was a calculated risk that the compartment you chose would be empty, but a reasonable one. The trains are fairly frequent, and the traffic is light at that time on a Saturday. If you add the Englishman's obsession with avoiding social contact whenever possible, it wasn't much of a gamble. Of course, the men joined you in your compartment not only to prevent any outsider boarding at Greenwich, but also to isolate you at Deptford station until the train was on the point of leaving. To my mind, that is what proves conclusively that it was a concerted attempt to discredit you.'

'I'm glad you think so.'

'Oh, I do, despite my homily to Mr er . . . just now. The girl must have been a few doors down. She got out as soon as the train stopped at Deptford, and when she saw there was no one else left to board the train, she signalled to an accomplice in your carriage. I think you said one of them was looking out of the window?'

'Yes, he stuck his head out while the train was still moving.'

Marshall was scanning rapidly through Bragg's notes, his finger moving down the margin as he did so.

'Yes, I have it,' he said with satisfaction. 'So as soon as there was no possibility of an outsider's becoming involved, the men left the compartment and boarded the train lower down . . . And you say that the last one handed up Miss Jessop into your compartment. A touch of artistry there; the kind of gentlemanly gesture that would allay your suspicions. Then, of course, they left the train promptly on reaching London Bridge, to ensure that a satisfactory furore was created. Indeed, some of them may even have got into the next compartment, to stir up a reaction to Miss Jessop's cries.'

'That's all very well,' said Bragg irritably, 'but where does it get us?'

'You must bear with me,' said Marshall reproachfully. 'Yesterday morning I was fishing for trout in Hampshire.'

'I'm sorry,' Bragg mumbled.

'That's quite all right. When a barrister of the eminence of Sir Rufus Stone calls for assistance, we lesser mortals are apt to come running. Nevertheless, I cannot pretend to have assimilated the facts thoroughly yet.'

'They're all there as far as I know.'

'Yes. Well, as I was saying, we shall have some time before the trial to establish further facts about these people, so tomorrow's hearing is largely a tactical matter for us.'

'I doubt if we'll ever find out about the men involved,' said Bragg. 'I reckon they'd vanished before the constable started asking for witnesses.'

'Nevertheless, we have the name and address of the girl, which you say is authentic enough. We shall just have to extract what information we can from her.'

'You won't get much,' Bragg said gloomily.

'We'll get enough. My chief concern is to decide what to do with you.' Marshall gave a disarming smile. 'We generally assume that policemen make good witnesses, but in my experience, they do not often do so in their own defence. And in a case such as this, there are layers of prejudice to peel back before you can expose the mind of a jury – or even a magistrate – to the light of the objective truth. For a start, I detect that you are a countryman. Now, it is an unquestioned assumption of any town-dweller, that our rustic brethren live in a bucolic bliss which is untrammelled by considerations of morality.'

'Well,' said Bragg with a laugh, 'there was a rumour that the vicar of our parish had an unusual fondness for the churchyard goat!'

'Goat?'

'They had a big nanny goat to keep down the grass in the churchyard. They would tie her to each gravestone in turn, and she'd eat all the grass within reach. And the vicar would milk her. But he'd never let anyone watch. He'd lead her into her shed, and close the door. Many's the time we crept up and listened – and some damned funny noises there were too! Then one day she was gone. The old women said she'd been taken by the devil. My old dad wouldn't have any of that. He reckoned the old goat's sight had got so bad, she couldn't tell what was grass, and what was gravestone; so she wore her teeth out. She was no good for her job then, and Dad said the vicar got rid of her quietly, so as not to upset the children. That wasn't the general opinion, though, and the parish council replaced her with a young billy goat . . . but he was never as good.'

Marshall laughed merrily. 'You see what I mean. Tell a story like that, and they wouldn't need to call witnesses! . . I was about to say, "Let us get back to a more sober consideration of the position", but I hate to play on words. Are you a drinking man, Mr Bragg?'

'If I said I wasn't, my belly would call me a liar.'

'How much do you drink?'

'I suppose four pints of beer a day.'

'Regularly?'

'It varies, obviously. I generally have a drink at lunchtime, and always a beer with my supper. If I go out to the pub in the evening, I could easily get through another two or three.'

'And would you be inebriated after such an amount?' asked Marshall.

'Not unless I sloshed them down, one after the other.'

'Do you drink spirits?'

'Not often.'

'Now last Saturday was warm and humid.' Marshall referred again to Bragg's notes. 'You say that was the reason why you went to Greenwich. How much did you drink that day?'

'Let's see. A couple of pints on the boat, and two more in the Grapes. Then I had one at the refreshment kiosk before the band concert, and another after it. Oh, and I had one while I was waiting for the boat back.'

'So that is seven pints of beer within – what shall we say – an eight-hour period?'

'I suppose that's fair.'

'And your body is habituated to no more than four pints a day. Moreover, from your account, you had eaten very little since breakfast that morning.'

'Now just a minute . . . ' began Bragg.

Marshall held up his hand. 'I am merely outlining what the prosecution will undoubtedly put to you with much greater force.'

He sat silent for some moments, twiddling with a pencil on his desk, his brow furrowed. 'The most effective defence I can remember, in a case such as this,' he said slowly, 'was where we were able to demonstrate that the defendant's sexual proclivities tended exclusively towards his own sex.'

'Not bloody likely!' exclaimed Bragg, wrathfully.

'I didn't think it of you, for a moment,' said Marshall with a reassuring smile. 'The next best thing is having the wife give evidence of a frequent and satisfactory marital connection. Do I take it that your wife would be able to give such evidence?'

'I haven't got a wife,' replied Bragg shortly.

'I'm sorry. You have the look of a married man.'

'I was married for a couple of years in the early seventies. My wife died in childbirth – the child too.'

'And you didn't marry again?'

'I never fancied anyone enough.'

'Don't you have a paramour?' Marshall persisted.

'No.'

'Even a regular *fille de nuit* would help.'

'Look here,' said Bragg in exasperation, 'I'm a policeman, not a frigging whoremonger. Once you start pawing women around, you're finished as a copper. They can put the squeeze on you, any time they like . . . Blast it! That's what this case is all about, isn't it?'

'So to get off a rape charge, you've got to be assiduously promiscuous, or a sodomite!' Morton said with a laugh.

'That's about the size of it,' replied Bragg.

'Well, if it's any comfort to you, Charlton Marshall is very well thought of in the profession. I spoke to a barrister who was at Trinity with me. He's just started to practise at the criminal bar, and he says Marshall is head and shoulders above the other young QCs.'

'I expect he'll do his best,' said Bragg gruffly. 'Now, what have you got for me?'

'You were, of course, perfectly right about the cart. I tracked down a vet, who saw it stationary in George Street about five o'clock. He was quite certain about the horse.'

'Did he see the men?'

'He said there were three in addition to the driver. One of them was "asleep" on the cart.'

'Does that tally?' asked Bragg. 'The constable said there were four or five, and the carter they found last Sunday said three men plus the driver.'

'If you take the constable as having seen five in all, then it does. When they were in George Street, they would have sent a man to reconnoitre, but Foster would still be on the cart. When they'd disposed of Foster, the scout would have taken his place.'

'Good. Have you heard from the Whitechapel police yet?'

'Not yet.'

'If there's nothing by the beginning of next week, you'd better go round the hay merchants yourself. Drop a word to the

Met boys first, won't you?'

'Yes, I'll do that.'

'We've got to follow that lead for all it's worth; we have precious little else.'

'We did get a telegram from the Cardiff police. It must have cost a fortune! I had to leave the original with Inspector Cotton. He's keeping a fatherly eye on the cases I'm suposely running. However, I did make some notes.'

'Be careful what you tell Cotton. He'd kill any enquiry that would help me, like he'd tread on a cockroach.'

'Don't worry. So far as he's concerned, I'm investigating the Foster murder in blinkers.'

'Right. Then what did the telegram say?'

'It appears that Dic Penderyn was a Welsh patriot, if that's the right word.' Morton took a fold of paper from his pocket. 'He was hanged at eight o'clock on Saturday the thirteenth of August eighteen thirty-one . . . You can't say they're not thorough in the Cardiff police!'

'Probably they sympathize with him. What had he done?'

'He was somehow mixed up with riots in Merthyr Tydfil. The miners seem to have marched on the town centre, and attacked the house of the government official there. Troops were called out next day, and the rioters attacked them too, and seized some of their muskets. The soldiers fired into the crowd, and several people were killed. After that, the insurrection developed quite spectacularly. The rioters ambushed an ammunition party in the hills, and even disarmed the Swansea Yeomanry.'

'Quite a to-do,' remarked Bragg. 'It was never in any of the history books I read.'

'It was probably regarded as an unimportant local disturbance when it was all over, but at the time the government seems to have panicked. They obviously decided to hang a few people to cow the populace, and one they picked on was Dic Penderyn.'

'Which no doubt transformed him from a patriot into a martyr . . . But all this happened sixty years ago. Why have people got to remember him now?'

'Perhaps there's a revival of Welsh nationalism,' said

Morton. 'If there is, the newspapers have been remarkably silent about it. I'll do a little research.'

'It might be worth another telegram to Cardiff.'

'Very well. Anything else?'

'I can't think of any.' Bragg stood up, and to Morton's surprise, held out his hand. 'If they don't let me out after tomorrow's hearing, I know you'll do your best.'

Morton squeezed his hand, wordlessly, and stumbled down the stairs into the darkening street. For the first time in his life, he felt that more was asked of him than he could possibly perform. He recalled his annoyance at Bragg's explosion of dismay on being told that he had been appointed to take over his cases. But it had been totally justified; he was a mere apprentice, his growing confidence entirely dependent on the presence of his master. It was Bragg who had the expertise, the instinctive feel for the right tactics, for when to bring pressure, and when to let things develop. It was pointless to tell himself that this was the fruit of long experience. He needed it now. He wouldn't be able to run to Bragg for advice any more, and he wouldn't get it from Cotton. Everybody else was prepared to play along with the Special Branch. The Foster case would gently die, and Bragg would rot in prison . . . Rubbish! He was getting maudlin. There was still time, even if they did remand Bragg in custody. One thing was sure: he'd do everything he could, officially or unofficially, to see that it didn't happen.

He bounded up the stairs to his rooms with a lighter heart. His manservant met him in the hall.

'There's a cold supper in the dining-room, as you requested, Master James, and you'll find some letters on the table in the drawing-room.'

'Thank you, Chambers.'

There were two envelopes reposing on a silver salver, both with round feminine handwriting. He picked one up, and opened it. It was from Catherine Marsden. She asked him to be early at court next morning, as she was bringing a photographer to try to get a snapshot of the Jessop girl. Brilliant! Why hadn't he thought of that himself? With a sudden access of optimism, he picked up the other envelope. It was heavy vellum, in a light shade of mauve, and was delicately scented. Morton smiled as he opened it. Yes, it was from Helga.

12, St James's Square,
London W
26 August

My dear James,
   We journeyed back to London yesterday after a deluge of
rain. It was to me a great sadness to leave your beautiful Priory
and your charming family.
   Now Karl tells me that he must be away from London for
some days. He has taken ship from Weymouth to study the
cows of Jersey. I hope that you will rescue me from being
marooned in my rooms till he returns. I have no other
acquaintance in this rather frightening city.

   Yours,
   Helga

At least Viennese girls didn't go in for mock modesty, thought
Morton. The weekend itself would have to depend on the
outcome of Bragg's trial, but at the very least Friday evening
was free. He could take her to the concert of German music at
the St James's Hall. No one could look askance at his escorting
her to a public entertainment without companions. Not that a
widow needed a chaperone in the same way as an unmarried
girl. There was Karl to consider, of course; but he could hardly
object to his cousin's going to a perfectly innocent concert.

   Morton smiled in anticipation, and sitting down at his
escritoire, began to scribble a reply.

11

When Morton arrived at the court, he could see that Catherine
was already there. She was dressed in the blue tailor-
made, white jabot and perky little hat that for her were
just as much a uniform as the City clerk's morning coat
and bowler.

'Good morning, Miss Marsden,' he greeted her. 'A bit windy
this morning, isn't it?'

'I feel I shall be lifted up any moment and carried over the
rooftops,' she replied with a smile. 'I want you to meet Aubrey
Rivington. He's the photographer I mentioned in my note.'

'Ah yes. How do you do?' Morton took an instant dislike to
the man. Apart from his fluttering yellow locks and sketchy
beard, he was wearing a green velvet smoking-jacket with a
floppy orange bow at the neck.

'It's a stroke of pure genius to get a likeness of the girl,'
Morton remarked, turning to Catherine. 'But surely it will be
difficult?'

'Well, of course it's different from doing it in my studio,' said
Rivington. 'The wind may interfere with my magnesium gun.
Still, it's nice and sunny on this side of the street, so I think we
have a good chance.' He spoke in a soft mincing voice that
dwelt fractionally too long on every vowel.

'Aubrey is our foremost society photographer,' said Catherine with a smile. 'If it can be done at all, Aubrey will do it.'

'Shouldn't you be erecting your equipment?' asked Morton.
He thought he saw a flicker of amusement cross Catherine's
face, instantly extinquished.

'Yes, Aubrey,' she agreed. 'We don't know when she will
come.'

'Very well.' He picked up a tripod that had been lying by the wall, and set it up about ten feet from the steps of the court. Then he took a large plate-camera from a canvas bag, and secured it on the tripod. 'Which way will she come?' he asked.

'Oh, my goodness!' exclaimed Catherine. 'I hadn't thought of that. A photo of the back of her head wouldn't be much use.'

'I should think it will be all right where it is,' said Morton. 'If she's coming from home, she'll come from the Elephant and Castle. But more than likely she'll be with the prosecution people, going over her evidence. In either case she'll come from the Borough High Street end.'

'And if not?' asked Catherine.

'Then we'll have to try to get her to turn round.'

Rivington had now disappeared under the black cloth at the back of his camera, and was pulling and pushing the lens, to get his focus. He looked, thought Morton, for all the world like a strange five-legged monster picking its nose.

'Catherine dear,' he called, appearing briefly from under the drapery, 'could you go and stand at the foot of the steps? Just a little beyond their centre, and in the middle of the pavement . . . a little further back . . . just where you would begin to turn to go up into the court . . . That's right. Stay there a moment, dear.' He disappeared again, and twiddled briefly with the lens. 'That's lovely! You can come back now, Cathy.' He turned to Morton. 'The girl will be in focus from well the other side of the steps, to about three feet this side. So if she comes from behind us, I wouldn't want you to cause her to turn round until she's just about to go up the steps.'

'We shall have to conceal the camera,' said Catherine. 'If she sees it, she could easily hide her face, and we would have wasted our time.'

'We could stand in front of it,' said Morton, 'close together as if we were talking, then jump apart at the last moment.'

'You'd better tell me what she looks like,' Rivington said plaintively.

'I haven't any idea,' replied Catherine in dismay.

'Nor have I,' Morton admitted. 'The only person on our side who has seen her is Sergeant Bragg. Damnation! How thoughtless can one become? I should never have allowed him to come to court on his own this morning.'

'Don't worry.' Catherine brushed a speck of fluff from his sleeve. 'We can only do our best.'

The echo of Bragg's last remark to him only increased Morton's irritation. They stood and watched the trickle of clerks and policemen going up the steps, with an occasional barrister, his large dolly-bag slung over his shoulder. The other two were now chattering about mutual acquaintances . . . Society butterflies by the sound of it. Morton was surprised at Catherine; somehow he hadn't been prepared for this shallow side, and he was becoming more angry by the moment at the way the photographer fawned on her. He turned his head away from them, and saw Bragg striding firmly across the road.

'Good morning,' he said in a taut voice, raising his hat to Catherine. 'What's going on?'

'Thank goodness you've come!' Catherine said, with a reassuring smile. 'We intend to take a photograph of Miss Jessop, as she goes into court. We've just realized that none of us knows what she looks like.'

'I'm not sure I do either,' said Bragg. 'Still, it's a good notion. I'll just pop inside, to show them I've not scarpered, then I'll be back.'

By the time Rivington had loaded a plate into his camera, Bragg had returned.

'Miss Marsden and I are going to stand in front of the camera, to screen it,' said Morton. 'Mr Rivington will tell us when to pull apart.'

'Then I'd better stand with him,' said Bragg. 'It will look natural. As soon as I see her, I'll tell you.'

They took up their positions, Catherine next to Morton. With her full skirt, he noted, she amply screened the tripod; she was tall, too, for a girl, every bit of five foot eight or nine. She glanced up and caught him gazing at her, then smiled and tucked her arm beneath his.

'That's better,' she said.

'Watch out,' cried Bragg. 'There's a group of people coming along now. I can't make them all out. I think there's a woman with them . . . Yes, there is. I can't see her face, the man with her keeps leaning inwards to talk to her . . . I wish to God she'd look up . . . It's them! It must be. That's the prosecuting solicitor talking to her.'

'I can't see her face,' wailed Rivington.

Morton swivelled round. The girl was walking sedately, her hands crossed before her, her head bowed. He released Catherine's arm, and they stepped apart . . . She was walking like a bloody nun, thought Morton . . . Only two more paces, and they'd be turning into the court. Then the solicitor drew to one side, so that his client could mount the steps first. Morton took a deep breath.

'Jessop!' he shouted.

The girl looked up, startled. There was a sizzling flash as the magnesium gun went off, and a click.

'Lovely, lovely!' gurgled Rivington, deftly removing the plate. 'Oh, I know it's going to be there, I just know it!'

'Now, Aubrey,' said Catherine urgently. 'You go straight back and develop that plate. Send me some prints as quickly as you can, and lock the plate up in your bank. Do you understand? It's very important.'

There was a surprising number of people in court, thought Morton, even a scattering in the public gallery. It was probably as good a diversion as any other, if you'd nothing to do. He had gained access to the back of the court by showing his warrant card, while Catherine was on the press bench, with two male reporters. The court had been opened, and the magistrate, high on the dais under the royal arms, was leafing through his papers. There was a group of men on the left side of the lawyers' benches, in the well of the court. Three of them wore a barrister's wig and gown. The right-hand one, on the front bench, must be Charlton Marshall. He exuded an air of alert confidence, and the sheen of his silk gown contrasted with the dingy stuff of the junior's to the left of him. Morton was amused to note that the junior was, by a considerable number of years, Marshall's senior. They were talking quietly together, the junior making an occasional gesture to emphasize a point. On the row behind them sat the pimply solicitor's clerk, still obviously bewildered; and beside him was a young barrister, presumably a pupil, wearing an unsullied white wig and an expression of aloof disdain on his face.

On the right-hand end of the front bench sat the prosecuting solicitor, isolated and alone. In his frock coat he looked amateurish and vulnerable. Presumably that was the intention. He appeared to feel it, too, for he leaned over to Marshall with a sycophantic smile, and said, 'I am not accustomed to having my accused defended by so illustrious a counsel.'

'Nonsense, man,' replied Marshall with a wolfish smile. 'It's perfectly straightforward. Just follow the rules of evidence, and there's no difficulty in the world.'

Morton found it difficult to decide whether the prosecutor was reassured by the words, or disconcerted by the smile. At all events, he withdrew and began to fiddle with the documents in front of him.

The magistrate now leaned forward to his clerk, and the latter rose portentously to his feet. 'The case of Joseph Bragg,' he announced.

There was a scrabble of feet at the back of the dock, and Bragg came into view, staring straight in front of him. He stood with his hands grasping the rail, and Morton could see the knuckles showing white.

'You are Joseph Bragg?' asked the clerk.

'Yes, sir.'

'I am going to read the charges to you. Since, however, these are indictable offences, I shall not require you to plead to them. Do you understand?'

'Yes.'

The clerk took up the charge sheet, and cleared his throat. 'Joseph Bragg, you are firstly charged that on Saturday the twenty-second of August in the year of Our Lord eighteen hundred and ninety-one, you did feloniously attempt to rape a female person, to wit Mary Jessop.' He glared at Bragg, lest he should dare to declare his innocence.

'You are secondly charged that on Saturday the twenty-second of August in the year of Our Lord eighteen hundred and ninety-one, you did assault the said Mary Jessop with intent to commit a felony.'

'You are thirdly charged that on Saturday the twenty-second

of August in the year of Our Lord eighteen hundred and ninety-one, you did commit an indecent assault on a female person, to wit, the said Mary Jessop. Do you understand the charges?'

'Yes.'

'Then you may sit down.' The clerk subsided into his chair, his moment of glory over.

'I take it, Mr Philpot,' said the magistrate in his high-pitched voice, 'that these are in the nature of alternative charges.'

'They are indeed, your worship.'

'I thought so.' He looked over his glasses towards the dock, and smiled thinly. 'I felt it might be of some comfort to the defendant, to establish that at the outset.' He settled himself in his ornate chair, and dipped his pen in the ink-well. 'Yes, Mr Philpot?'

The prosecuting solicitor rose to his feet with a sideways look at Marshall.

'Your worship,' he began in a subdued voice, 'the facts that underlie these three charges are in no way complicated. Nor do they differ in essence from the many cases you must have heard, involving attacks on helpless women. And the eminence of counsel for the defence is not occasioned by any difficulty you would encounter in construing the applicable law. You will hear during the evidence that the defendant claimed to be a police officer, and indeed that has been established as being the truth. You will recall that I submitted a missive from one of his superiors acknowledging as much.' He broke off, as the magistrate began to hunt through his bundle.

'Ah yes. I have it.' The magistrate read the document carefully, then laid it precisely on the top left-hand corner of his desk. He wrote briefly in the large book in front of him.

'Proceed,' he said.

Philpot had been thrown out of his stride by the interruption, and now had recourse to reading from his notes.

'Your worship,' he went on, 'the prosecution submits that the defendant's profession should have no influence on your consideration of the evidence. No assumption should be made that because the defendant is engaged in enforcing the law, he would therefore not break the law. In my submission he should be dealt with as would any other citizen, faced with these charges.' Philpot glanced across at Marshall, somnolent in his place, and appeared to draw comfort from the spectacle.

'Your worship,' he said in a more confident voice, 'the complainant, a young woman of gentle upbringing, was returning home from Deptford on the evening of the day in question. She proceeded to the railway station, and boarded a train to take her to Charing Cross. You will hear that the only other occupant of the compartment she entered was the defendant . . . ' He hesitated. 'And I do not think the fact is disputed.' He glanced round at Bragg, sitting stony-faced in the dock.

'Your worship will be told that as she sat down in the corner furthest away from the defendant, he made a remark to her. A remark to which she made the briefest reply consistent with decorum. You will hear that as soon as the train drew out of Deptford station, the defendant crossed over to her, and seizing her wrists, attempted to force intimacies on her. She resisted and cried for help. You will hear how he redoubled his efforts, tearing her garments, and injuring her in the process. You will be told how, upon the train's arrival at London Bridge station, the occupants of the neighbouring compartment detained him, and how he was subsequently arrested by the police. You will also hear evidence from a nursing sister at Guy's Hospital, who examined the complainant after the alleged attack.'

Philpot paused, and picked up another piece of paper. 'Your worship, although the defendant ought, in my submission, to be treated as would any other subject of the Crown, your worship might consider that public policy requires an altogether higher standard to be applied to those whose duty it is to protect us from lawbreakers. Your worship might feel that, as with Caesar's wife, society cannot tolerate even a suspicion of guilt in the guardians of her peace. Whichever view your worship takes, it is my submission that if there is the slightest doubt in your mind as to the weight of the evidence, you should err on the side of the complainant, and send this case for trial to the assize.'

The magistrate appeared about to take issue over the suggestion that he could err, then thought better of it.

'Your worship, I call Mary Jessop.'

'Call Mary Jessop,' repeated the usher.

A policeman opened the door to the corridor. 'Mary Jessop,' he called.

She had shed her cloak, and now appeared in a plain brown dress with a bodice buttoned high at the neck, and a beige frill around the throat. Her hair was drawn back into a bun on the nape of her neck; on her head was a small brown and beige hat, trimmed with ribbon and flowers. She was decidedly plain, thought Morton. It was a wonder they hadn't chosen someone prettier, the whole episode would have seemed more likely then. But he had to admit that she looked weak and defenceless, with her slight body and pale face. And from the murmur that ran round the court, it was obvious that she had the public's sympathy. She read the oath in a soft well-modulated voice, as if she were an intimate of the Almighty.

'Miss Jessop,' began Philpot, his deep voice mellifluous, 'I am going to take you through the events of Saturday the twenty-second of this month. I do not wish to cause you any distress, so please do not hurry. And if you feel the need to sit down at any time, please say so.'

Her murmured reply was inaudible to Morton.

'Is your name Mary Jessop?'

'It is.'

'And do you live at number twelve, St Mark's Road, Kennington?'

'I do.'

'Do you live there alone?'

'No. I live with my mother.'

'Have you any other relations?'

'No. My father is dead.'

She had been well rehearsed, thought Morton. Her voice was low, yet carrying perfectly, her face the picture of vulnerable purity. She just had to be an actress, the erring daughter turned out into the snow. He'd seen it scores of times.

'Will you tell the court where you had been on that Saturday evening?' asked Philpot, with a reassuring smile.

'I had been to a meeting of the British and Foreign Bible Society, at the Deptford Mission Hall.'

'Pause there,' Philpot instructed, holding up his hand. 'His worship has to take down what you are saying.'

'I'm sorry, sir.' Her voice was full of solicitude, and it extracted a friendly smile from the magistrate.

'And when the meeting was over, what did you do?'

'I went to the railway station, to catch a train home.'

'How many of you went to the station at that time?'

'I was alone. I sat at the back of the hall, because I wanted to be able to leave without delay.'

'Why was that?' asked Philpot.

'Because I had a long journey home.'

'How many minutes did you have to wait at the station?'

'A train was arriving as I came on to the platform . . . I thought I was very fortunate,' she added plaintively.

Marshall jerked up in his seat, as if about to raise an objection, then slumped down again.

'Did you board the train?'

'Yes. Some gentlemen were just leaving it, and one of them held the door open for me.'

'Were you alone in the compartment?'

'No. There was a man there, also.'

'Do you recognize that man in this court?'

A look of fear and revulsion crept over her face. She glanced at the dock, and pointed to Bragg.

'I am sorry, Miss Jessop,' Philpot said gently. 'However repugnant it may be to you, the law requires that you answer the question.'

'The defendant.' She bit her lower lip, and dropped her eyes to the floor.

'What happened then?'

'He spoke to me.'

'What did he say?'

'He remarked that I had only just succeeded in catching the train.'

'What did you reply?'

'I said "yes", and turned away to the window.'

'What happened then?'

'The train set off.'

'And then?'

'As soon as it had left the station, the . . . the defendant got up from his seat and came towards me.'

'Did he say anything?'

'He said, "What about a little cuddle?" I said, "No." Then he said, "Come on, be a sport," and sat down beside me.'

Philpot appeared to be wondering if he would manage to get his witness through her evidence. His voice became soothing, almost caressing. 'What happened then?'

'He put his arm round my neck, and . . . and began to pull open the front of my blouse.'

'Where exactly?'

'At the breast.' Her voice was trembling.

'What did you do?'

'I screamed for help, and begged him to stop.'

'And did he?'

'No. He held both my wrists in one hand, and began to pull at my shift. I tried to fight him off, but he was too strong. He tore open my clothes and . . . touched me.' She fumbled in her bag for a handkerchief.

'You can take a rest, if you like,' the magistrate said kindly. She dabbed at her eyes, and sniffed. 'No, I'll be all right, sir.'

'Then, usher, give the young lady a glass of water.'

There was a delay of some minutes, while a glass was filled and taken to her. She sipped delicately, then put the glass down on the edge of the witness-box.

'Are you ready to continue?' asked the magistrate.

'Yes, your worship.'

'The last thing I have is: "He touched me." '

'Thank you, your worship,' said Philpot, and turned back to his witness. 'What did the defendant do then?' he asked.

'It seemed to make him worse. He tried to kiss me. I got one hand free and scratched his face, but he seized it again, and began to pull my skirt up above my knee.' Her face bore witness to her determination to relive the nightmare, whatever pain it cost her.

'And then?'

'He stood up, and pushed me down on to the seat.'

'And all this time, what were you doing?'

'I was screaming, and struggling.'

'What happened then?'

'I felt him forcing his leg between my knees. I begged him to stop, but he continued, forcing my thighs wide apart.'

'What did you do?'

'I closed my eyes, and prayed for deliverance.'

'And then?'

'I felt him dragging at my underclothes. I managed to get one hand free, and struck at him again. Then I heard the train slowing, and I knew my prayer had been answered.'

'What happened when the train stopped?'

'I heard the door open, and looked up. He was still standing over me, holding my wrists. But there were people outside.'

'And then?'

'A policeman came, and I was helped off the train, and looked after.'

'Thank you, Miss Jessop.' Philpot resumed his seat.

Morton thought he detected a subtle change in her, as Marshall rose to his feet; a tensing of the muscles, a new wariness in the eyes.

'Miss Jessop,' he began urbanely, 'you said that your father is no longer alive.'

'That's right.'

'When did he die?'

'In June of eighteen eighty-eight.'

'What was his profession?'

'He was a Church of England clergyman.'

'And what was his last benefice?'

'St John's church, East Dulwich.'

'Can you tell me the name of the previous incumbent?'

'I don't know. I was only five when we moved there.'

'So you grew up in the vicarage?'

'Yes.'

'Did you have any brothers or sisters?'

'No.'

'Where did you go to school?'

'While I was small, I went to school near my home. Then I went to Dulwich High School.'

'And when did you leave?'

'When I was seventeen.'

'Can you tell me the name of the headmistress?'

'Yes. Miss Alger.'

'What did you do after leaving school?'

'I lived at home with my parents, and helped in the parish.'

'And how old were you when your father died?'

A gentle sadness tinged her face. 'Nineteen and a half,' she said softly.

'Where have you been living since then?'

'My father's death was very sudden, and we were left with little money. We knew the vicar of a church near Newcastle. He had at one time been curate to my father. He begged us to stay with them, out of the regard he had for my father.'

'His name?'

'Charles Firth.'

'And when did you leave the Firth abode?'

'Two months ago.'

'Why?'

'His family was growing, and we had become an embarrassment to him. My mother insisted, much against his wishes, that we should leave.'

'Where did you go to?'

'After several unfortunate experiences, we secured lodgings in the house where we now live.'

'Good,' Marshall drawled indifferently. He turned to his notes, then swung round briskly. 'Why were you in Deptford on your own?' he asked.

'My mother was unwell, and could not come.'

'Why didn't you stay at home with her?'

'I had looked forward to the meeting. There was a very inspiring speaker.'

'And how did you propose to get back to Kennington, at that time of night?'

'The train would have taken me to Charing Cross station. From there I would have taken a number three bus to Kennington Oval.'

'And from there?'

'It is a very short walk to my home.'

'What time did you expect to arrive there?'

'It would depend on how long I had to wait for a bus, but by half past ten, at the latest.'

'But by then it would have been dark for well over an hour,' exclaimed Marshall incredulously. 'Are you saying that you knowingly went to a meeting which would entail your journeying back across London, for some two hours, at night, and alone?'

'Yes.'

'Was not that exceedingly reckless?'

'I was in God's hands,' she said simply.

Marshall fixed her with a baleful stare. 'Miss Jessop, are you a virgin?'

There was a gasp from the court, and the magistrate looked up startled.

Philpot jumped to his feet. 'Your worship, that was an unnecessary and brutal question,' he protested.

The magistrate looked coldly at Marshall. 'I am bound to protect witnesses from gratuitous abuse by counsel,' he said. 'Would you kindly explain, Mr Marshall, why your question is relevant to the matters here under consideration?'

'I don't mind answering the question, your worship,' the girl interrupted. Philpot subsided anxiously, and the magistrate went back to his book.

'Could you please repeat the question?' she asked.

'Are you a virgin, Miss Jessop?'

'Yes,' she cried in a triumphant tone.

'Have you ever had physical intimacies with men?'

'Never.'

Marshall sat down, and the girl turned to go.

'One moment, Miss Jessop,' said the magistrate. 'You said in reply to the prosecution, that when the defendant first spoke to you, you made him an answer.'

'Yes, your worship.'

'Bearing in mind that a man's liberty is at stake, are you satisfied in your own mind that he could not have construed your answer as some kind of invitation?'

'Quite satisfied, your worship.'

'Very well. Thank you, Miss Jessop.'

She stepped down from the box, and walked sedately out of the court, her face showing nothing but resignation and compassion. A magnificent performance, thought Morton, and glanced over at the dock. Bragg's sagging shoulders eloquently displayed his dejection.

'I call Police Constable Fitch,' said Philpot.

The constable bustled into the witness-box with a no-nonsense air, and took the oath in a brisk gabble. 'Three seven two PC Fitch, railway police, attached to London Bridge station,' he announced, then half turned towards the magistrate.

'Constable Fitch, were you on duty on the evening of Saturday the twenty-second of this month?' asked Philpot.

'I was.' Fitch produced a note book from his top pocket.

'By all means use your notes to refresh your memory,' Philpot said hurriedly. 'Will you tell the court how soon after the incident you made that record?'

'About a half hour after the defendant was charged.'

Marshall looked across at Fitch, and made a note on his papers.

'Will you tell the court what happened on that evening?'

'At fifty-four minutes past eight o'clock, I was on duty at platform four, and I noticed a crowd gathering around the first carriage of a train that had just come in.' He paused while the magistrate laboriously recorded the information. 'I approached the disturbance, and saw through the open door of the compartment, a man whom I now recognize as the defendant.' He then turned towards the dock, to make a retrospective identification.

'He was standing between the legs of a young woman, whom I now know to be Mary Jessop. He was holding her wrists. Miss Jessop was half-lying on the seat.' He turned over a page of his note book, and waited till the scratching of the magistrate's pen ceased. 'The defendant said, "Constable, this young woman needs a doctor." Miss Jessop said, "He tried to rape me." I subsequently arrested the defendant, and charged him.' The constable put away his note book and turned to the prosecuting solicitor.

'What subsequently happened to Miss Jessop?' Philpot asked.

'I sent her, accompanied by another lady, to Guy's hospital.'

'And what was your purpose in that?'

'Partly to establish the extent of her injuries; and anyway, she was in a very nervous state.'

'Thank you, Officer.'

Marshall rose casually to his feet. 'Constable Fitch,' he asked, 'did you at any time see the defendant adjusting his dress?'

Fitch looked puzzled. 'I don't understand your question, sir,' he said.

'I mean in the sense of the notice in our urinals, which says, "Please adjust your dress before leaving." '

'I see, sir. No, I didn't.'

'Can you go further? Were the buttons on the fly of the defendant's trousers fastened all the time he was within your observation?'

'I'm sorry. I didn't notice.'

'You didn't notice whether they were fastened, or unfastened. But in view of the allegations, you would surely have noticed had they been undone?'

'Possibly.'

'Thank you, Constable. That is all.'

Philpot rose to his feet again, with a smile of growing confidence. 'Call Sister Becket.'

The nurse appeared in a starched white cap and collar, a blue cape thrown over her shoulders. She took the oath with composure.

'Are you Ethel Becket? asked Philpot. His right hand was now thrust into his trouser pocket, and he was patently addressing his questions to the press bench.

'Yes.'

'Are you a nursing sister at Guy's hospital?'

'I am.'

'Will you tell the court what happened on the night of the twenty-second of August?'

'I was on duty in the casualty ward. About ten o'clock, a woman brought in a young lady. She said a man had tried to rape her, and the police wanted us to make an examination of her.'

'And did you do so?'

'Yes.'

'What did you find?'

'Her blouse and shift were torn, and there was a three-inch scratch on her left breast.'

'Did you form an opinion as to how the injury might have occurred?'

'It could have been caused by the fingernail of someone opening her blouse roughly.'

'Had she any other injuries?'

'Yes. Both her wrists were red and tender.'

'What was her general condition?'

'She was almost in a state of hysteria. I gave her a sedative, and put her to bed.'

Philpot sat down, with a smile at Catherine.

'Sister Becket,' said Marshall crisply, 'you were told by Miss Jessop's companion that she had been the victim of a sexual assault.'

'Yes, sir.'

'Have you seen many victims of such attacks?'

'Oh yes, plenty.'

'How would you compare the condition of Miss Jessop, with the generality of such cases?'

'Well, like I said, she was very upset.'

'And her injuries?'

'I've seen much worse . . . but it depends how far they get, doesn't it?'

'You mean the attackers?'

'Yes.'

'You say there was a scratch on the left breast. Where exactly was it?'

'It began in the middle of the chest, and ran straight across, ending an inch above the nipple.'

'Is it possible that she could have inflicted such an injury on herself – deliberately?'

'Well . . . ' The nurse pursed her lips in thought. 'Yes, I suppose so.'

'Did you, Sister Becket, extend your examination beyond the breasts and the wrists?'

'No.'

'Why not?'

'Those were the injured areas.'

'Did you not give her an internal examination?'

'Well, I . . . '

'Surely in a rape case,' pursued Marshall, 'it is important to establish whether or not penetration had taken place?'

'But I was told he'd only tried it on.' The nurse was looking flustered now.

'Did you look for seminal stains on the girl's underwear?'

'No. She got into such a state while I was examining her, I had to put her to bed.'

'What time was that?'

'About half past ten.'

'Did you complete your examination next morning?'

'I didn't see her again. I went off duty at six.'

'I suggest to you, Sister Becket, that the examination you made was superficial in the extreme.'

'I did what was necessary,' said the nurse in an injured tone.

'I suggest that you accepted the version of events as told to you by Miss Jessop and her companion, without a vestige of independent critical observation.'

'It's not true.'

'And that your testimony should not be accepted by the court as emanating from an expert witness.'

'No.'

'At any rate, it is clear you are unable to assist the court in the matter of whether Miss Jessop was a virgin or not.' Marshall sat down without waiting for a reply.

Philpot stood, one hand resting elegantly on the edge of his desk, and waited for the magistrate to finish writing.

'Call Amelia Harding,' he said.

The woman was short, stout, and overbearing. Her coat was open in front, and Morton could see string after string of beads draped across her ample bosom.

'You are Amelia Harding?' asked Philpot.

'Of course I am,' the woman answered crossly.

Philpot smiled indulgently, and glanced across at Catherine. 'And do you live at three, Harrow Road, Sudbury?'

'I do.'

'And were you a passenger on a train from Dartford to Charing Cross on Saturday the twenty-second of August?'

'Yes, I was. And I think it's a disgrace that the police can't give us women better protection from the likes of him.' She shot a venomous glance at Bragg in the dock.

'Madam,' fluted the magistrate, 'please confine your remarks to answering the questions put to you, and do not address the court.'

The woman looked up rebelliously, her jaw set hard.

'Did you hear anything unusual during that journey?' asked Philpot.

'Indeed I did. We'd hardly pulled out of Deptford station when a girl's screams started coming from the next compartment.'

'Pause there,' instructed Philpot, his hand raised dramatically until the magistrate looked up from his book.

'Could you distinguish any words?' asked Philpot.

'Yes. She was shouting, "No. No. Please stop it." Then after some more screams, I heard, "Stop. Stop. Leave me alone." '

'What happened then?'

'Some of the men began knocking on the partition between the two compartments, but it made no difference.'

'And then what?'

'At London Bridge station we all got out and opened the door of the next compartment.'

'And what did you see?'

'He had her down on the seat, with her clothes up round her waist.'

'Your worship,' Marshall interposed, springing to his feet, 'I am reluctant to interrupt the examination by the prosecution of what is evidently a particularly recalcitrant witness; the more so as these are merely preliminary proceedings. However, I would like to be assured that the prejudicial comment in the last reply will not appear on the deposition.'

'Have no fear, Mr Marshall,' said the magistrate. 'My record merely says that the young woman was down on the seat.'

'Thank you, your worship.' Marshall half sat down, then rose again. 'Since there has been this interruption,' he said, 'might I suggest that it would be appropriate for the prosecution to establish that this witness's evidence is relevant to my client?' he sat down.

'Ah, yes. I apologize, your worship.' Philpot's smile was a little threadbare now.

'Mrs Harding,' he asked, 'do you recognize anyone in this court as being the man you saw in that compartment?'

'Yes,' she said defiantly. 'Him!' She flung out her arm in the direction of the dock.

'Now you said the young lady was down on the seat. Where was the defendant in relation to her?'

'He had her by the wrists and he was between her legs, just going to . . .'

'Madam!' cried the magistrate peremptorily. 'You really must stop colouring your answers by your own moral convictions, and merely reply to the question.'

'But he's asking me what I saw,' she protested vehemently.

'Yes. But we are concerned here with facts,' observed the magistrate drily, 'not with retribution.' He wrote briefly in his book, then nodded at Philpot.

'Did the police constable later ask you to do something?'

'Yes, he did, and I missed my train home through it.'

'What was that?'

'He asked me to take Miss Jessop to Guy's hospital.'

'And did you do so?'

'Of course I did,' she snorted.

'And did anything happen on the way?'

'We were nearly there, when Miss Jessop said she would have to stop.'

'Did she say why?'

'She said her drawers were coming down. She said he must have torn them.'

'What did she do?'

'We went into a doorway, and I screened her while she secured them with a safety pin I gave her.

'And did you see the garment?'

'Yes. It was badly torn at the waist.'

'Thank you.' Philpot sat down in relief.

Marshall rose slowly, and turning towards the witness-box studied Mrs Harding for some moments, while she gazed truculently back. Nevertheless, the tone of his first question was surprisingly mild.

'Why didn't you stop the train?'

'Well, I . . . '

'You heard screams from the next compartment as soon as the train left Deptford. Why did you not attempt to stop it?'

'One of the men said it was better to let it go on to London Bridge.'

'Some six minutes away? What reason did he give?'

'He said the train couldn't go back to the station because of the points.'

'I see. Would you recognize this man again?'

'I might. He was just an ordinary man.'

'You said that when the carriage door was opened, you saw the defendant standing in front of Miss Jessop,' observed Marshall pleasantly. 'Was there any dust on the defendant's trousers?'

'I don't know what you're suggesting,' she said suspiciously.

'I am not suggesting anything. Please reply to my question.'

'Well . . . no.'

'Mrs Harding, do you travel on trains frequently?'

'Very frequently,' she asserted.

'What would you say the distance is between the cushion of the seat, and the floor . . . eighteen, twenty inches?'

'I suppose so.'

'It is about at the back of the knee as you sit down, is it not?'

'Yes,' she replied cautiously.

'You are a married woman I take it?'

'Indeed I am!' she exclaimed indignantly.

'Then you must have some notion of where the male appendage of generation is to be found.'

There was consternation in court. Philpot bounced up. 'I protest,' he cried, swinging round towards the press bench. Mrs Harding seemed about to burst in outrage; the magistrate took off his spectacles reprovingly. But Marshall had already sat down. In the hubbub, Mrs Harding was bustled out of the court, red-faced and spluttering.

Morton caught Catherine's eye, and she smiled with satisfaction.

'That concludes my examination of the witnesses for the prosecution,' said Philpot, and sat down heavily.

Marshall did not rise immediately; he waited till the whispering and tittering had died away. Then he rose, the embodiment of authority and experience.

'Your worship,' he began in measured tones. 'It is axiomatic that no class of case demands more vigilance on the part of the judiciary, a more scrupulous weighing of the evidence, than does that of offences against women. A woman, according to that weighty authority, *Taylor on Evidence* . . . a woman has an innate love of the marvellous, and is often prone to exaggeration. Everyone involved with the administration of justice has experience of young women who, having committed an indiscretion, then throw the whole blame upon the man, reckless of the outcome of that course. Your worship, the purity of a woman is undoubtedly a jewel, but it is not a pearl beyond price. It would be abhorrent to all civilized principles, that a man should be incarcerated for life without overwhelming evidence of his guilt.

'Your worship, in my submission, not only is that degree of testimony lacking in this case; the whole story is absurd and unworthy of credence. Can one really imagine that any man would endeavour to force his attentions on a strange, and therefore presumably hostile, woman; on a train journey which cannot last longer than six minutes? A journey, moreover, which ends at a busy station, with the concomitant certainty of capture? Your worship, the case submitted by the prosecution is unsatisfactory throughout. The only direct evidence of the incident is that given by Miss Jessop. Now, she is said to be a woman of sensibility, gently brought up, jealous of her reputation. Yet she not only journeys from her home in Kennington to Deptford alone, through some of the most hazardous areas of London; but she returns thence after darkness has fallen. When challenged on the point, she indicated – with, you may feel, some presumption – that God would take care of her. A very laudable sentiment, no doubt; yet in reality, only the most feather-brained woman would hazard her person in such a way. But Miss Jessop is far from irrational. Your worship will recall her demeanour in the witness-box – controlled, lucid, rational. And according to her evidence, she met this unexpected assault in a most determined and resourceful way.

'After her "deliverance", she says she was helped down, and looked after. Now one might expect her, if an incident such as she described had occurred, to be in a state of shock. You will remember that the prosecution questioned Constable Fitch about her condition. In his reply, he said that she was in a very nervous state. No more than that. Your worship, the assault is alleged to have taken place before nine o'clock. After the elapse of somewhat more than an hour, Miss Jessop suddenly became hysterical. You will recall that Sister Becket was unable to complete her examination, and had to put Miss Jessop to bed under sedation. It is my submission that this hysteria was wholly spurious, and that it was designed to limit the evidence seen by the nursing sister to that which would support Miss Jessop's allegations, and no more. I suggest that if a full examination of her body had been undertaken, it would have demonstrated that Miss Jessop is not the sanctified virgin she pretends to be.

'Let us consider again the curious episode of the torn nether garment. Your worship will recall that Miss Jessop said she felt the defendant dragging at her underwear, just before the train pulled into London Bridge station. The court is invited to suppose that the drawers were damaged at that point. Thereafter Miss Jessop was helped down from the train, walked down to the waiting-room, stayed there for the best part of an hour, walked the considerable distance from the platform to the station entrance, and thence almost to Guy's hospital, before the damaged state of the garment manifested itself. This cannot have been less than a quarter of a mile, and yet Mrs Harding was emphatic that the drawers were badly torn at the waist. Your worship may feel that the only conclusion to be drawn from this evidence is that the garment had been deliberately torn by the complainant in order to provide corroborative evidence of the alleged attack; and had been secured in some way until what she regarded as a suitable moment arrived. Your worship, the court is presented with a dilemma. If Miss Jessop's story can be relied on, she did indeed become suddenly hysterical; if she did become belatedly hysterical, can she be accepted as a credible witness?

'And what of the evidence in corroboration of the allegations? I have already dealt with the torn underwear, and submit that no reliance should be placed on it. Mrs Harding says that she heard cries, but was unable to see what was in truth occurring in the next compartment. Both she and the constable deposed that the defendant was standing between the complainant's legs, holding her wrists. His clothing was not in disarray, or soiled. There is no evidence whatever to show that he had in any way made such dispositions as would facilitate his sexual penetration of this woman's body. The constable stated that my client shouted: "This woman needs a doctor." I suggest that my client's posture was entirely consistent with his endeavouring to restrain a woman who appeared, in the course of a brainstorm, to be doing damage to her own person. In my submission this incident was manufactured by this young woman, for reasons which at the moment remain obscure.

'Your worship, the defendant is a public servant of long standing, and of the highest integrity. The prosecution have, very properly, furnished evidence of that. Your worship, in my submission there is no evidence which would justify your placing my client on trial for his liberty, and I invite you to discharge him.'

There was a surprised hum of conversation in the court, as Marshall sat down. The magistrate held a whispered conversation with his clerk; Marshall's junior had turned round, and was discussing a point with the pupil. To Morton it was like the interval at a play. Catherine was talking to one of the other reporters, her face tense; Bragg sat erect, preparing for the worst.

'Silence,' called the clerk, and the chatter faded away. The magistrate cleared his throat, and surveyed the court.

'I have listened with great interest to the submission made on behalf of the defendant,' he began. 'And I comprehend the dilemma which has been urged on me by learned counsel. It is not in dispute that, until these allegations were made, the defendant has enjoyed a spotless reputation. I am bound to add, however, that the complainant has also lived a blameless life, so far as the evidence goes. The prosecution has not produced a testimonial to that effect, but Miss Jessop is not on trial, and the need did not arise. The defence has made certain insinuations, but they are not evidence; and while, if they were proved, they might affect the outcome of this trial, they afford no compelling reason why it should not proceed. My function is circumscribed, and my duty limited. I am required to determine whether, in my judgement, the evidence adduced might convict the defendant in the minds of a jury of twelve reasonable men . . . and I do so find. The defendant is committed for trial at the Central Criminal Court – I believe that was what your clerk requested, was it not, Mr Marshall?'

'If your worship pleases.' Marshall was on his feet in an instant. 'I would like to apply for bail to be renewed. My client was bailed at the earlier proceedings, and has acted with the utmost propriety. I am instructed to say that Sir Rufus Stone of Counsel is prepared to offer himself as surety for his due appearance.'

The magistrate was obviously impressed. He leaned towards his clerk. 'What were the terms?' he asked.

'Own recognizance of twenty pounds.'

'Very well. Bail continued as before.'

'The court will rise,' bawled the clerk. The magistrate gathered his papers together, and withdrew.

Bragg had disappeared, so Morton strolled over to Catherine.

'What a charade!' she exclaimed wrathfully. 'That girl was obviously a fraud. No woman would have been deceived for a moment. Her hairstyle was ten years out of date, and her gown was ages old. That style of dress went out six years ago to my knowledge. Nobody would go out dressed like that nowadays.'

'Not even if they were poor?' asked Morton.

'Don't be stupid,' Catherine snorted.

At that moment Bragg wandered into the well of the court, and, as they crossed to him, Marshall joined them.

'I'm sorry I didn't give you the satisfaction of going into the witness-box,' he chuckled. 'I decided you'd be too much of a liability.'

'Thank you for keeping me out of prison, anyway,' said Bragg huskily, holding out his hand.

'And you'll stay out, mark my words. No virgin would

135

describe her ordeal with such relish! Anyway, you've got the address of the vicarage and the school, it's up to you now.' He patted Bragg on the shoulder and, followed by his acolytes, left the court.

'I'll get some photographs of the Jessop girl to you on Monday,' said Catherine. 'I must rush now. I shall have to write something for tomorrow's *City Press*, and a paragraph for the *Star* . . . Don't worry, I'll say the minimum.'

'I suppose she has to,' Bragg muttered at her retreating back.

'The other two reporters certainly will. However, there is no need for you to be in London when the news breaks. My mother insists that you come down to The Priory for the weekend.'

'I couldn't trouble . . .'

'Nonsense. It's all settled. I'll call for you at nine o'clock tomorrow morning. By lunchtime you'll be in the country, shaking the creases out of your soul.'

'You are so good to me,' said Helga, taking Morton's arm and pressing against him. 'Let's walk home, it's not far.'

'If you insist.'

'I do. I am so excited, and the wind is exhilarating.'

'It will ruffle your hair,' Morton said teasingly.

'What do I care? Oh, I love Mozart, especially *Serail*. How clever of you! *Seufzt Tag und Nacht und weinte gar, Wollt 'gern erlöset sein,'* she sang, and pulled away from him, searching his face with mocking eyes. '*Woll' gern erlöset sein.*'

'You have no need to be freed,' Morton laughed.

'Ah, you do not understand, James. It is not that the maiden in the castle wishes to be at liberty, it is the moment of rescue she longs for; to have her shining knight storm the castle, and tear her away by force. That is the excitement. She does not concern herself beyond it.'

'That sounds much less urbane than Mozart.'

'Of course. He knew nothing of a woman's passion, only of his own.'

'I wouldn't contest the point. What does a mere Englishman know of such things?'

She smiled at him provocatively. 'Shall I see you tomorrow?'

she asked.

'Alas, no. My boss, Sergeant Bragg, has been falsely charged with rape. He was released on bail today, and I'm taking him off to the Priory tomorrow, away from the newspaper reporters.'

'I so loved being at that great house,' said Helga dreamily. 'Especially knowing that it will be yours one day.'

'I'm glad.' For a moment Morton was tempted to invite her also. But it wouldn't be fair to Bragg.

'And after the weekend?' asked Helga.

'I shall be fully involved for a few days in clearing up this murder case.'

'It will so soon be solved?'

'I hope so. And then I shall be at your service.'

'Good! And Karl, was he right about the label?'

'It was written in Welsh certainly, but it seems quite irrelevant to our enquiries . . . I must thank Karl, nevertheless.'

'If you are ever free from your so important duties.' Helga pouted at him, then smiled mischievously. 'We are becoming solemn. Let us run!' She lifted the hem of her dress, and began to race down the street, her cloak fluttering behind her. Morton gave chase, and came up with her just as the cloak slipped from her shoulders. He made a grab at her, but she broke from him, skipping up a flight of steps and through a doorway. Morton looked down at the cloak in his hands. She must mean him to follow . . . As he entered the hallway, he could hear her heels clattering on the marble stairs, then ceasing. He came to a landing with a half-open door, and pushed through it. She was standing facing him, the skin of her bosom creamy in the gas-light. Morton stood irresolute for a moment; then she came towards him, and put her arms around his neck.

'My bold knight,' she whispered.

He held her, then took the jewelled comb from her hair, so that it cascaded softly down over her shoulders. She looked up questioningly.

'Beautiful,' he murmured, stroking it gently. Then he took the end of the ribbon which held her dress at the shoulder, and began to tug.

'No!' she said, pulling his hand down to her breast. 'Not here . . . My bedroom . . . '

12

'Your son tells me that you are going to America soon,' remarked Bragg.

'That's right,' Lady Morton replied in her soft New England voice, then glanced mischievously towards her husband at the other end of the dinner table. 'I like to go back every year, to restore my mental balance. My father was the Ambassador of the United States to the Court of St James, so even though I am American, I was mostly brought up here.'

'Come, Mother,' said Morton with a smile, 'you're more English than American by now.'

'Ah, but that's where you're wrong . . . Though I have to admit that I've lived longer in England than anywhere else; and I do love its traditions and ceremonials, and, of course, its beautiful old buildings. I must have been exceptionally fortunate. I was presented at Court in 'fifty-seven, before Prince Albert died, and while it was still lively and full of fun. And when my handsome cavalry major proposed marriage, I felt I'd reached the pinnacle of happiness.'

'And hadn't you?' Bragg asked.

'Oh I had! I had!' exclaimed Lady Morton. 'And I would not have you think that there has been much declension from that peak. Rather I have reached a plateau of maturity, of lush green grass studded with the rocks of Harry's absences abroad, of houses . . . of children . . . '

'Mamma!' protested Emily.

'Oh yes,' her mother smiled fondly at her. 'In a few years you will know, all too well, what I mean.'

'No, I shan't,' said Emily rebelliously. 'I shall arrange things better than you did.'

'Perhaps you will,' replied her mother, the smile fading.

Bragg sensed that the pleasant intimate conversation was in danger of degenerating into a family wrangle. 'What do you mean by "restoring your mental balance"?' he asked.

'I flatter myself it's not just a matter of going to see the place where I was born,' Lady Morton replied pensively, 'like some Irish-American millionaire visiting Dublin out of curiosity. Nor is it mere indulgence, though it must seem like it to some people. The children seem equally at home with both cultures, but although I feel I have adapted well to life here, there are aspects of English society that I find uncongenial. Those that affect me personally are trivial indeed, and yet after a time they assume an importance to me which goes far beyond their true significance. It is then that I flee across the Atlantic, to bathe in the spring of America's culture, and return with my sense of proportion restored.'

'What is it about life in England that irks you?' Bragg asked.

'I expect it's the difference between the exhilarating turmoil of an expanding country, and the staid, stratified society of Europe. Let me give you an example. Try as I will, I cannot accustom myself to the way the English working classes hold people like us at a distance. I want to get to know everyone around me; to be acquainted with carpenters and farmers, equally with bankers and politicians. But they won't have it. There's a stubborn determination among the lower classes in England to prevent any intimacy with people they regard as their betters.'

'That's nonsense, Lottie,' observed Sir Henry mildly. 'It's a matter of each side having a proper respect for the other.'

'Anyway,' Morton interposed, 'there would always be difficulties in a friendship that smacked of being imposed from above.'

'I'm not talking of close friendship,' his mother replied, 'but of getting by harmoniously. What I find irritating is the way everyone in England conspires to foster the delusion that the nobility and gentry are some kind of superior caste.'

'Mamma is perfectly right,' said Emily. 'Take old Mrs Smith, for instance. She's been in bed with a fever, and her husband is so rheumaticky he can hardly walk. On Wednesday, I was silly enough to tell him that next morning Mamma and I were going to come down with some delicacies to tempt her appetite. When we got there, the house was scrubbed and shining, and poor Mrs Smith was back in bed, exhausted. We would have done more good if we had stayed away.'

'People have their pride, Emily,' said Sir Henry. 'You should always remember that. She wouldn't have wanted you to see her cottage in disorder.'

'But in America we don't have that kind of pride in our station in life,' said his wife. 'We are rich or poor, lucky or unlucky; but deep down, we know we are all as good as each other.'

'It's very deep down, with some of the moneyed people we've met,' remarked Morton. 'If you ask me, the American idea of equality is just as great a delusion.'

'Well, the sixteenth of September can't come too quickly for me,' exclaimed Emily. 'I'm bored to death here. There's nothing to do, and we don't meet anyone interesting.'

'But it's hardly a week since Karl and Helga were here,' protested Morton. 'Didn't you find them entertaining?'

'It wasn't like the old times. Karl isn't as much fun as he used to be; and he was away most of the time. He went to Rochester one day, and he was at Portsmouth for another two. Despite all his pretences, he takes this silly agricultural job of his very seriously.'

'And so he should,' said Morton. 'But surely you found Helga good company?'

'She's all right, but she's nothing like so effervescent when there aren't any men around.'

'Emily!' her mother rebuked her.

'Well it's true. She asked me endless questions about The Priory, and the family – particularly about James. I got the feeling she was going to make a bid for the whole job lot.'

Morton laughed merrily. 'Wouldn't you fancy Helga as a sister-in-law?' he asked.

Emily frowned defiantly. 'I wouldn't want any brother of mine married to another man's mistress,' she declared.

'My daughter loves to shock,' Lady Morton assured Bragg in embarrassment.

'But you must have noticed, too, Mamma, the proprietorial way they looked at each other, when they thought they weren't observed.'

'Don't be stupid, Em,' exclaimed Morton irritably. 'They are first cousins, after all. And I happen to know that they not only have separate rooms in St James's Square, they even live in different buildings.'

'That doesn't prove anything,' Emily retorted with a toss of her head. 'Miss Dobson, in the village, seems very respectable and nice; but no one believes it's her step-brother that comes to stay with her.'

'I'm quite sure you are not supposed to be aware of such things,' said her mother firmly. 'I think it's time we withdrew, and left the men to their port.' She rose, acknowledging the men's bows, and Emily followed her through the door, a contrary smile on her lips.

'I have a mystery of my own that might interest you,' Sir Henry said, as the ladies disappeared. 'I'll just get something from my study . . . Please carry on.'

The butler leaned deferentially over Bragg's shoulder. 'Port, sir?' he asked.

'Can I have a glass of beer?'

'Certainly, sir.'

'All this wine makes me dry.'

'Well, you've undoubtedly been initiated as a member of the family this evening,' said Morton with a grin.

'Your sister's something of a tearaway, then?'

'That's certainly true. I think Mother is perplexed as to how she is going to turn her into a normal, marriageable young lady.'

'Better a tomboy than a cowed nonentity,' grunted Bragg.

'She'll be better when she's been to America. She'll be able to do unconventional things like riding astride instead of side-saddle, and she'll have had her fill of parties for a while. I'm not surprised at her feeling rebellious, living down here in the country.'

'I like a girl with a bit of spirit,' remarked Bragg. 'I can well understand how a man would indulge a daughter like that.'

'Cigar, sir?' The butler proffered a box of Havanas.

'No thanks. I'll stick to my pipe.' Bragg produced his tobacco pouch, and began to cut thin slices of twist with his juice-stained knife.

'Here we are!' Sir Henry resumed his seat, and taking a cigar from the butler, rolled it at his ear to test its condition. 'That's excellent,' he said, giving it to the butler to cut. 'See we've enough to drink, Hemmings, and then you can be off.'

'Thank you, sir.' The butler poured two glasses of port, and set the decanter at Sir Henry's elbow. Then, indicating to Bragg that there was more beer on the sideboard, he quietly withdrew.

'Good. I didn't want to discuss this in front of Hemmings, since it concerns someone who lives on the estate.' Sir Henry took an appreciative sip of his port, and leaned back.

'The circumstances are brief, as with all good stories,' he said. 'Last evening, as dusk was falling, one of the keepers was out near Ashley Copse, when he heard a shot. He ran over and caught George Trump with a gun in his hand. He was just in the act of retrieving a pigeon that he'd shot.'

'That's a tricky one,' said Morton with a smile. 'A pigeon isn't within the definition of game, so you won't be able to charge him with poaching.'

'I was sure that would please you,' remarked his father sardonically. 'However, that is not the point of my story. The bird was not a common wood pigeon, but a homing pigeon; and attached to its leg was a cylinder containing this message.' He placed a small square of paper on the table before Bragg, and Morton came round to peer over his shoulder. Four lines had been printed on it with a blunt pencil:

> Pontifex
> Glengal B
> Cutler S
> Grove Ben

'What do you make of that?' asked Sir Henry.

'I can't say it means anything to me,' replied Bragg. 'They are obviously names of people.'

'I've half a mind I've seen one of those names recently,'

remarked Morton thoughtfully. 'Glengal . . . Glengal . . . I know, it was in *The Times*. Do you still keep the old newspapers, sir?'

'They're in the library. Why don't we adjourn there? I'll just tell the ladies that we won't be joining them.'

Bragg was soon ensconced in a leather armchair with a large glass of brandy, while Morton riffled through a pile of papers. 'I think this is the one,' he said, and dropped into a chair opposite. He scanned the pages rapidly, then began to read intently.

'I was right,' he announced. 'It's mentioned in the report of the Amalgamated Society of Engineers' meeting last Wednesday night.'

'Did you find what you were looking for?' his father asked, coming in.

'Yes, sir. There was a trade-union meeting on Wednesday. Karl and I went to it, for a lark. At the end, the crowd hoisted the speaker shoulder-high, shouting for a strike. We didn't follow them, but according to this report, they marched to a foundry in Beech Street, belonging to Glengal Brass Works. The gates were shut on them, and they besieged the works for two hours. It seems they only dispersed when the union official promised to call a strike from Monday.'

'That's tomorrow,' grunted Bragg.

'I'm very much afraid, sir,' said Morton, 'that you must not even contemplate taking proceedings against George Trump. On the contrary, you should do all you can to hush up the incident.'

'Why's that, my boy?' asked Sir Henry with a frown.

'I think Sergeant Bragg ought to explain.'

'There have been some very curious happenings at public meetings recently,' said Bragg. 'At the beginning they were political meetings aimed at the new voters, but increasingly trade-union meetings as well. There seems to be a well-organized faction which turns a perfectly ordinary, uncontroversial meeting into a violent demonstration. We have been keeping watch on the situation for some weeks, and now the Special Branch has taken over. So you will realize that it has become a matter of considerable concern to the government.'

'But what difference does this make to George Trump?' asked Sir Henry in perplexity. 'Are you saying that the name "Glengal B" on this paper is more than just a coincidence?'

'It could be.'

'Equally, it could merely be somebody called Bertram Glengal,' Sir Henry countered. 'After all, there's an S. Cutler and a Ben Grove.'

'You're probably right, sir,' conceded Bragg. 'Nevertheless, I would prefer it if the fact that this pigeon has been brought down could be kept quiet, until we can definitely establish that it has no bearing on our enquiries.'

'How long will that take?' asked Sir Henry.

'It's not possible to say. A week, two weeks – a month.'

'We can't keep it hanging over Trump like that.'

'Come on, sir,' urged Morton. 'You wouldn't even succeed with a charge of trespass . . . and it would be a pity to spoil his record over a miserable pigeon.'

'It's amazing,' complained Sir Henry, 'that something always turns up to save the necks of my son's disreputable acquaintances . . . Very well.'

It was Sunday afternoon, and Bragg was sitting on the terrace in the hot sun, enjoying a pipe. Morton had gone to see his brother; the rest of the family had excused themselves and gone about their various activities. Bragg glanced at the exquisite china coffee cup on the table, and smiled to himself. To think that he, a carrier's son from the depths of the countryside, should be staying in a great house like this! How his mother would delight in hearing about it. He would have to remember every detail, what they ate, what the ladies wore and, above all, how the house compared with their local manor. Even if he were able to describe it, she would never be able to comprehend the mellow richness of it all. But she would be so proud! He hugged himself with gratification. Joe Bragg, from Turner's Puddle, an honoured guest in such a household! . . . And more than just a guest – one of the family. That was what young Morton had said. It was amazing that a bare twenty-four hours here could have so lifted his spirits. And yet to have such people treating him as an equal, as if no rape charge were hanging over him, could hardly fail to restore his self-esteem. It was Lady Morton who made the difference, of course; it was always the womenfolk who set the tone of a household . . . Yet it wasn't really that they treated him as an equal. That would have been patently false, and would have come through as condescension. Rather it was that they welcomed him as Joe Bragg, that the inequality was of no importance . . . And it wasn't as if he was there on sufferance, because their son worked under him . . . He must try to tell her how grateful he was, before he left. Really, they'd devoted the whole weekend to him. There weren't any other guests to overawe him, and that must be rare in a house like this. She'd put him in a room that was cosy and homely and had explained that they didn't dress for dinner when they were just family. And it had all been done on the off-chance that he would still be at liberty. Well, one thing was sure: they wouldn't go to that trouble for many people . . . It wasn't surprising that Morton was different from the ordinary run of young nobs, coming from such a background. Not that he was by any stretch of the imagination a mother's boy. But her ideas must have rubbed off on him, particularly with his father being away so much. It was less surprising, now, to find him working as an ordinary copper . . . And yet the likelihood was that he would inherit this vast house and the land around as far as you could see. From his chair, Bragg could see the flint wall of the medieval hall, with a warm red brick wall running down to his right, and the grey limestone of the main house behind him. It ought to be intimidating, but it wasn't . . .

'I'm sorry to have been so long.' Morton appeared through the french windows. 'I've arranged for a trap, so that we can pursue this elusive pigeon of yours.'

'Why mine?' asked Bragg, knocking out his pipe.

'I have a feeling that it's going to be the key that unlocks every door.'

'God knows we need one.'

They were soon bowling along a narrow lane. The leaves of the trees looked dusty and dejected after the long dry summer. Bragg glimpsed orange clusters of rowan berries. To have them taking colour so early meant a hard winter – or so the country folk would say.

'We're going to see George Trump,' said Morton. 'He's the village blacksmith, and although he gets most of his work from us, he owns his own business. That gives him a special status, as you can imagine. As well as being the blacksmith, he is known to be an inveterate poacher, though he's never been caught red-handed till now.'

'That's what you meant about not spoiling his record, is it?'

'Yes.'

'Your father described him as one of your disreputable acquaintances.'

Morton laughed. 'He was just leg-pulling. It's really a great joke between us. You see, I was taught to shoot by the head keeper; but by the time I was sixteen, I'd got tired of standing in a line, blasting driven birds out of the sky. So I began to go rough shooting on my own. Stalking your quarry takes much more skill, and it gives them a sporting chance, too. Anyway, it isn't quite right to say that George Trump had never been caught poaching, because I did just that, one autumn evening. I followed him, in the shelter of a gully, and came up on him just as he was setting a snare.'

'What did you do?' asked Bragg.

'I couldn't have turned him in; the village would never have forgiven me. But I made him promise to teach me all he knew about poaching, as the price of my silence. You're the first person I've told since that day . . . Here we are.'

Morton guided the pony down a cart track beside a thatched cottage, with a corrugated-iron smithy behind it. A bearded man in shirt sleeves emerged from the back door. To Bragg he seemed surprisingly slight for a smith.

'Afternoon, Master James. I got your message.'

They jumped down from the trap. 'George, this is my boss, Sergeant Bragg.'

Trump put out a dirt-ingrained hand.

'I gather that you introduced Mr Morton to poaching,' said Bragg.

'Yes,' grinned Trump. 'It spoiled it for me, though. The keepers weren't really going to try, once it got out that I had the young master in tow.'

'They've caught you now, though,' said Morton. 'You ought to be ashamed of yourself.'

'I am, though,' Trump replied with a rueful smile. 'I just couldn't resist it, Master James. It were coming fast and low. I couldn't rightly make out what it were in the dusk, but I knew it wasn't a game bird. There was never pheasant came on so fierce. It was the shot of a lifetime. I just upped the gun, and let fly without thinking . . . but I got it, that's something.'

'Sergeant Bragg and I are interested in that pigeon, so I'll do a deal with you; if you say nothing about it to anyone but us, I'll see you don't get charged.'

'Seems I win both ends up,' replied Trump with a smile. 'Mind you, the keeper won't have kept his mouth shut.'

'Which one was it?'

'Bert Abbott.'

'I'm sure I can persuade him to say nothing more.'

'Well, I'm your man, then.'

'Where exactly were you when you shot it?' asked Morton.

'At the top end of the copse. I was standing under that big elm tree, by the spring.'

'I know it. And from what direction did the bird approach you?'

'There was a terrible wind that night, and it was flying about twenty foot off the ground, down the fields.'

'Following the line of the Downs?'

'That's right. I suppose it had come down low to get into some shelter.'

'What direction was the wind coming from?' asked Bragg.

'Sittingbourne way.'

'That would be north-east,' said Morton.

'Sir Henry said the pigeon had a cylinder on its leg,' remarked Bragg. 'What was it like?'

'Come and see for yourself; 'tis still in the wash-house.' He led the way to some outbuildings.

'Oh, the pigeon as well! I'm surprised they let you keep it.'

'Why not? Pigeons is vermin – 'twouldn't have been fair.'

'Not this pigeon, I think,' murmured Bragg. 'And this is the cylinder . . . aluminium, with a screw lid. Made for very special messages, I'd say, wouldn't you?' He turned it in his hands.

'There are bits of wax on it, here. Was it sealed when you picked up the bird?'

'Yes.'

'Was there any marking impressed in the wax?'

'I can't rightly say. I'd only just seen the cylinder, when Bert Abbott had me by the collar.'

'Who opened it, do you know?'

'Abbott did. He were that in a rage, he had it off and undone in a blink. I reckon he thought he would hang me, with what was inside it.'

'Was there just the one piece of paper in it?'

'So far as I know.'

'Right,' said Bragg, 'we'll take charge of this.' He tossed it in the air. 'Astonishingly light, isn't it, for a metal?'

'Is that a mark on the base?' asked Morton.

Bragg peered at it. 'There's something stamped on the bottom, but I can't make it out. Here, lad, your eyes are younger than mine.'

'It's not very clear,' said Morton, taking it out into the sunlight. 'It looks a bit like a crown. Let's hope you've not brought down a Queen's Messenger, George!'

'Christ!' Trump's eyes widened. 'How many years d'you get for that?'

'Life, I should think,' said Bragg laconically. 'Unless it amounts to treason – then you'd swing all right.'

'You're kidding me on, I hope,' said Trump, swallowing hard.

'Maybe. Is there anyone around here that knows about racing pigeons?'

'The rector would be your best bet,' replied Trump. 'That's if he's out of Sunday school by now.'

They found the rector at the bottom of the glebe field. He was squatting in a large pigeon loft, talking to the birds.

'I won't be a moment,' he called softly, disengaging a pigeon from the grey fringe of hair over his ear, and placing it on a perch. He scattered grains of wheat on the floor of the loft, then backed out on all fours.

'I'd like to move them nearer the house,' he said, brushing at his white-spattered broadcloth, 'but Mildred won't hear of it

'. . . Good to see you, James. Will you be down for evensong? I'd like you to read the lessons if you are.'

'I'm sorry, sir, but we have to get back to London. We've come to consult you professionally.'

'Goodness me, James. How splendid! And is this the lucky girl's father?'

'No, no,' said Morton, with a laugh. 'I mean our profession, not yours. We have a body in the trap outside, that we'd like to ask you a few questions about.'

'You know, James,' the rector twittered, as they walked to the road, 'I know very little about death. I leave that side of things to the curate . . . Oh my dear boy! The trap's empty! . . . Ah, I see now; you are having a little fun at my expense.'

'By no means,' replied Morton with a smile, as he produced the dead pigeon from under the seat.

'That was wicked of you, James,' the rector admonished. 'I thought for a moment that my horse must have run down some unfortunate, while he was bringing me home from the lodge dinner last night. Ah well,' he chortled, 'I shan't need to revise my heretical views on the resurrection of the body, after all! Now what have we here?' He began to smooth the ruffled feathers of the bird, stroking them till they gleamed iridescent in the sunlight.

'What can you tell us about it, sir?' asked Bragg.

'She's a racing pigeon, of course,' said the rector, 'and a particularly fine one at that, well muscled – and look at those wings!' He extended one wing by pulling at its tip. 'See how perfect the feathers are. She's in the pink of condition . . . What vandal had the temerity to destroy this glorious creature?' he demanded.

'I'd better not tell you,' said Morton, 'or you might curse him with bell, book and candle.'

'Have you any idea where it might have come from?' asked Bragg.

'As to that, anywhere in the British Isles. That isn't the interesting question. What you should be asking, is "Where was it going to?" The answer to that would be "Straight home." See, its crop is empty, so it's almost certain that it was racing at the time it was killed – it reduces the body-weight, you see.'

'Are you saying they always race towards their home?' asked Morton.

'That is correct. The sport is dependent entirely on the pigeon's homing instinct. They don't really race against each other, they race against the clock; and their only motivation is the desire to get back home as quickly as they can.'

'So how do you decide which bird has won?'

'All the birds are sent in baskets, by train, to one spot, and are released simultaneously. They fly home, and we record the moment of arrival with a special clock. Then we work out the speed in yards per minute. That is what matters.'

'Would they be raced in a high wind, such as the gale you had on Friday evening?'

The rector looked shocked. 'By no means. It would be the height of folly to risk valuable birds in such weather.'

'Would it surprise you to know,' asked Bragg, 'that there was a cylinder containing a message attached to its leg?'

'Not at all. It could just as easily be used as a carrier-pigeon. Wherever it was released, it would fly straight back home.'

'And where is home?'

'Certainly not in England. This is a breed which is used all over the Continent, but very rarely indeed over here.'

'The Continent?' exclaimed Morton in surprise. 'Have you any idea where?'

'None. A beautiful specimen like this could fly up to six or seven hundred miles. That at least sets a rough limit for you.'

They hurried back to The Priory and Morton took down an atlas from the library shelf. He found a map of Europe, and laid a ruler across it.

'Allowing for minor variations,' he remarked, 'and assuming that the rector meant they fly in a straight line, the course that pigeon was following could have taken it over France, Belgium, Luxembourg, the southern tip of Germany, Switzerland, Austria and Italy!'

'That gives us plenty of choice, anyway,' Bragg said. 'We can't even set the extreme limit of its flight until we know where it was released. Even then, the rector only gave its range within a hundred miles.'

'Yes, but we must assume, if it really is relevant to our

150

enquiries, that it was released near London.'

'I suppose so. I wonder if the gale could have blown it off course. It might have been heading across the North Sea to Holland or Norway. I tell you what, lad, we keep this under our hats for the moment. Your crack about a Queen's Messenger may be too near the truth for comfort. We can't afford to be found showing every Tom, Dick and Harry a secret message from the Foreign Office to one of our embassies abroad. We'd both be in the crap then.'

13

Morton went up to the duty desk at Whitechapel police station, and introduced himself. 'I'm wondering if you've managed to trace the hay cart,' he said.

'What cart's that?' asked the sergeant.

'The one which may have been used in the Allhallows murder. Constable Goff saw it in Royal Mint Street, and we've traced two more people who saw it in the vicinity of Trinity Square that morning.'

'I've heard something about it, only I've been sick for a fortnight. What were we going to do for you?'

'Sergeant Bragg came in on the twenty-second, and arranged with the sergeant on duty that you would keep an eye open for it in Whitechapel High Street.'

The sergeant's eyes narrowed. 'He's the one that's up for rape, isn't he?'

'He's certainly been charged with it, but I'm quite certain he's not guilty,' Morton said firmly.

'I remember they were saying that he'd been here just before he done it.'

'I've told you,' Morton said angrily, 'someone has him set.'

'All right. All right.' The sergeant retreated to the corner, and consulted a large note book. 'Large flat lorry, drawn by a big grey stallion. That the one?'

'Yes.'

'No reports of sightings yet.'

'I think I'll go and talk to the hay merchants myself. Can you tell me who they are?'

'Well, there's George Brown and Son, in Half Moon Passage, and Warrens at the Aldgate end of the High Street.'

'Thank you.'

'Do you still want us to keep a lookout?'

'No. Don't bother any more.'

Warrens seemed to be a large establishment, to judge by the tangle of carts outside its premises. Morton ducked under a horse's nose, and pushed his way into the office. The only occupant was a lanky young man, with a cigarette drooping from one corner of his mouth. He was standing by the counter, sorting a stack of bills into various piles.

'Yes?' he asked tersely.

'Mr Warren, please.'

'Sorry mate, he's not in.'

'What time does he arrive?'

'He don't. He's an old man, an' he stays at home wiv 'is housekeeper. I'm the manager, you'll 'ave to put up wiv me, mate.'

'Very well. I'm a police officer.'

The man looked up from his pile of bills to glance at Morton's warrant card, his face screwed up to keep the cigarette smoke from his eyes.

'So what's up, then?' he asked uninterestedly.

'We are trying to trace a hay lorry, drawn by a big grey stallion. We think you might be able to help.'

'Come off it, mate. We 'ave 'undreds of 'em in and aht of 'ere. You don't reckon we give each one a look-see do you?'

'It was a very striking shire horse, about eighteen hands, with a white star on its forehead, and white stockings on only three of its legs.'

'And what 'elp would it be if we'd seen it?'

'We'd like to know who it belongs to, for a start.'

The young man blew sharply from the corner of his mouth to dislodge the ash from his cigarette. 'I dunno of none like that. Your best bet is to turn up at five in the morning, and 'ang around.' He turned dismissively, and began to impale some of the bills on a spike.

'Thank you, I'll do that,' Morton said lamely, and went out to the street. He was furious with himself. The man had treated him with an offhandedness that verged on contempt, and he'd been unable to deal with it. He'd been sent off like an importunate schoolboy, and he'd submitted like one. Bragg would have been round the counter at the first sign of insolence, and shaken the truth from the man. He went over the interview in his mind, trying to determine the point at which it had gone wrong, the moment when he should have seized the initiative. It ought to be at the point where you announced that you were a policeman. If they treated you with disdain after that, there was nothing for it but to get rough, and convince them that they'd better co-operate. He'd seen Bragg do it a score of times, and it rarely failed. He would thrust out his head, and hunch his shoulders, so that the mass of his body appeared to increase. Then, hands at the ready, he would walk slowly towards his victim like an angry grizzly, growling menacingly. Most people's nerve cracked before this threat of physical injury . . . Or perhaps it was a kind of convention, a sham encounter, where the police had to appear threatening enough to justify the submission. Whichever it was, he could never bring if off. No one would believe in his posturings: he was too young and too refined-looking. If he tried it, he'd probably end up in a real fight. Morton sighed with irritation. He'd just have to accept it, which in this case probably meant ' 'anging around'.

He turned down a passage by the Half Moon public house, and found himself in a courtyard. There was a large pile of hay at one end, and a gang of men was engaged in loading it on to small carts. A short wiry man in a tweed lounge suit stood watching them critically.

'Mr Brown?' asked Morton.

'I'm Brown the son,' replied the man genially. 'If you want Brown, George, you'll have to go inside.'

'I'm sure you'll do splendidly,' said Morton. 'I'm a police officer, and I'm looking for someone with a good memory for horses.'

'Well, we see plenty, and no mistake. Here lads, knock off for a minute, will you?'

Morton was soon surrounded by sweating dusty men, grinning at their good fortune.

'I am a policeman,' he began again. 'We are looking for a particular horse and cart, which has been involved in a fatal accident. We have a good description of it, and we're trying to locate the owner.'

'Where did it happen?' asked one of the men.

'In Trinity Square. The cart was a big flat lorry, but the horse is what sticks in the memory. It's a shire stallion, very big – about eighteen hands, we're told. Instead of the usual white flash down the nose, it has a big white star in the middle of its forehead, and it doesn't have a white stocking on its off-side hind leg.'

'Why come to us?' asked Brown.

'We are working on the theory that it was a cart used to bring hay from the country to merchants like you.'

'It needn't be,' broke in another man. 'There are plenty of lorries like that down Millwall and Limehouse way, round the docks.'

'Wot was the horse's markings, again?' asked another.

'White star on the forehead, white stockings on all the feet, except the hind off side.'

'Yes. I seen that horse,' said the man, conviction growing in his face. 'I seen it last week . . . Mon- . . . no, Tuesday. I took that load down to Cottmans' at Stepney Green.'

'Are you sure?' asked Morton.

''Course I'm sure. I watered my horse at the trough on the green. He was there for about twenty minutes.'

'What time was that?'

'Around a quarter to six.'

'What was his driver like?'

'Little bloke, nothin' special . . . Had a limp.'

By the first post Bragg received a thick square envelope, addressed in writing he did not recognize. He turned it over hesitantly, but it didn't seem to be any kind of official communication. He took a deep breath, and slit it open with his knife. Out slid Mary Jessop! It was her to the life, startled, looking up at Morton's shout. No sorrowful compassion there; it was the look of a predator, tense, alert, cruel. That Rivington chap might be effeminate, but he knew his trade. Bragg picked up Catherine's note. She had merely written 'Good luck!' Well, she was worth having on your side and no mistake.

He hadn't asked for breakfast in his own room, so perforce he took it in the kitchen with Mrs Jenks. Her pent-up curiosity about the letter was so palpable, that for once he took refuge behind his paper. He escaped as quickly as he could, and walked briskly along the congested streets to London Bridge station. There he caught a train to East Dulwich. He could see the spire of the church before the train had stopped. It was squat and dark, probing the sky assertively, declaring itself the immutable symbol of the Only Truth. He was glad to lose it behind the houses as he walked; but now and again he would glimpse it, ominous, through a gap in the buildings. As he neared the end of the street, he could see a large board school, like a fortress behind its high brick wall. He counted five floors to it, and it was topped by a small spire of its own, echoing that on the church close by. This must be the school Mary Jessop went to as a child. But no one there would remember her from the photograph in his pocket.

He turned the corner, his heart thumping. There was the church, screened by trees, and facing a pleasant green. Close to, there was nothing menacing about it. The spire was clad in brown scalloped tiles, and surmounted by a gold cross. The church must be fairly new, for the sandstone still showed clean and warm in the sunlight . . . That must be the vicarage, on the other side of the road; an imposing villa, with a wrought-iron balcony. She didn't belong there – not the Mary Jessop of the photo. Bragg pushed through a gate into the churchyard, and walked along the gravelled path. There seemed to be nobody about, so he went into the porch and opened the church door. He was startled at the strong smell of incense that met him. It was more like a Catholic church, and yet he was sure she'd said her father was Church of England. What a fantastic bit of luck it would be, he thought excitedly, if they'd picked the wrong religion. He strode back to the notice board in the porch. No. Here was a circular, headed 'Diocese of Southwark'. Oh well, it was too much to expect that they'd make such an elementary mistake. He wandered back into the church, looking for a verger, but it was empty . . . It wasn't really his idea of a church. Apart from the incense, it didn't have a proper chancel; instead there was a shallow rounded apse. There was virtually no stained glass either, and the clear light was reflected from bare, white-plastered walls. And yet it had a harmony, a peace. He sat in a pew, and let the scented stillness settle round him. He'd never been much of a one for churchgoing, for the black cassocks and mumbo jumbo. And when his wife died, he'd vowed never to set foot in church again. Nor had he, except by way of duty. Now here he was, *in extremis,* looking up at a crucifix. If only he could reach out his arms, have his burden lifted from him . . . but that wasn't what Christianity was about. He felt tears of self-pity pricking at his eyelids, and stumbled into the sunshine.

'You may well sniff!' A spare, erect old man was addressing him from a bench on the edge of the green. He looked every inch a retired army officer.

'It's a disgrace, all this papism and idolatry! I've written to the bishop, but he tells me it's what the parish wants. What does he know about it?' he snorted.

'Are you a parishioner, then?' asked Bragg.

'Well, I am, and I'm not,' said the man crossly. 'I live in the parish, I can't remedy that. But I won't set foot in the church again, not while they have those candles and incense . . . I come and sit here for some part of every day, to remind them that God is not mocked.'

'Wasn't it always like this?'

'It was not!' exclaimed the man. 'It used to be a proper place of Christian worship, not a forum for papistical pageantry. And it's all been done by this vicar. First the candles, then the crucifix hanging from the roof, then the incense . . . I hear they're going to have tinkling bells in the Holy Communion soon. It's blasphemy, that's what it is.'

'Did you know the previous vicar?'

'Mr Jessop? I was his warden. He'd turn in his grave if he knew what was going on now.'

'You must have known his daughter, too.'

'Of course I did.'

'Is this a picture of her?' Bragg extracted the photograph from his pocket.

'I haven't got my specs,' said the man, peering at it short-sightedly. 'No. I don't know who that is, but it can't be

Mary Jessop. She had a hare lip.'

Bragg took his farewell of the old man, and walked away across the green. His elation and relief seemed to run counter to each other, and he sat down on a bench to clarify his thoughts. The old man had seemed definite enough, and if he was right about the hare lip, no further proof was needed. But his attitude to the new regime at the church was very extreme, and old people were notoriously unreliable. Bragg decided it would be folly to act on the old man's unsupported word, and go back to London proclaiming that he was cleared. He must get corroboration; and it would be easy enough. He took out his watch. Twenty minutes to twelve. As good a time as any to call on a headmistress on holiday. He got directions from a cheerful young woman with a perambulator, and set off down the tree-lined avenue with more spring in his step than he could remember.

He found the entrance to the school without difficulty, and walked along its rhododendron-bordered drive till he came to a side path, which bore a sign to the headmistress's house. He followed it, and mounted the steps of what was a very substantial villa. He was about to pull the bell, when he heard a voice calling from behind him.

'Hello!'

She was wearing a bright day dress, and carrying a trug full of roses. Bragg raised his hat, and turned down the steps to meet her.

'Miss Alger?'

'Yes. I was just gathering some flowers,' she said with a warm smile. 'They are so beautiful at this time of year.'

'Miss Alger, I am a police officer. I want to ask you about one of your pupils.'

A cloud passed over her face, and Bragg sensed the strength beneath her charm. 'I will do anything I can to help, of course,' she said warily.

'It's about Mary Jessop.'

'One of my former pupils,' she smiled in relief. 'She was one of my very first girls. The school was only opened in eighteen seventy-eight, and in the early years the numbers were small. We were really just a large family.'

'What kind of girl was she?' asked Bragg.

'Considering her unfortunate disfigurement, she turned out very well.'

'You mean the hare lip?'

'Yes. She overcame the handicap through remarkable perseverance; and though it was obvious she would never marry, she has made a useful life for herself by sheer determination. We still correspond regularly.'

'Where does she live?'

'In Worthing. She teaches at a small private infants' school.'

'And her mother?'

'She lives with her. Can you tell me what your interest is in Miss Jessop?'

Bragg smiled. 'We only want to eliminate her from our enquiries, and you seem to have done that already. Perhaps you would tell me if this photograph is of Miss Jessop or not?'

She took the photo, and studied it intently. 'Most assuredly not,' she said. 'This girl has not the faintest resemblance to Mary Jessop.'

14

Constable Passey looked at his watch in the light from the street lamp, and shivered. Twenty minutes past four. Over another hour and a half to go. When he'd started his shift, last evening, it was still very warm; and he'd put on only a thin shirt under his tunic. But in the night it had turned cold, with a clear sky and a waning moon. And with it had come the mist. He'd stood for a time in Bishopsgate, watching silvery wraiths dancing on the grids that ventilated the sewers. Then they had been swallowed up in the silent veil edging up from the river. The first of September, and already a touch of autumn.

He turned, and resumed the steady pace that would take him round his beat in half an hour. Goodness knows, they had enough mist at home in Norfolk, particularly out on the fens. But it was different there, with that great open sky. Here, you never seemed to get used to the light. Your eyes were just accustoming themselves to the shadows, when you came on the jack-o-lantern of a street lamp, then plunged into darkness again. And if you kept your eyes upwards, following the line of the rooftops, you were sure to bump into a pillar-box.

He opened the shutter of his lantern, and walked with measured tread down the alley that gave access to St Ethelburga's graveyard. The sergeant called this one 'Beelzebub's beat', because it had six churches, a synagogue, and the Wesleyan Hall in it. But you shouldn't joke about these things, it was unlucky . . . He could see the outline of the church now, squat and insignificant. They had finer churches than this in Norfolk, by a long way; better than any in the City, barring St Pauls. And still with proper graveyards as well. Here they'd turned them all into public open spaces; taken away the headstones, and grassed them over . . . Desecration, his mother had called it, when he'd told her. Only the presence of one or two chest tombs showed it was still consecrated ground. He shone his lantern around. Nothing was disturbed. Margaret Poynter still slept as soundly as she had done since sixteen hundred and thirty-six. On the summer evenings, he'd amused himself by trying to make out the words chiselled on the tombs. Not that he'd made much progress with the older ones; the letters were mostly worn off, and they were in Latin anyway. He crossed the grass to the gate . . . It wasn't right for the living to walk over the bones of the dead. His mother had always drummed it into him, not to tread on the graves. It was sacrilege. They didn't seem to care here. He'd seen youngsters sitting on Margaret Poynter's tomb, eating jellied eels and drinking beer. It might mean nothing to them, but somebody would have to pay for it, one day. He quickened his step, and was relieved to see the diffused glow of a street lamp again . . . Mind you, they used to say that only them buried inside the church itself, were sure of heaven. Those in the graveyard could be pulled down to hell, if the devil had a mind. It was true enough, too. They'd built that office building partly on the old churchyard of St Andrews; and it was cracking all down that corner – sinking down . . . Best not to think of it.

Here was Great St Helens, his favourite churchyard. Nice and open, with a few shrubs to soften the outline of the railings. It was presided over by Joseph Lems, in his grey stone tomb by the west door: *A citizen of London, departed this life 21st September 1686.* Constable Passey opened the shutter of his lantern again. Now, if he were on the day shift, he wouldn't swap this beat with anybody. This was where the office girls came in the summer, to eat their lunch. They looked a treat, too, with their bouncy breasts and slim ankles . . . shouldn't think such thoughts here, it was blasphemy . . . Hello, something odd . . . a dark blob on old Joseph's tomb. It hadn't been there an hour ago . . . He walked apprehensively down the path, shining the beam of his lantern towards the tomb – then stopped in his tracks. Through the swirls of mist, he could see an outline . . . a shoulder, the profile of a head, white marble in the gloom, hands clasped in prayer. A worm of fear crawled up his spine . . . Old Joe risen from his tomb? . . . Was it the Last Judgement? . . . Constable Passey dropped his lantern, and began to run . . .

It had gone six o'clock by the time Morton arrived at Great St Helens. He had been summoned because of the label tied round one wrist of the corpse, its message as indecipherable as the other. The uniformed branch had closed off the entrance to the churchyard, lest an early cleaner or workman should disturb them. The body was still as it had been found, and Constable Passey, smelling strongly of whisky, had given him an account of its discovery. Now Morton was walking around the tomb, making notes in his book. It was a man of about forty, with dark hair and whiskers. He was not particularly tall, but nevertheless well-built. The body was on its back, and naked. It was arranged as a recumbent effigy, and the wrists were tied with string, to hold the palms of the hands together. The legs and feet were laid parallel, and round the neck was a noose, cutting into the flesh. There was no obvious sign of a wound. If you didn't look at the face, you could think he'd fallen asleep . . . It would save a lot of trouble, Morton thought, if someone could take a photograph of the body. The only photos he'd seen in police files had been taken in the mortuary. He thought of nancy-boy Rivington being summoned to this one, and smiled derisively. When he had completed his observation, Morton carefully cut the label from the wrist; then, instructing the uniformed men to get the corpse to the mortuary, he went home to breakfast.

He was modestly pleased with himself. He'd taken a firm control of the proceedings, and everyone had done as he directed, without demur. He'd made an unhurried examination of the body, and had detailed sketches of its position. Now he had to wait for the pathologist's report before he could take it any further. No doubt he'd be appointed coroner's officer, because of the label . . . Damnation! He should have looked around the graveyard itself in case the murderers had left traces. To the alarm of Mrs Chambers, he jumped up from his grilled kidneys and dashed downstairs.

He managed to get there before the street-sweepers, although the body had gone and the churchyard was reopened. He carefully examined the area of ground around the tomb. It was bone-hard with the drought and there was no hope of finding footprints. He couldn't see any wheel marks either. But they could have got the body almost to the tomb, on the paved roadway. They wouldn't need a big cart this time, either; a costermonger's barrow would have sufficed. An empty match-box had been crushed into the grass, a few inches from the foot of the tomb. Morton examined it carefully, but it suggested nothing to him. They were hardly likely to have stayed for a smoke after the deed. Probably the box had been tossed there by some passer-by; at most, the murderers might have trodden on it. He put the box in his pocket, in case Bragg should deduce something from it, and made a more general search of the area. Then, satisfied that there was nothing more to discover, he set off for the fifth division police station.

Sergeant Griffith greeted him with a smile. 'How d'you get on with the Cardiff police, boyo?' he asked.

'They were very helpful, thank you, sir. It seems that Dic Penderyn was a Welsh patriot, who was executed by the authorities in eighteen thirty-one.'

'Can't say I've ever heard of him, myself,' said Griffith. 'What's the point of putting him on a label?'

'I don't know, but we've got another.'

'Another label?'

'Another corpse, complete with label – here.'

'Dear goodness,' Griffith said, 'what is it this time? "Buddu-goliaeth i Cymru Fydd".' A troubled look spread across his face, and he put the label on the desk in front of him.

'Can you not translate it?' asked Morton. 'Is it not Welsh?'

'Oh, I can translate it, more's the pity,' Griffith said heavily. 'It means "Victory to Wales of the future".'

'What can that be about?'

'I don't know. But I don't like the sound of it.'

Bragg received a note from Morton by the mid-morning post which told him about the sighting of the horse on Stepney

Green. Conscious of his straitened finances, he walked to Whitechapel, and took a tram along the Mile End Road. There was little point, he reflected, in wandering around the streets at random. If they were accurate, the facts relayed by Morton were significant in themselves. The two drivers had been at the horse trough around a quarter to six, for some twenty minutes. There was no suggestion that they had arranged to meet, or, indeed, that there had been any conversation between them. But nobody needed twenty minutes to water a horse. They'd just been putting on time, both of them. That could mean only one thing. The driver of the grey had got back from a job a bit earlier than he'd expected, and rather than risk having to go out again that evening, he had wasted a bit of time on Stepney Green. Allowing for the time necessary to unharness the horse and get him bedded down, the factory or warehouse or whatever-it-was couldn't be far off.

He sat on a bench near the horse trough and scrutinized every horse that went by. He soon realized, however, that the vehicles stopping at the trough obscured his view of those going down the other side of the road. He therefore took up a position in the bow window of the King's Head opposite. There he had a clear view of six busy road junctions. It was as much as he could do to keep them all under continual surveillance. He would become interested in an incident that was totally irrelevant to his purpose; and in that time half a dozen greys could have gone down one of the other roads. He decided continuously to sweep the whole area with his gaze; and to make it impossible for him to be distracted, he would move his head in a circular motion. This worked very well, but it excited the interest of the other men in the bar. On receiving a distinctly suspicious look from the waiter who brought his food, Bragg gave a sickly smile, and said: 'My neck's bad, I've got to keep it moving.' Unlikely as it was, the explanation succeeded in diverting attention from him.

By four o'clock he was beginning to lose hope. From the start, he'd been concerned by the description of the driver as 'a little bloke'. But the identification of the horse had been so positive as to outweigh everything else . . . If he'd been able to question Brown's driver himself, he might have learned of other places where drivers lost time. Not that he would say much in front of his boss. He'd probably be in trouble already. Anyway it wasn't possible to watch more than one place at a time . . . By five o'clock, Bragg's head was swimming. He wasn't sure whether it was the beer he'd drunk, or the result of waving it around in circles. Whatever the reason, he was no longer sure whether he was concentrating or not. He made a last careful scrutiny of the area, then paid his reckoning and went out into the steet. He picked his way across the road and sat down again by the trough. He began another survey from his new vantage point . . . Nothing of interest. There was a grey going away from him, on the other side of the road. A big one too, if one could judge by its rump, but it was pulling a small wagon . . . Even as he thought it, Bragg realized how stupid he'd been. The cart was of no significance. A factory would use whatever vehicle was best suited to the load. He sprang to his feet, and began dodging back across the road again. By the time he got there, the wagon had disappeared. But there was only one street it could have gone into. He ran frantically after it, reaching the opening breathless and sweating. But there it was, clip clopping sedately along. He mustn't get too close, the driver might look round and see him. It certainly wasn't the bearded man who had been driving the murder cart. Bragg had a moment of doubt. After all, two of the three important details were wrong. He must get a good look at the horse, even if it meant risking discovery. He quickened his pace, just as the driver checked for an approaching van. Then the wagon pulled right, into a side street, and Bragg had a clear view of the horse's feet. They tallied! It was almost certain! He waited till the wagon had disappeared, then ran to the corner. It was now stationary by the entrance to a works. He walked casually along the opposite side of the street, merely glancing across as he passed. The driver was lifting a nosebag over the horse's head. They would be there for some time, at least.

Bragg crossed obliquely, risking a brief look back. The driver was going into the works, walking with a distinct limp. There was no one else in the street, so Bragg turned round and strolled back. Now that he was approaching the horse head-on, he could see the white star on its forehead and its powerful shoulders. It was certainly a magnificent animal. It was nuzzling in its bag contentedly, shaking its head to keep off the flies. As he came up to it, Bragg whispered 'Jewel' as loudly as he dared, and saw the horse prick up his ears. There was no doubt whatever, now. All he had to do was to follow it for the rest of the afternoon. He concealed himself in a doorway in the factory wall, and waited. After half an hour, the driver emerged, removed the nosebag, took the horse by the bridle, and led it into the works. Bragg waited ten minutes, then walked slowly back. As he peered through the entrance he could see the horse, now unhitched from the wagon, being led to stables at the top end of the yard. So this was where it belonged. Bragg took a couple of quick steps through the gateway. On the left was an office, and above it was a board with the name 'Samuel Cutler & Co. Engineers'.

Dr Burney straightened up with a sigh, as Morton entered. 'I've done four already today,' he said, his loose mouth hanging open in a fatuous grin. 'There seems to be an epidemic of sudden death at the moment, though fortunately not all of them murders most foul.'

'Have you looked at the man found in Great St Helens this morning?' asked Morton.

'I've practically finished. I've just asked my assistant to bring in some tea while I have a break. Would you like some?'

'No, thank you,' replied Morton in revulsion.

'You'll be wanting to know my conclusions, I suppose?'

'It would be very helpful.'

'The coroner showed me your preliminary report. So this one had a label similar to the body found in Allhallows?'

'That's right.'

'Well, you will know what to make of that, I dare say. From my point of view, this corpse, though it met its end in a less gruesome way, is every bit as interesting . . . Ah, thank you John.' He took a large pottery mug of tea from his assistant, and sipped noisily. Then he beckoned Morton over to the grey slate slab on which the body lay. It was more a carcase, for the abdomen and chest had been opened up and the organs removed, leaving a bloody cavity. Morton felt sour bile rising at the back of his throat.

'I think I will have some tea,' he mumbled.

'Splendid!' Burney smiled at him approvingly. 'You're getting quite case-hardened nowadays. Well now, to business . . . ' He took a gulp from his cup, and set it down. 'There is no indication that this man was tortured, but he was quite deliberately murdered, just as the other was. The wrists were tied together, you will remember, with this relatively fine cord. In my view, that was done after death. But look here . . . ' He ran the tip of a probe around the inside of the left wrist. 'You see that weal, and the abrasions on the outside? That was clearly caused before death, probably as a result of his being bound with a rope considerably stronger than this. There are also minor abrasions on the ankles, which could have been caused by a rope; trousers would have prevented more obvious injuries. There is a very significant linear bruising, here, across the right biceps; and a less well-defined bruise on the corresponding part of the left arm. These injuries are all consistent with his having been tied to, say, a chair.'

'While he was alive,' remarked Morton.

'Oh yes. Indeed they may partly have been caused by his struggling to escape . . . Over here,' he pointed behind the left ear, 'is an area of boggy swelling, which suggests that he was struck from behind with some object like a weighted stick. There is no fracturing of the skull, although the scalp is split. I would say that the force was enough to stun him temporarily.'

'Long enough for the attackers to overpower him?'

'Yes. Without that friendly tap, he might have given them some trouble. You wouldn't call him a big man, but the muscular development of the torso is considerable, and he would appear to have been in excellent health.'

'Can you say how long they kept him, before hanging him?' asked Morton.

Burney's sagging mouth took on a mischievous grin. 'Now you come near the heart of the mystery,' he said. 'But to answer the first part of your question, I would say that the blow to the head was inflicted several hours before death. As to the cause of death, however, I am firmly of the opinion that he did not die by being hanged.'

'But the noose?'

Burney bent over the head. 'You can see where the rope ran around the neck,' he said, tracing the line with his probe. 'And look where it goes upwards, just behind the right ear. That is a typical suspension point, and yet there's no vital reaction in the tissues. He was hanged all right, but not until after he was dead.'

'Good God! What did he die of, then?'

'Manual strangulation,' pronounced Burney gleefully. 'There's no shadow of doubt about it; all the classic signs – fracture of the hyoid bone, blood oozing into the tissues around the voice-box, fingernail marks on the front and back of the neck. The dissection was a pleasure to do. I'll show you if you like.'

Morton glanced at the mound of entrails on the table by the sink. 'I'll take your word for it,' he said hurriedly. 'What time was he killed, do you think?'

'It's not easy to be precise. The body temperature is not so accurate a guide in cases of asphyxiation – say between two and three this morning.'

'So he was strangled while he was conscious and bound to a chair?'

'I would think it in the highest degree unlikely that they untied him, to give him a sporting chance.'

'And yet they didn't torture him,' Morton mused.

'Perhaps he'd already told them what they wanted to know.'

'But why hang him, when he was already dead?' asked Morton.

'I can only surmise that the murderers have a sense of the dramatic. It's all a piece with draping Constable Foster over the railings . . . assuming, that is, they were both murdered by the same people.'

Morton dropped into Bragg's lodgings that evening, and told him of the new development.

'So now we have two murders that aren't what they seem?' remarked Bragg, rubbing slices of tobacco lovingly between his palms.

'One wonders how far their sense of drama extends. By providing the new label, though, they were making sure that we'd link the two cases.'

'It begins to look more political by the minute. The Home Office will try to hush this one up, too, I shouldn't wonder.'

'That reminds me,' said Morton. 'We are both summoned to the coroner's chambers at eight o'clock tomorrow morning.'

'Obviously he doesn't keep City hours. Good for him!'

'My enthusiasm for people is in direct relationship with the amount of sleep they let me get.'

'I take it that doesn't extend to the fair sex,' said Bragg slyly, feeding tobacco with his finger into the bowl of his pipe . . . 'I'd be a lot happier if we knew who the chap on the tomb was.'

'I have a vague idea that I've seen him, or his likeness, somewhere before,' Morton said thoughtfully, 'but I can't pin him down. Moreover, I have a persistent feeling that we could have been indirectly responsible for his death.'

'How do you make that out?'

'If you remember, we came to the conclusion that Foster had been killed as a warning to someone, perhaps to the police. Once we'd had the message translated, however, it didn't mean much to us. But it might have done to somebody else. It could be that the murderers wanted that first message publicized; we prevented it by insisting Catherine didn't write anything.'

'Look here, lad,' said Bragg firmly. 'You can't take a personal responsibility for what the other side does. You'll never make a policeman if you do . . . So you think they intended to ensure it gets into the newspapers this time?'

'What better way than to assassinate a public figure, whose death can't be hushed up?'

'Hmn.' Bragg began to light his pipe, sending great spurts of smoke across the room. 'What is happening about publicity?'

'So far, we've taken the same line as in the Foster case.'

'Which is to keep the lid on . . . Well, let's leave it that way, even if it doesn't suit Sir Rufus. If you are right, then the very necessity for the second murder and the second message shows they are under some pressure.'

There was a rap on the door, Mrs Jenks poked her head in. 'Miss Marsden has come to see you, Mr Bragg. I thought as how it would be all right if I brought her up.'

'Show her in.' Bragg bounded to his feet, and enfolded Catherine in a bearlike hug. 'It's not her!' he exclaimed, 'Mary Jessop has a hare lip!' He waltzed her a turn around the room, before releasing her, astonished and amused. 'If it hadn't been for your photo,' said Bragg, 'we'd never have been sure. But two separate people in Dulwich have confirmed it.'

'Good! I'm glad. Actually, I've come to ask you to lend me one of the prints,' she replied with a mysterious smile. 'I didn't keep one for myself.'

'Now don't hold me in suspense,' said Bragg. 'What are you up to?'

'I wasn't going to say anything, in case we were disappointed, but after today I can see that you are not worried any longer.'

'I'm not worried, no. But by God, I'd like to find out who she really is.'

'That's precisely what I hope to do,' said Catherine. 'The crime reporter of the *Star* had a vague recollection of a case some years ago, where a girl accosted a man in a train and threatened to accuse him of rape if he didn't give her money. He refused to pay her and she carried out her threat. It turned out that the man had been . . . ' she faltered, and blushed, 'dreadfully wounded, in India . . . and he couldn't have.'

'Bad luck!' Bragg observed sardonically.

'Anyway, she was sent to prison for eighteen months. I don't know to which. But I've tracked down *The Times* report of the trial. Her name was given as Fanny Gregory. I intend to go round the prisons, till I find someone who knew her, and see if they recognize the photo of Mary Jessop.'

'You will be careful, won't you?' said Morton quietly. 'We've had a second murder.'

'In the City?'

'Yes. And it's obviously connected with the one at Allhallows.'

'Why didn't you tell me earlier?' asked Catherine indignantly. 'I shall be lucky to catch the early edition, now.'

'We aren't releasing details to the press.'

'But this is absurd!' cried Catherine rebelliously. 'You can't keep it suppressed for ever.'

'Not for ever,' said Bragg. 'Just long enough to let us find the murderers. When we do, you shall be the first to have the whole story.'

'That sounds suspiciously like a qualification,' Catherine said warily. 'The reporters on the *Star* are already curious, because of my enquiries about Fanny Gregory. I can't keep them off for ever.'

'Do you know their political correspondent?' asked Morton.

'Why, yes. It's John Roberts.'

'He sounds Welsh. Is he?'

'Not noticeably so. Does it matter?'

'Probably not. It might even be an advantage. Do you think you could persuade him to help us?'

'I don't mind trying, if it's important enough.'

'Where would we be able to find him? The House isn't sitting at the moment.'

'He'll be down at the office now. He's always there till they've put the paper to bed, in case some juicy piece of political gossip comes in.'

'Would he talk to us this evening?'

Catherine looked surprised. 'I don't see why not, if it's as urgent as all that. But I warn you, he'll probably want a *quid pro quo*.' She got to her feet.

'I won't come with you,' Bragg said, knocking out his pipe in the empty grate. 'I've a mind to have a walk up Bishopsgate way.'

As they walked to the cab rank, Morton told Catherine about the discovery of the body, and the conclusions of Dr Burney. He watched her face grow grave, and felt her hand tighten on his arm.

'But what is it all about?' she asked.

'We don't know. I'm hoping that your friend Roberts will be able to put in another piece of the jigsaw puzzle.'

On being introduced to him, however, Morton began to have doubts. His eyes were bloodshot, his speech was slurred, and he smelled strongly of brandy.

'Cymru Fydd? Yes, I've heard of it. The Wild Welsh playing at Owain Glyndwr.' He seemed disinclined to expand on this cryptic utterance.

'Is it a political party?' asked Catherine.

'Not a party, not even a movement . . . an illusion.' He began to rummage in the bottom drawer of his desk. 'Will you have a drink?' he asked, pulling out a new bottle of brandy.

'Not at the moment,' Morton replied and pulled a face at Catherine. She ignored him, however.

'Who is involved in it?' she asked.

Roberts concentrated on splashing a generous measure of brandy into a tumbler, then swung back to them. 'Tom Ellis, the Member for Merioneth; he's the leading light. He's attracted a gaggle of squawking geese from the Welsh-speaking constituencies.'

'There's a slogan going around, which translates as "Victory to Wales of the future",' said Morton. 'What kind of victory is it they seek?'

'A victory of the Celts. They long to be like the Irish, to find a Welsh Parnell, to achieve Home Rule. They think they can saw Wales off from England, and punt it across the Irish Sea.'

'Are you saying that it's not a serious political movement?' asked Catherine.

'They're serious enough, some of them. But it will never come to anything. They should stick to rugby football; they're good at that.'

'Where can I get hold of Tom Ellis?' asked Morton.

'He's down in his constituency. Your best bet is David George, the new Liberal member for Caernarvon. He seems a bit of a lightweight, but he's one of Ellis's disciples . . . and he never goes home.' He scribbled an address on a piece of paper, and handed it to Morton. 'That's where he lives, in London; though whether you'll find him there, is anyone's guess.'

15

'So it could be a group of Welsh terrorists?' said Bragg. 'Interesting.'

They were sitting in the waiting-room of Sir Rufus Stone's chambers.

'I never thought of the Welsh as being fanatical about anything, except beer and singing,' he went on. 'But I suppose anybody can get worked up about their own patch of ground.'

'I don't believe they are,' said Morton. 'You don't see reports in the newspapers about murders and burnings such as occur in Ireland.'

'Maybe,' replied Bragg. 'But everything has to have a beginning. You remember our Mr Crisp? He was very bitter about the unions being manipulated by socialist politicians in England. Why shouldn't nationalist politicians manipulate the Welsh people in the same way? It all smacks of it, to me. They did name Dic Penderyn in the first message, and he seems to be a kind of martyr – a fairly recent one too.'

'I suppose so. It seems odd, though, that they should have reached the stage of publicized murder so quickly. From what I've been able to discover, the people of Wales are more concerned to get control of their religious affairs than to fight for political freedom.'

'You know,' Bragg mused, 'I reckon there's an educated mind behind it all. You remember that there was a brass plate in Allhallows church, with the figure of a knight engraved on it? He had his hands and feet crossed, which seems to mean that he was a crusader, or something. Now poor old Foster had his hands and feet crossed, as near as they could manage it. I walked up to Great St Helens last evening, and inside the church there are several tombs with effigies on them. Their legs, however, are stretched down side by side, and their hands are placed with palms together.'

'Just like the man we found on the tomb,' observed Morton.

'Right. Whatever is going on, I think someone is having a little fun in the process – a little intellectual amusement.'

'Sir Rufus will see you now, gentlemen,' the clerk interrupted. 'I think you know the way.'

The coroner heard their account of developments in silence, then rose from his desk and took his accustomed stance in front of the fireplace.

'We shall have to adjourn it,' he said abruptly.

'What's that?' asked Bragg.

'The inquest, you blockhead, the inquest. Well now, Bragg,' he said assertively, 'it's time you stopped sulking in your tent, and got back to work. You can forget about the charge against you. If you like I'll get you reinstated.'

'I'd prefer to leave things as they are, for the moment,' said Bragg. 'I wouldn't want to alert our quarry.'

'Dammit, Bragg, it's action I want.'

'You shall have it, sir. But if we go blundering in, we shall lose our chance of wresting the initiative from these people.'

'What proposals do you have?' asked the coroner. 'Mind you, if I don't approve, I shall veto them.'

'It's clear now that whoever is behind these murders, there is a link between them and Samuel Cutler's works in Stepney. You recall the names on the square of paper? I think they were in a particular order. According to this morning's paper, there's a complete strike of engineers at Glengal Brass, and the works is closed.'

'So?' grunted the coroner impatiently.

'If I am right, then Cutler's are next in line for labour trouble. I want to try to get a job there before it happens, so that I can look around.'

Sir Rufus pursed his lips thoughtfully. 'Makes sense,' he pronounced. 'I think I can help you there. I got to know old Sam very well, when I was advising on the setting up of the engineering employers' federation. Be back here at three o'clock this afternoon. I'll get my clerk to ring and have him attend.'

Bragg and Morton walked from the Temple to Beech Street, where a crowd had gathered around the gates of the Glengal works. They were mostly onlookers – messenger boys and clerks from the offices around. Some, however, were unskilled workers at the foundry, who had been laid off because of the strike. They were standing around sullenly, or arguing with the pickets at the gate. A policeman was standing on the pavement near by, so Bragg shielded his face with his hat as they pushed through the entrance, and into the yard. They went up a steep flight of wooden stairs to an office overlooking the street. A young man in waistcoat and linen sleeve-protectors was staring through the window.

'Could I see the boss, please?' asked Bragg peremptorily.

'I don't know if Mr Crossley is in yet,' replied the lad, his eyes glued to the scene outside.

'Find out then,' snarled Bragg. 'Tell him we're police officers.'

The young man reluctantly turned away from the window, and disappeared through a doorway. After a few moments he emerged, and ushered them into a large airy office, with a good carpet on the floor. A smartly dressed man turned from the window, and held out his hand.

'Hello,' he said, 'I'm Crossley, the manager of this works.' The perfunctory smile faded as his eyes drifted back to the window. 'Just look at them,' he exclaimed. 'I don't understand it.'

'In a way, that's what we've come to see you about, sir,' said Bragg.

'The strike, you mean?' asked Crossley.

'Rather the events leading up to it.'

'Well, there weren't any events, to speak of. The union organizer just came up last Thursday afternoon, and said there was to be a strike, starting from Monday.'

'What reason did he give, sir?' asked Morton.

'He didn't give a reason, or none that would hold water. He more or less said that was what his members wanted and that was how it was going to be. It will destroy us. We'd just got a big order from America . . . I don't know how we shall meet it.'

'Have you got other works?' asked Bragg.

'Yes, we have three others in Millwall, but this is the only brass foundry.'

'Are the men on strike at the other factories?'

'No, thank God!'

'Then why here?'

'I don't know.' Crossley sighed despondently. 'They gave me no proper explanation. They haven't any grievances that I know of, they are well-paid, we have full order-books, so their jobs are secure – which is more than can be said for a lot of engineering firms.'

'Surely there had to be a pretext, or they'd never have got the men out?' remarked Morton.

'That's the right word for it. He said it was to protect his members' jobs against dilution by semi-skilled men. I understand their concern, and I have a certain amount of sympathy with it. But it just doesn't apply to us. We haven't brought in new machinery to replace skilled men. The engineers we employ are all pattern-makers. You can't get machines to do their work, and well they know it.'

'Have Pontifex had any trouble?' asked Bragg.

'Pontifex and Wood? Yes, they've had strikes off and on, for a month now. They're not competitors of ours, of course . . . Mind you, I wouldn't wish this on anybody.'

Bragg and Morton mounted the steps of the substantial terraced house near Westminster Abbey and rang the bell. They waited for some minutes, but nothing happened.

'Your reporter friend was right about his not being in,' remarked Bragg, giving a series of fierce tugs on the bell. There was still no response from within. Then they heard a window pushed open above their heads.

'Who's there?' cried a powerful voice.

Bragg backed down a couple of steps, out of the shadow of the porch. The dishevelled head of a man was poking out of a second-storey window.

'Police,' he called. 'Are you David George?'

'Lloyd George,' said the man automatically, 'I like to be known as Lloyd George.'

'We want to have a few words with you.'

The man gazed down irresolutely for a moment, then nodded and slammed the window shut. Even now, the house remained silent, and Bragg was about to renew his assault on the bell when they heard steps crossing the hall. Lloyd George opened the door warily, and took them upstairs to a sitting-room. As he hurried on ahead of them, Bragg saw him sweep a lady's handbag behind a cushion.

'I can't spare you long,' said Lloyd George. 'I'm in the middle of writing a speech.'

'I gather you are a friend and disciple of Tom Ellis, the MP for Merioneth,' said Bragg.

'Disciple, is it?' Lloyd George exclaimed wrathfully. 'You can tell your informant that I'm nobody's disciple. Friend I may be, but only as a politician, not as an individual.'

'And what might that mean, sir?'

'Political friendships are ephemeral, matters of mutual convenience. They seldom survive the loss of self-interest.'

'At least you're refreshingly frank.'

'I'm a lawyer. I know better than to try and deceive the police. Now perhaps you'd be so kind as to tell me what it is you want.'

'I'm told you are a supporter of Cymru Fydd. Can you tell me about it?'

'Cymru Fydd,' repeated Lloyd George, correcting Bragg's pronunciation. 'What is it you wish to know?'

'What kind of organization is it?'

'I would say "organization" is altogether too grand a word. As you will have gathered from the title, it's a group which, amongst other things, is concerned with the preservation of the Welsh language. Our native tongue is in danger of disappearing altogether, under the weight of barbarian English.' His smile robbed his words of their sting.

'Would you say this group was nationalist in character?' asked Bragg.

'It depends what you mean by the word. It's nationalist in so far as it seeks to preserve the culture of the Welsh people, but it

177

has nothing to do with the rebirth of the Welsh nation.'

'We're told that Cymru Fydd means "Wales of the future". That doesn't seem to square with what you've just told us,' said Bragg.

'We Welsh are Celts, romantics. We need a rallying cry, we respond to emotion.'

'So what does "Wales of the future" imply?'

'What every man wishes it to imply,' replied Lloyd George with a shrug. 'Some people look to a future where nothing but Welsh will be spoken throughout the principality, and where we will be freed from the monstrous irrelevance of the Church of Wales.'

'And others, no doubt, hope for political independence?'

'Devolution,' Lloyd George countered. 'The opportunity to run our own affairs under the Crown.'

'And what are your own views?'

'I am the elected representative of the people of Caernarvon,' Lloyd George replied cryptically.

'You are also the political correspondent for a newspaper, whose title, when translated, means "the Welsh Nation",' said Morton.

'That is a matter of public record.'

'And is it not correct that, together with Tom Ellis, you own the Welsh National Newspaper Company?'

Lloyd George looked uncomfortable. 'Yes, well, that's true, that's true.'

'And isn't your newspaper called the *Trumpet of Freedom?*'

'Yes, yes.'

'Do you still say that you are not agitating for independence for Wales?'

'Look you, I don't give a damn about Welsh Home Rule,' burst out Lloyd George irritably, 'or any variation on that theme. I formed an association with Tom Ellis, certainly, because I wanted to be a Member of Parliament. I've spoken on Home Rule platforms, because I needed a cause. How else was I going to be noticed? But now I've been elected, I've got more important things to occupy me.'

Bragg felt the concealed handbag against his thigh, and smiled.

'You surely can't abandon your views,' said Morton. 'You wouldn't be re-elected if you did.'

'Of course I continue to pay lip-service to them. But you don't think I could found my career on Welsh affairs, do you? Let me explain the situation to you. Wales is solidly Liberal. But if the Liberals are returned to power, they will have their hands full with an Irish Home Rule Bill. That means we can fulminate in the House about autonomy for Wales, and strike what attitudes we like, without there being the slightest danger that it will lead to a change in the present position. Moreover, the elders of the party don't mind, because it keeps our constituents happy.'

'Do you think anyone connected with Cymru Fydd would go as far as violence,' asked Bragg, 'perhaps in the hope of bringing their feelings to the attention of the general public?'

'Not a chance!' replied Lloyd George scornfully. 'Most of them don't aspire to anything more dynamic than dressing up in sheets and reciting interminable odes in Welsh.'

'What do you make of this?' Bragg passed him the second label. 'We're told it means "Victory to Wales of the future".'

Lloyd George smiled triumphantly.'Well your informant is as ignorant as the person who wrote this. In the Welsh language, not only do inanimate objects have a sex, but we have mutation of letters, also. If you were going to write "Victory to Wales of the future", the C of Cymru would become a G – "Buddugoliaeth i Gymru Fydd". It is quite impossible that a member of the movement could have made such an elementary mistake.'

'It was good of you to come at such short notice, Samuel,' Sir Rufus said expansively. 'I'm sure it won't be time wasted.'

'I never thought it would,' replied Cutler shortly. He was about sixty years old, with heavy whiskers, and a severe face.

'I'm not going to bother you with details that don't concern you,' said Sir Rufus. 'But we have reason to believe that your business is about to be disrupted.'

Cutler looked up sharply, with a mixture of truculence and defiance. 'Not if I can stop it, it won't.'

'That's why I've called you here. If the experience of other people is anything to go by, you would be unable to prevent it. These two gentlemen are police officers, who have been involved in certain enquiries which are, at the moment, still confidential. They will explain as far as they can, and answer any questions that are proper at this stage.'

Cutler transferred his hostile gaze to the policemen.

'We are investigating two very serious crimes,' said Bragg, 'which are almost certainly related. During the course of our enquiries, a piece of paper came into our possession, on which four names were written. The first was Pontifex, the second Glengal Brass, and the third was that of your own firm. The fourth, Ben Grove, we haven't yet traced.'

'It means nothing to me,' said Cutler tersely. 'The others I know, of course.'

'Then you'll be aware that there is a strike at the Glengal brass foundry, called by the engineers' union. I spoke to the works manager this morning. He's completely stumped at the union's action, because it has been called on a pretext which has no relevance to the kind of work done in his foundry. It is represented as a demonstration against the dilution of skilled workers; but he says it hasn't happened, and couldn't happen, in his works.'

'I suppose that's right enough,' murmured Cutler.

'When he challenged the union organizer, he was told that a meeting of the membership had demanded a strike. Now Constable Morton, here, was at that meeting, and in his view it was manipulated by a small faction – probably outside the union.'

'For what purpose?' asked Cutler.

'We don't know. Perhaps they wanted to bring Glengal to a standstill, perhaps it is part of a wider campaign. But whatever the reason, the Beech Street foundry is closed.'

'And why do you think it will spread to my factory?'

'We know there has been disruption at Pontifex and Wood, over a prolonged period . . . '

'Aye, I know,' interjected Cutler. 'And we've benefited from it. I'll not complain.'

'We also have reason to believe that men involved in the conspiracy are already employed at your Stepney works.'

'What!' exclaimed Cutler, half rising from his chair. 'I'll soon send them packing! Who are they?'

'Now that's just what you must not do, Samuel,' said Sir Rufus soothingly. 'If I'd merely wanted to warn you, I wouldn't have needed to drag you here. What we want is your co-operation.'

'Co-operation?'

'Yes. Go on, Sergeant.'

'I would like you to take me on as an employee at Stepney, so that I can identify the trouble-makers, and perhaps find out what is behind it all. Then, when the disruption starts, we shall be able to arrest those responsible, and help you to bring it to an end.'

'If you go arresting union men, we shall have trouble, and no mistake.'

'I don't think they'll turn out to be members of a union,' said Bragg. 'But naturally we would consult you before we made a move.'

'It's a big works,' said Cutler doubtfully. 'If you were in the wrong spot, you might never hear what was going on.'

'Has there been trouble in any department, recently?'

'Well, not trouble exactly,' replied Cutler, glaring at Bragg as if daring him to contradict. 'We've had some damned poor work in the despatch department that's cost us a pretty penny.'

'What happened?' asked Bragg.

'We were sending a consignment of finished work to one of our customers in London, only it ended up in Glasgow. It had been addressed to another customer of ours, up there. I took it as a genuine mistake – only it never arrived at their works. We found out later that it had been sent to Glasgow goods station, for collection by the customer. That's a thing we never do, but still . . . We asked for the consignment to be returned, of course, only to be told that it had been collected! They sent us a docket with a signature on it, but our Glasgow customer swore it wasn't any of their people.'

'So the goods vanished?' asked Bragg.

'Aye, they did. It's been dead money for two months now, and we shall have to replace them at our own expense. Our customer is going mad.'

'But in order to collect them,' said Bragg, 'someone must have had a copy of the consignment note.'

'I know . . . ' Cutler pondered gloomily for a moment. 'All right. I'll do what I can to help. But I can't engage you as a policeman.'

'The despatch department will do very well,' said Bragg. 'I used to work in a shipping office, so I know the ropes. I'd like you to tell the works manager what's happening, and make sure he keeps his mouth shut.'

'I'd stake my life on Alf Webb's discretion.'

'That's good,' said Bragg drily. 'I reckon I shall have to.'

Bragg threaded his way through the clogged traffic at the Bank with a light heart. For the last fortnight his spirits had been crushed by the black despair sitting on his shoulders. Now, suddenly, he felt confident that the case against him would fall apart, that he would regain his position in life. He made a silent vow never to take anything for granted again . . . And over and above that, he could see his way forward with the investigation. Once more, patient police work had paid off. He smiled with satisfaction as he recalled the coroner's gibe. 'A hit-and-miss proceeding', he'd called it. Well, it wouldn't do any harm for him to be taken down a peg or two; he was a bit bumptious at times. Mind you, there'd never been a coroner like him. He really got stuck in, and he had contacts in all kinds of unlikely places. They'd never have persuaded old Sam Cutler without him.

Bragg paused and looked up at the weather vane on the Royal Exchange. A grasshopper spitted on a golden needle. That's what he would be, if he didn't watch out. These people killed like a fox in a hen run, without compunction, without even necessity. If the conspirators at Cutler's rumbled him, he wouldn't last long. He'd be under a runaway cart, or the hook of a crane would just happen to catch his head. He might even end up on a tomb . . . Good God! He'd been acting like a fool, parading himself at the Glengal works that morning. He'd screened himself from the policeman and hadn't even thought about the pickets. The conspirators would be sure to have someone there, to keep the strikers from flagging. And no doubt they'd have orders to report comings and goings to their bosses. Well, one thing was sure: a brown dust-coat wasn't going to be enough to disguise him . . . Could he back out, and send young Morton? After all, he was supposed to be in charge of the case . . . No, they'd gobble him up, as soon as spit. And what the hell did he know, anyway, apart from German and French and not to eat peas off your knife?

Bragg found that he was standing by a shop window, decorated with sponges and badger shaving brushes. Of course! Toni's Emporium. He'd promised to come back, too.

'Ah, ze Capitano Marittimo,' the barber greeted him as he pushed open the door.

'You were right about the moustache,' said Bragg. 'Get rid of it.'

The barber ushered him to a chair, winking at one of his assistants. 'Ze Eenglish wife ees not kind, yes? You weesh to pliz her.' He tucked a cover round Bragg's neck, and quickly snipped at his moustache, as if afraid he would change his mind. Then he spread lather along the denuded upper lip.

'No hot towels this time,' warned Bragg.

'So sorree,' the man said with a grin. He seized Bragg by the tip of his nose, and removed one half of the lather with a careless backhand flick. This was worse than the dentist, Bragg thought, and he closed his eyes till he felt his face being patted dry.

'You like?' The barber was holding a hand mirror, to show his side-face. He certainly looked changed. But was it enough? If he were honest, he just looked like Joe Bragg, with his moustache off.

'Can you make me look, er . . . different?'

'Pliz, you liv it to Toni.' He spread out his hands like a magician doing the three-card trick. 'I maka you look young for ze beautiful Eenglish wife. First I cut ze 'air, zen we see.'

The chair jolted upright, and Bragg was soon lulled by the grasshopper chirping of the scissors and the caress of the comb. He should be thinking about tomorrow, not drifting off like a Chinese with an opium pipe. He must at least know what he wanted to achieve. The gentle fingers leaned his head towards his left shoulder, and the chirping began again by his right ear. The main thing was to identify the conspirators . . . Funny, keeping calling them that, but it was the best he could do. He hadn't any idea what was behind it all. Establishing that must be the second objective. Once he got them in clink, he'd make them sing all right. Not that the men at Cutler's were likely to know a lot. They'd just be monkeys . . . gorillas more like it. The brains behind it all was probably sitting at a big office desk, not half a mile away, his feet on a turkey carpet, a big cigar in his mouth. If you caused enough disruption in a rival firm, you could capture some of its customers; maybe buy it up cheap . . . It was a damned rough way to go about it, but you'd see your hands were clean. And the City was Jesuitical enough not to enquire too closely into the means, if the end put money in their pockets.

'You like?'

Bragg opened his eyes, and gazed at his new face in the mirror. He now had a side parting, his hair was cropped close at the back and sides, and his sideboards barely extended below the tops of his ears. His first reaction was one of revulsion. It just wasn't him! But that was exactly the point.

'Maka you look young,' urged the barber.

'Yes . . . ' Bragg moved his head around experimentally, and watched his reflection in the big mirror opposite. 'Yes, I like it.'

'Ees a leetle grey just 'ere,' murmured the barber. 'Shall I take eet out?'

'What?' exclaimed Bragg in alarm. 'Not bloody likely!'

'No, no,' said the barber, in a wheedling voice. 'A leetle colour, that ees all.'

'Do what you like,' Bragg said in resignation.

The barber half filled an enamel bowl with warm water, then bustled over to a cupboard in the corner, and took out a glass bottle. He carefully measured out some black liquid from it, and poured it into the bowl. Immediately there was a hissing effervescence, and white vapours rose from the mixture.

'Ees all right,' the barber assured him. 'Ze water, 'ee is not pure.'

At least the fizzing had died away now, leaving a white scum on the surface. The barber carefully skimmed this off with a spoon. 'Ees new,' he said with a reassuring smile, and dropped a small sponge into the black liquid that remained. Then taking some forceps, such as Bragg had seen in Dr Burney's dissecting room, he retrieved the sponge and began to dab at Bragg's hair.

'God, what a stink!' cried Bragg.

'Ees all right, eet will go.'

His head was now saturated with the clammy, evil-smelling liquid, and some was trickling down his forehead into the corner of his eye. The barber was watching the clock intently, like a doctor counting a patient's heartbeat.

'Now we wash,' he announced, pushing Bragg's head over the basin. Soon his hair was being vigorously towelled dry, and combed into place.

He looked in the mirror apprehensively. Who the devil was that, staring out at him? Instead of dark-brown, his hair was jet-black; his face looked pallid and thin, shorn of its moustache and sideboards. He looked as if he'd just escaped from a dago prison . . . But at least he didn't stink any more.

'Ees all right?' enquired the barber anxiously.

Bragg burst into laughter. 'Ees fine,' he replied.

'Kip ze 'at off till 'ee ees dry,' the barber advised, as Bragg tipped him. 'Ave good night wiz ze Eenglish wife!'

As Bragg emerged, he could see that a trestle table had been erected in the paved area behind the Royal Exchange. It was covered with piles of that week's edition of *Tit-Bits*. A poster was hanging from the edge of the table, and Bragg bent to look at it. The name of the magazine was blazoned across the top, and underneath was reproduced a black-and-white sketch of a man's head. Below it was an exhortation.

CLAIM YOUR £1 NOW
Jenkin Apthorp is in the CITY today.
Be the first to challenge him!
Say
'You are Jenkin Apthorp.
Here is my copy of Tit-Bits,
I claim my £1'
CLAIM YOUR £1 NOW

The man at the table held out a copy in Bragg's direction, but he shook his head. Bloody disgusting, cluttering up the streets of the City with displays like that . . . Dear God! They were all over the place. He could see another in front of the Bank of England, and yet another by the Mansion House. Surely to God the police hadn't given permission for this? He walked up Princes Street, and found another stall in Lothbury. The ploy seemed to be working, more's the pity; plenty of people were walking along with a *Tit-Bits* under their arm, peering at each other. They'd get rid of all they could sell, without Jenkin Apthorp turning up at all. Come to think of it, that would be fraud . . .

'Excuse me.' A young woman was standing at his elbow. 'You are Jenkin Apthorp.' She glanced down at the magazine in her hand. 'Here is my copy of *Tit-Bits*. I claim my one pound.'

Bragg smiled down at her in embarrassment. 'No, I'm not, miss.'

'Aren't you?' she asked, disappointed. 'I was sure it was you.'

'No. Sorry.'

He crossed over into Moorgate. Damned silly business. It was all right at the seaside, with ice cream cornets, and candy floss; but here, in the sober heart of the world's commercial centre, it was nothing short of an outrage.

'Right, mate. I got you.' Bragg's way was blocked by a large grinning workman. 'You are Jenkin Whatever-'is-blasted-name. 'Ere's my bleeding *Tit-Bits,* an' I'll 'ave my quid, ta very much.'

'I'm not him.'

'Come off it, mate. Give us the money.'

'I tell you, I'm not Jenkin Apthorp,' said Bragg firmly.

'Well, if you're not, who bloody is?' grumbled the man as he walked away.

This was absurd, thought Bragg. It turned the streets of London into a circus; and all to sell a few more copies of a weekly muck-raker . . . All right, so he read it himself; it still didn't have to be smeared all over the face of the City. There was another stall right in the middle of Moorgate station's forecourt. People seemed to be queueing for the blasted things. Mainly women here, middle-class, office girls, wives of tradesmen, all acting out of character – and just for a miserable sovereign. One burly woman, with a *Tit-Bits* clamped firmly under her elbow, was waiting impatiently for her change. Then, looking around, she saw Bragg and let out a whoop of triumph. She began running towards him, followed by several others. Bragg sighed with ill-natured resignation, and prepared to meet the charge.

'You're him!' she panted, seizing his arm.

'No. I'm not.'

'Go away! I saw him first,' shouted the woman, striking out with her umbrella.

He felt his other arm grasped, and someone was holding on to his coat. All around, he could hear the name 'Jenkin Apthorp' being screamed at him.

'I tell you, it's not me,' he shouted, trying to dislodge the women.

'It is him, isn't it?' the first woman appealed to the crowd. 'Look at his picture.'

'Yes, yes . . . Apthorp . . . money . . . *Tit-Bits* . . . claim . . . pound.'

They were tearing at his clothes now, dragging him down. He struggled, trying to make his voice heard above the din. 'All right – somebody's already claimed the pound.'

There was a momentary lull, then the burly woman shook her umbrella at him threateningly. 'It doesn't say only one person can get it,' she screamed. 'You're cheating us!' She began to beat him about the head. He squirmed to free himself, while blows rained down on him from all sides.

'Blame them!' he shouted, nodding his head towards the stall. 'It's their fault.'

For a moment, his captors relaxed their hold, and he tore his arms free. The women were now streaming towards the stall, brandishing their umbrellas and swinging their handbags. Bragg retrieved his trampled hat, and battered his way through the remnant at a run.

After this, Cutler's would be a kindergarten!

'Ah James, I fear I shall never make a gentleman of you.'

Morton propped himself on one elbow, and gazed at Helga's glowing face. 'I would hope you didn't need to,' he said with a smile.

'Ah, but I do! What gentleman would burst unheralded into a lady's room . . . and drag her, protesting, to bed?'

'Now I know that you are teasing!'

'You English have no finesse,' she pouted. 'One minute you are telling me that you will not see me for days, the next you are pounding at my door.'

'I couldn't foresee how things would change. Sergeant Bragg will be taking over his cases again. The girl who accused him isn't who she pretends to be.'

'Nevertheless, it is not flattering to me. A gentleman would have considered that I could be otherwise occupied, that there might be other men who would find my company engaging. You come bursting in, like a great lumbering ox,' she dug him in the ribs. 'Quite confident I'll be waiting for you.'

'I wish you could always be waiting for me,' said Morton softly.

Helga laid a finger over his lips. 'If you are meaning what I suspect, then I must definitely discourage you.'

'But Helga, I love you,' Morton protested.

'A proposal of marriage is much too important to be considered in bed,' she said teasingly. 'In any case, I am not sure that I would be good for you . . . But perhaps it is not marriage that you are considering.'

'You are the only person I've ever wanted to marry.'

'And I would entrust my reputation, in this way, to no one else.' She put up her arms, and pulled him down to her. *'Liebchen,'* she murmured, ruffling his hair. 'Come again to me on Sunday. By then we will both have had time to think.'

'But you will be serious, won't you?'

She looked into his eyes. 'At this moment,' she said gravely, 'I long to be part of you always, whatever it is you propose.'

16

Bragg rose early, and dressed himself in an old coat and a pair of trousers with ragged bottoms. To complete the picture of an out-of-work clerk, he added a shirt collar scrubbed threadbare and a bedraggled tie. The previous evening, Toni's efforts to rejuvenate Bragg had merely confirmed Mrs Jenks's suspicions about his goings-on with young girls. Now her outrage was turned to bewilderment, but his glare fended off her anxious reproaches. Immediately after breakfast, he took a tram to Stepney Green, and walked the quarter-mile to Cutler's works along with a score of other workmen.

Alf Webb, the works manager, proved to be a powerful chunky man, on whom the smart clothes sat ill. His accent, also, proclaimed that he had originated on the shop floor.

'Mr Cutler told me why you are here,' he said briskly. 'Any help you need, let me know.'

'Thank you.'

'I thought we'd best not put you in the despatch department itself, because you'd be stuck there. I expect you'd rather be able to move around a bit.'

'Good idea.'

'We decided it would be best to say you were a temporary clerk brought in to do a job for me. I shall instruct you to collate the despatch notes with the invoices, and then compare them with debtors. It will look as if I'm doing a check on the accounts department, to satisfy myself that our credit control is working properly. On that footing, you should be able to go anywhere.'

'I can see that it would cover the despatch and accounts departments,' said Bragg. 'But what about the factory floor?'

'Every invoice is prepared from a job card. If you want to go

189

in the machine shops, you'll have to say that you are checking the invoice back to the job card.'

'Good. What kind of work do you do here?' asked Bragg.

'General engineering – mainly milling and finishing. Now here's a list of the managers and foremen in the various departments. Is there anything else you'd like me to do?'

'Just let it be known that I'm reporting only to you . . . Oh, and make a particular point of telling them that I'm not to be allowed anywhere near cash.'

'Right. And we'll call you Jack Jones, shall we?'

Bragg spent half an hour in the accounts department, being shown how an invoice was compiled, and the consequent entries in the company's books. It was a large office, with a dozen clerks in it. The manager was a nervous, myopic man, who regarded Bragg with apprehension. He constantly paced about the office, peering over the shoulders of his staff. Bragg had hoped he might start some chatter amongst the clerks, but there was no chance of that. He therefore gathered up a bundle of invoices and shambled over to the despatch department. The factory buildings had been laid out to gain the maximum advantage from the ground, which sloped gently towards the road. On the highest part were the machine shops, which occupied the whole of the back of the site. On the right-hand side of the central yard were stables and storage buildings. Opposite them were the packing sheds and despatch department. The finished goods could be pushed on a trolley from the works into the packing shed; and from there, still on the same level, they emerged on to the loading ramp by the despatch office. By then, they were five feet or so above the yard, a comfortable height to get a cart alongside.

Bragg stood for a time watching some men load a flat lorry. They seemed cheerful enough, their talk confined to the usual ribald banter. But if any disaffection had been fomented, it was more likely to be on the shop floor, among the skilled men. As Bragg turned into the despatch office, the pipe nearly dropped from his mouth. Behind a desk in the corner sprawled a big man with a full black beard, bulging brown eyes, and a completely bald head.

'Whaddya want?' he barked.

'I'm Jones, Mr Ruddick,' stammered Bragg timidly. 'I've got to go through the despatch notes.'

'Oh. I've heard of you. All right. They're in that cardboard box in the corner.'

'I've got to start with last October,' Bragg said, dropping his eyes before Ruddick's challenging gaze.

'They're all in one ruddy great heap. You'll have to sort out the ones you want. You can sit at that table over there.'

Bragg saw that the table was in the back corner, pushed against the wall. If he sat there, he would see little or nothing. He walked quietly over, and pulled it away from the wall, taking the chair round behind it.

'Whaddya do that for?' demanded Ruddick, belligerently.

'I've seen enough of walls in my time,' replied Bragg, tipping the contents of the box on to the table.

Ruddick eyed him speculatively. 'Well, just keep out of my way.'

Bragg occupied himself with arranging the despatch notes into number order; observing, as he did so, the people who came into the office, and listening intently to everything that was said. By eleven o'clock, he had completed the sorting, and had seen nothing that was remotely abnormal. Nevertheless, he was certain that Ruddick had been the driver of the cart that had carried Foster to his death. He was the only known suspect, and must be watched at all costs. In order to justify his continued presence, Bragg took a foolscap sheet of paper, and began to enter on it the details of every despatch note. He had laboriously completed three sheets, when Ruddick crossed over to him.

'Take a walk,' he ordered, jerking his head towards the door.

Bragg looked up in surprise, then meekly did as he was told. He could see from the doorway that three men were crossing the yard, towards the office. Two were talking animatedly together, while the third trailed ten yards behind. They weren't very skilful in concealing their intentions, thought Bragg. Probably they were local bludgers, recruited for the job but knowing nothing of what was behind it. He stood by the loading-bay, lighting his pipe, as the three men passed close by him. One of them had a heavy Welsh accent. So that was another piece of the jigsaw in place. Bragg mentally absolved David George, even though he had been lying through his teeth. Indeed, things were coming together a treat, for unless he was much mistaken, the grey coming into the yard was Jewel. He wandered across as the driver pulled to a halt and jumped down.

'Fine animal,' Bragg remarked.

'He's shifted some weight in his time,' agreed the man in a broad north-country voice.

'Do you drive him all the time?'

'I do that.'

'Any chance of borrowing him for next weekend?' asked Bragg. 'I've got some furniture to shift.'

'Not likely! They'd have my guts for garters if they found out.'

'It's worth a couple of quid,' Bragg persisted.

'No. I'm not risking losing my job . . . not that it'll last long, the way things are going.'

'Why's that?'

'There's some talk of a strike. If that happens, we'll all be laid off straight away.'

'What are they striking about?' asked Bragg.

'God knows. The bloody engineers are all for themselves. They don't give a tuppenny cuss about anybody else,' the driver said gloomily.

'What's the despatch foreman like to work for?'

'Albert Ruddick? He's all right I suppose. A real hard nut, but he seems to know his job.'

'Has he been here long?'

'No. About six weeks. He was right lucky. He'd just called in to see if there was a job for him, when a paint drum rolled off the loading ramp on to Sam Brett. Ruddick just walked into his job. Still, he's all right, if you don't cross him.'

'Who are those men coming out of the office?' asked Bragg.

'Him at the front is Taffy Evans, he's a packer. Behind him is Dick Cousins, he's a labourer in the paint shop – I don't know what he's doing over here. I can't remember the name of the other one. He sweeps up the swarf in the main machine shop.'

The unknown man was crossing towards them. Bragg leaned

on the shaft of the cart, puffing at his pipe, and memorizing his features.

'Where do you come from, Jones?' the man asked with a twisted smile.

'Hampshire,' replied Bragg briefly.

'Is Jones your real name, then?'

'It will do as well as any.' Bragg knocked out his pipe against the cart and began to amble back to the office.

'How d'you get this job?' asked the man, falling into step beside him.

'I was recommended.'

'By the Prisoners' Aid Society, I'll be bound,' said the man with a sneering laugh.

'It's no concern of yours,' replied Bragg defensively.

'Come on, mate. You done a stretch, ain't you? What was it, a twoer?'

Bragg halted. 'If you must know,' he said with a whine, 'I was given eighteen months for something I didn't do.'

The man laughed derisively. 'They all say that. Where did they send you?'

'Winchester.'

'I got a two-stretch at the Scrubs, for grievous bodily harm,' said the man perkily. 'The difference between you and me – I done it!'

Bragg began to move on, and the man caught his arm. ' 'Ere, what did they catch you for?'

'I used to work at a laundry. On the manager's instructions I put certain items in the books as cash expenses. When they found out they were false, he said I must have taken the money.'

'Hard cheese. Still, I expect you'd had a bit for yourself.'

Bragg allowed a small smile to cross his lips.

' 'Ere you are, mate.' The man pressed a golden sovereign into his palm. 'There's another for you, if you don't find nothin' in them records till next week.'

The prison governor smiled primly at Catherine.

'We haven't the slightest objection to an article on the British

193

prison system, Miss Marsden,' he said. 'And if you should decide to write it around Holloway, I would be glad to offer you every facility. I cannot spare you much time at the moment, but if you were to come back on' – he glanced at the calendar on the wall – 'next Wednesday afternoon, I could explain what we are trying to achieve here. Afterwards I could take you on a tour of one of the wings.'

'Thank you. I shall have to get my editor's approval first, but I'm sure he will be delighted.'

Catherine began to rise, then checked. 'Oh, there is one other thing. The article would also contain comments on Holloway from a former inmate – most of them remarkably commendatory. I would, however, like to be satisfied that this woman has, in fact, been imprisoned here and is not just deceiving us.'

'It would be an unusual imposture,' said the governor with a smile. 'What is her name?'

'The name she gave us is Fanny Gregory,' said Catherine. 'And here is a photograph of her.'

The governor looked at it carefully. 'I can't say that I recognize her,' he said. 'But that is hardly surprising. There are three hundred women here, and their appearance is somewhat different from the way they look outside. However,' he rose to his feet, and crossed to a cupboard in the corner, 'as an example of how modern our system is, there will be a photograph in our records, if she's been here.' He flipped over the pages of an indexed ledger. 'Yes,' he said, 'I have her. I'll just get the file.' He went into the outer office, and in a moment was back with a thin manila folder. He compared the photograph stuck inside the cover with that provided by Catherine, then placed them before her.

'I don't think there is any doubt about it,' he said with a self-satisfied smirk. 'It is obviously the same young woman . . . So unless I hear from you to the contrary. I will expect you next Wednesday afternoon. Shall we say immediately after lunch? That will give us plenty of time.'

Promptly at six o'clock, Bragg put away his lists and nodding goodnight to Ruddick, slouched out of the office and across the yard. Once through the gates, he trudged up the lane, away from the main road, till he came to the doorway that had concealed him two days before. He bent down, as if picking a cigarette-end out of the gutter, and seeing no one was about, he slipped into its shelter. It must be a side entrance to the factory, and from the look of the accumulated rubbish was seldom used. Before long there was a steady stream of men leaving the works, some of them coming towards him. Bragg squatted down in the doorway, his head on his knees. To the casual pedestrian, he would pass for a tramp or a drunk. And yet he had a clear view of the main gate through the gap between his knees and his hat brim.

After half an hour Bragg was thinking of abandoning his vigil. His ham bones were almost through to the pavement, and he could feel the imprint of the bricks on his back. There was always another day . . . though it seemed no more than one. He wondered if there was yet another exit from the works. He hadn't seen one, but he'd not been able to explore every part of the premises. He dragged himself to his feet, and began to ease his cramped limbs. Then he flattened himself into the doorway again. The unmistakable figure of Ruddick had emerged from the main gate and was striding briskly away from him. Once he had turned the corner, Bragg hobbled in pursuit, afraid of losing him. Gradually his circulation returned and he broke into a painful trot. He reached the corner just in time to see Ruddick turn right at the main road. He was going up to Stepney Green. If he got a tram there, Bragg would have to try and board it too. It was either that, or slog after it on foot; he'd never get a cab down here. Then, just as he was reconciling himself to a punishing marathon, Bragg saw the foreman mount the steps of the King's Head.

He moved cautiously, waiting until a couple of workmen went in, and following close behind them. He found himself in the public bar at the back of the building. He glanced quickly around. Ruddick wasn't here. Then Bragg remembered that there was a central bar serving both rooms. During his long vigil, two days before, he'd seen them playing darts in here. So he should be able to look the other way, through the bar, and into the parlour. Bragg edged forward, keeping in the shadows, his hat well over his face. He ordered a pint in a hoarse whisper and, raising his glass, surveyed the parlour over its rim. Ruddick was sitting alone at a small table, half-turned away from Bragg. Moreover, he'd put his hat on the table by the other chair. So he was expecting to meet someone. Bragg felt excitement growing inside him. He mustn't be seen now; it would spoil everything. He withdrew to a back table, watching the small square of the parlour over the heads of the two workmen. He was considering whether or not to risk getting another beer when he saw that a man had approached Ruddick's table. He spoke briefly, and Ruddick moved his hat. The man sat down and ordered a drink from the waiter. Beyond what seemed to be a polite enquiry as to whether the seat was taken, neither man took the slightest interest in the other. The newcomer was young, well-dressed, and good-looking; he really didn't belong in a mediocre pub like this. It must be a prearranged meeting. It must! Each man gazed around the room, yet meticulously avoided looking at the other. Well, it was only good manners – yet something was odd about it. Bragg watched carefully as Ruddick took a drink of his beer. That was it! The glass had been at his lips for a good few seconds, yet the level of the beer was virtually the same. And he could have emptied it in a gulp. Now the other man raised his wine glass, his fingers concealing his mouth. It must be the longest sip on record! So they were talking to each other behind their glasses. If only he could overhear them . . . But if they were going to such extremes of concealment, their voices would be low. Even if he edged his way into the parlour, he wouldn't be able to get close enough. He ducked his head as Ruddick got to his feet, and came towards the bar. He heard the thud of his glass on the bar, a brisk 'Goodnight', and the sound of his receding feet. The other man was still sipping his wine. It might be possible to get close to him, in case he had other people to meet. Equally it might be dangerous. They had been facing each other across the bar for twenty minutes. If the man had noticed him, it would seem very odd for him suddenly to pop up in the parlour. Then the man stood up, leaving the half-full glass on the table. Bragg dashed into the passage, and saw him going down the steps to the street. The man waved his arm, and a hansom, waiting by the horse trough, came across the road. The man sprang into it, and the cabby flicked his horse into a trot. He knew full well where he was going, without being told. Bragg looked around for a cab, but there was none. Already the hansom was at the end of the road. If he chased after it, he would stick out like a whore in a nunnery. Shrugging his shoulders philosophically, Bragg turned back, and remounted the steps of the pub.

Bragg had finished his supper and was relaxing by the kitchen fire. It was cool in the evening of late, and he was glad to resume his old routine. He'd taken off his collar and jacket, and put on his carpet slippers, and his pipe was drawing nicely. Mrs Jenks seemed reassured by it, despite his grotesque appearance. But although she studiously avoided asking questions, she couldn't refrain from darting occasional disapproving glances at him. He had just picked up a library book when there was a knocking on the front door above.

Bragg went up the narrow back stairs, wondering how servants could ever manage to carry trays of food up them. He opened the door to find Catherine Marsden standing there. She gave a gasp of alarm on seeing him.

'Come in, lass,' said Bragg. 'I think we'll go into my room.'

Even as he was helping her out of her coat, there was another tattoo on the door, and Morton came bounding upstairs.

'I could see Miss Marsden from the top of the street,' he panted. 'I ran like mad, but I couldn't catch her . . . Well, well! I like the new décor. A touch of yellow in the cheeks and you could pass for an inscrutable oriental gentleman!'

'That's enough of your cheek, lad,' said Bragg with a smile. 'You're getting above yourself, with all this independence . . . Quite a council of war. Well now, Miss Marsden, since you were here first, you shall begin.'

'I went to Holloway prison today, and saw the governor on the pretext of writing an article about the prison. I showed him the photograph, and he compared it with one on his file. There is no doubt whatever that our Mary Jessop is their Fanny Gregory.'

'Good, good!' said Bragg. 'I'd dearly love to be able to pull her in.'

'Can you not do so?' asked Catherine.

'I'd have to lay on information before the same magistrate that sent me for trial to the Old Bailey. It would be amusing, but we've more important things afoot at the moment.'

'Would you like me to leave?' asked Catherine, wrinkling up her nose.

'No, lass, You've earned your right to listen.'

'You wouldn't deny me the pleasure of escorting you home?' Morton asked with gentle raillery.

'I'll allow you to find me a cab,' said Catherine in an aloof tone, 'but I've no time for socializing. I have a busy few days ahead of me. Tomorrow I've got an interview with the Lady Mayoress; on Saturday I'm going to see the Master of the Worshipful Company of Vintners, for a new series I'm doing . . .'

'You should have started with the Skinners,' Bragg broke in. 'You might have got yourself a fur coat for the winter.'

'On Sunday, there's a memorial service at St Pauls,' went on Catherine, 'and on Monday, believe it or not, I'm doing a piece on the exhibition of the Royal Engineers' Balloon Section at the Artillery Ground.'

Morton raised his arms in surrender. 'Very well, Miss Marsden. If I cannot be your escort, I will gladly be your lackey.'

Catherine bridled, and Bragg intervened. 'Have they identified the man on the tomb yet?' he asked.

'Yes,' said Morton. 'He wasn't a famous person at all, he was a Special Branch man. Major Redman rang the commissioner, and said that one of their men was missing. They sent someone to the mortuary and identified him.'

'Was he on the job they pinched from us?' asked Bragg.

'They didn't say, but I assume so.'

'Well, well. The highly-trained specialists can come a cropper as easily as the amateurs, can they? Have they asked the coroner to drop that one as well?'

'Not that I'm aware of.'

'They wouldn't, would they,' Bragg chuckled sardonically.

'Not when it's one of theirs. What are we doing on that case?'

'We've had men out at four o'clock for the last two mornings, stopping passers-by,' said Morton. 'We haven't had any luck so far. In addition, I've been going round the area today, questioning residents – not that there are many, apart from the rector and a few caretakers. It's all offices there.'

'Well, if it's the same people as murdered Foster, I may save you a bit of drudgery. I spent today in the company of the man who drove his tumbril.'

Morton whistled. 'You mean that he works at Cutler's?'

'He does. But even more to the point, he's only worked there for six weeks. He's the foreman of the despatch department. They seem to have murdered his predecessor to get him in.'

Catherine gasped in horror. 'How could they do such a thing?' she exclaimed.

'It's a measure of how ruthless they are, and the importance of the objective that they're trying to achieve.'

'I can't think anything is worth the wanton taking of three lives.'

'Those are only the ones we know about,' said Bragg grimly. 'Anyway, I also got a good look at three other men, who seem to be in it with Ruddick. So here's where you reach for glory, lad. I want you to bring some men down tomorrow, and arrest them.'

Morton grinned with anticipation. 'How many shall we need?' he asked.

'They are big rough men, and they'll put up a fight. I'd say ten plain-clothes officers to make the arrests, and five uniformed men on the outside, in case things go wrong. As far as I can make out, there's only the main gate, and a side door that opens on to the same street. But have a look round yourself tomorrow morning.'

'I shall have to ask Inspector Cotton,' said Morton dubiously.

'Well, let's say we move at three o'clock. That should give you enough time to convince him. I shall be in the despatch office, on the left of the main gate, by the loading ramp. I want a couple of men there first, to arrest Ruddick. Put three men inside the entrance to stop anybody leaving. If I were you, I'd close the gate in case anyone tries to escape by cart. As soon as we have Ruddick, we pick up Taffy Evans in the packing shed, behind the despatch office. I shall need a couple of men for that. Then on to the paint shop for Dick Cousins – another couple there. As the men hand the prisoners over to the uniformed boys, I want them to go to the main machine shop. There's another man there, whose name I don't know. We shall have to leave him till last, and the alarm may have been raised by then, so we shall need all available men there. It's a big workshop, and I wouldn't want him to get away.'

The grin had faded from Morton's face, and he looked through his notes with care. 'Warrants?' he asked.

Bragg tossed him a sheet of paper. 'Here are enough details for the three whose names we know. The last one we'll have to take on suspicion.'

'Tomorrow is going to be a busy day,' Morton remarked with a smile.

'Oh, and that reminds me. Ring Pontifex, Glengal and Cutler's on the telephone. Ask them for a list of their principal customers, and the names of the people they regard as their main competitors. And see you get them by tomorrow evening.'

17

Bragg was irritated to find a peremptory summons from the coroner by his breakfast plate. He had no choice but to go, yet he was afraid his late arrival at Cutler's might arouse suspicion. Then he remembered the sovereign in his waistcoat pocket. They would only think that he was delaying his work, as they'd requested.

Sir Rufus was in ebullient mood. 'It's a good thing you're not going into the witness-box,' he remarked. 'You look like a body-snatcher! Well, I told you we'd beat those pen-pushing nincompoops. I've written to the commissioner insisting that you be reinstated as my officer forthwith.'

'I don't understand,' said Bragg.

Sir Rufus took up his favourite stance in front of the fireplace. 'You won't have forgotten that according to the script of this abominable melodrama, you were due to be put away for life. Well, yesterday the prosecution were to have seen their main witness, Mary Jessop, but she did not arrive. They sent out to Kennington for her, only to find that she and her mother had decamped that morning, without saying where they were going; and, indeed, without paying the rent. The prosecution, very properly, informed Charlton Marshall, and told him that they were dropping the charges against you.'

Bragg felt a wave of relief surging over him. 'Could they reinstate them if they found her?' he asked.

'I wouldn't think there is the remotest chance of that. Between you and me, counsel for the prosecution wasn't any too sanguine of success, once he'd seen the papers. I think he felt the case should have been thrown out by the magistrate.'

'Why then, I'll go back to being a policeman again,' Bragg

said with a smile. 'I've identified our suspects at Cutler's, and we shall be picking them up this afternoon.'

'Good, good. And what about the Great St Helens corpse, eh? Perhaps Special Branch won't be so arrogant in future.' Bragg detected a blend of malice and gratification in the coroner's tone.

'Have you been approached by the Home Office to keep that murder quiet?' asked Bragg.

'Indeed not,' said Sir Rufus triumphantly. 'The shiny-bottomed brigade soon flee the field when the shells start falling around them.'

'What about the inquest?'

'I shall open it on Thursday of next week. If you are successful this afternoon, we'll be able to show them how it should be done.'

Bragg took a hansom to Old Jewry. The sergeant on duty gave a look of shocked surprise at the change in his appearance, then held out his hand.

'I'm gladder than I can say, Joe. We've just this minute sent out young Alf Glover to find you. Inspector Cotton wants you to go up as soon as you arrive.'

'Thanks, Bill.' Bragg leapt up the stairs in elation, and rapped on Cotton's door.

'Christ Almighty, Bragg,' exclaimed Cotton. 'Whatever have you been doing to yourself? You look like an off-season ice cream seller . . . Still, I suppose it made things easier. Not that I doubted for one minute the woman was lying. But as the last commissioner used to say, "Justice is a perverse mistress, only half related to truth." ' He leaned back in his chair, his hands clasped behind his head. In just such a posture he'd gloated over Bragg's discomfiture at their last meeting.

'I gather you wanted to see me, sir,' Bragg said abruptly.

'Yes. As soon as we heard the news, Sir William instructed me to reinstate you. Your holiday's over, Bragg. You can take back the cases that Morton's been minding for you.'

'Thank you, sir. Then I'll take charge of this afternoon's operation to arrest the Foster murder suspects.'

Cotton looked up suspiciously. 'Morton came to see me about that. In my view his proposals were much too elaborate for mere suspicion, so I scaled them down.'

'I see.'

'To my mind, four men will be ample.'

'Four won't be anywhere near enough,' said Bragg. 'I've seen those men; they are big labouring types, real bruisers. It could take three or four men to make certain of each one.'

'And how comes it that you are so well acquainted with them, Bragg?' enquired Cotton with heavy sarcasm. 'Been moving in criminal circles recently?'

'I took a job at Cutler's, yes. Nothing against that, is there? . . . It was just chance that I realized the despatch foreman tallied with the description of one of the wanted men.'

'And you just happened to pass the information on to your lad, Morton? And just chanced to let him know what you thought would be needed for the job?'

'I was doing my duty as a citizen.'

'Like bloody hell, you were,' snarled Cotton. 'I won't be made a monkey of by buggers like you.'

'My concern,' replied Bragg evenly, 'is to ensure that we capture the murderers of two policemen, one of them from our own force. I imagine the Home Office won't look too kindly on us if we let them escape.'

'I've told you, I'll use my own judgement as to the number of men required.'

'Very well, sir. I will let you have a written statement of my estimate of the force required, and ask you to initial it.'

'I'll do no such thing! By Christ, Bragg, you'll push me too far one day!'

'Very good, sir.' Bragg turned to go, then retraced his steps. 'Would you see that Constable Foster's widow gets this?' He placed the sovereign from his waistcoat pocket on the desk. 'If it belongs to anyone, it belongs to her.'

Bragg grew more anxious by the minute as three o'clock approached. His late arrival had caused no comment, but something was making Ruddick uneasy. Several times he had left the office for prolonged periods, and when he was there he seemed to be brooding darkly. Bragg worked his way diligently through another batch of despatch notes, seemingly oblivious of the tension. Could it be, he wondered, that it was linked to the flight of Mary Jessop? If so they might scarper before Morton arrived. He surreptitiously felt the handcuffs in his pocket. If Ruddick looked like running he'd have to jump him, and take his chance . . . Even if they came, it might mean only five men, including himself. With a lot of luck they could do it, but it would entail grabbing them unawares, one by one. Bragg examined the despatch office carefully. It had brick walls, and a stout door with an old-fashioned lock. The only window was by the door. It should be possible to keep the prisoners here, once they were handcuffed. One man should be enough to prevent escapes.

Three o'clock. Bragg glanced out of the window, and saw Morton and two other detectives strolling casually towards the building.

'Mr Ruddick,' he called, 'what's RGF stand for?'

'What?' Ruddick asked truculently.

'RGF. It appears on quite a number of despatch notes.'

'Mind your own bloody business.'

Morton's shadow was now over the window. A few more seconds, and Ruddick would be trapped.

'I haven't found the despatch note for the consignment that went to Glasgow in error,' said Bragg, getting to his feet and coming round to the front of the table.

'I thought we told you not to bother about that,' snarled Ruddick.

At that moment the door opened, and the three detectives burst in.

'Albert Ruddick,' said Morton crisply, 'I have a warrant for your arrest on a charge of murdering William Foster on August the sixteenth.'

The tableau held for a long moment, then with a roar of anger, Ruddick leapt on to his desk, and launched himself feet first towards the open door. His momentum carried him between the detectives, but he missed his footing on landing, and as he stumbled, Morton jumped on his back. For a moment they swayed together, then one of the detectives, who was holding an injured shoulder, lashed out with his foot at

Ruddick's crotch, and he collapsed in agony on the floor.

'Right. Put the darbies on him, and you, lad, with the feet, lock him in here and stand guard outside.' Bragg turned to Morton. 'How many men have we?'

'Seven, plus you.'

'Two men only on the gate then. Send one man to the paint shop, over there. Now you, Edgley, get up by the main machine shop there. Nobody is to leave. If anyone gets by you, the lads on the gate should grab him, so you stay there.'

Bragg watched as his dispositions were effected. Nobody in the works seemed to have realized what was happening. He beckoned to Morton and the remaining two detectives, and they walked quietly through to the packing-shed. Bragg opened the door a crack. Taffy Evans and two of his mates were busy nailing up a wooden crate. Bragg motioned the two detectives to stay by the door.

'If it gets rough,' he whispered, 'come bloody quick. And watch those claw hammers.'

He shambled across to the men, a piece of pink paper clutched in his hand. As soon as they were in conversation, Morton crept round behind them, and with a lunge seized Evans's arms and twisted them behind his back. Bragg had the cuffs on him in a flash.

'Police!' cried Bragg in warning, to the other men. 'Evan Evans, I have a warrant for your arrest on a charge of murdering . . . ' The rest was lost in an incomprehensible flood of invective. Bragg ordered one of the men at the door to lock Evans in the office, and then join the man near the main factory. He took Morton and the other officer towards the paint shop. By now the yard men were aware that something was afoot. They had stopped working, and stood gazing at the detectives. How long would it be before they intervened? The paint shop was a small building, and only two men were there, daubing some castings with green paint. The policemen entered silently, and were standing in a semi-circle around the bench, before they were noticed.

'Dick Cousins?' asked Bragg.

The man swung round, the blood draining from his face in alarm.

'I have a warrant for your arrest, on a charge of . . . ' With a moan the man's knees buckled, and he fell to the floor in a faint.

'Get the cuffs on,' directed Bragg. 'Don't take any chances; and when he comes round, stick him in with the others.'

At that moment, they heard the shrill blast of a police whistle. Dashing to the door, they could see the figure of a man twisting free of the outstretched fingers of a policeman, and running towards them. At the sight of Bragg, he veered away to the centre of the yard. Suddenly there was a ring of policemen edging inwards, with the man half-crouched in the middle, looking for an opening. Then he made his spring, trying to crash past an oldish, ponderous-looking policeman. Surprisingly, the officer seemed to make no attempt to grapple with the man, but as he passed, pivoted on his left toe and unleashed a vicious kick. There was the loud crack of an ankle bone breaking, and the man crashed to the ground. The policeman was on him like a lurcher on to a hare.

'Well done, men!' called Bragg. 'Now see you don't lose them.' He beckoned to Morton. 'Take them to Seething Lane, and have them charged. Organize a rota of men to interrogate them; but tell them to go easy until the vet and the van driver have identified them – after that I don't care how much they hammer them . . . Oh, and you'd better go up to Old Jewry, and report to Inspector Cotton. I shall have to eat humble pie there. I didn't know we'd recruited half the Arsenal football team.'

Bragg crossed the yard to the works manager's office, and Crossley insisted on taking him to see Samuel Cutler. The old man was almost smiling.

'That was a good job done,' he said. 'I watched from up here, and if I hadn't known in advance, I wouldn't have realized what you were about. They never had a chance.'

'Those four men in your employ,' replied Bragg, 'impaled one of our constables alive on some railings. You don't give men like that a chance.'

'Did they, by God? We owe you a lot, Sergeant. Do you think there'll be a strike now?'

'If there's no reason for one, I'm hopeful that none will now be fomented. But we still don't know what's at the bottom of it all. Who would stand to gain if you and Glengal and Pontifex were put out of business?'

The old man pondered for a while. 'Oddly enough, no one. At least no one in England. Of course, some of the minor jobs would go to other firms here, but not the important work. Each of those firms is a specialist in its own field, and no one else can touch them for quality.'

'What do they do?' asked Bragg.

'Glengal Brass make the finest castings you can get, Pontifex and Wood do gear-cutting, and we specialize in machining to very fine tolerances. The only other firms who can turn out work of comparable quality are abroad – in Switzerland or America.'

'Have you had any approaches from people wanting to buy your business?' asked Bragg.

'I have not,' replied Cutler emphatically. 'And if I did, they'd get damned short shrift.'

Bragg got back to his office to find Morton poring over handwritten lists he had received from the three firms.

'Well, at least they're all jumping to it,' Bragg remarked. 'According to old Cutler, the only people who would benefit if those three firms went out of business would be the Swiss and the Americans.'

'That seems to be borne out by the lists of competitors,' Morton replied. 'None of them mentions a British firm . . . And don't forget the pigeon. It could have been pointed straight at Switzerland.'

'What about their customers?'

'I've just been looking at that. There seems to be only one customer common to all three, and that's the Royal Gun Factory.'

'That's odd,' said Bragg. 'When you were crossing Cutlers' yard, I wanted to distract Ruddick's attention. My eyes fell on a despatch note with RGF on it, and I asked him about it. He told me to mind my own business.' Bragg reached for the telephone instrument, and pressed the signal bell. 'Get me Mr Crossley, the works manager of Samuel Cutler & Co. at Stepney.' He sat drumming his fingers on the desk till the bell rang, and he picked up the ear-piece.

'Mr Crossley?' he asked. 'I wonder if you can help me. You remember the consignment that went to Glasgow, and got lost? Where should it have gone to? . . . I see . . . No, just an idea. Thanks.'

Bragg put down the telephone thoughfully. 'I think you are on to something,' he said. 'Our friend Ruddick deliberately diverted a consignment of work from Cutler's, and it disappeared into thin air. It seems it should have gone to the Royal Gun Factory, at the Royal Woolwich Dockyard.'

18

The Royal Gun Factory's premises proved to be an insignificant brick shed, with a corrugated-iron roof. It was tucked away at one corner of the dockyard, and the only thing that distinguished it from a dozen others, was a small brass plate with the letters RGF engraved on it. Bragg and Morton were received by a jacketless clerk, with tattooed snakes rippling up his bare arms. He sat them in a cramped corner of the office, and gave them tin mugs of tea while they waited.

'We're not in the City now, lad,' muttered Bragg, staring round at the cluttered deal tables, and the dusty floor strewn with cigarette-ends.

The boss proved to be a pleasant, fresh-faced man, with a relaxed manner. A trifle donnish, Morton thought, with his spectacles and the diffidence he showed in welcoming them. Not a man used to exercising authority – but at least his chairs had been dusted.

'I'm surprised to find you down here, Mr Worseley,' said Bragg.

'This is just a temporary office, which we are using for the development phase. You see that building there?' He crossed to the window, and pointed out a huge warehouse near the river. 'We are fitting that out for next year, when we take over all production from the Royal Laboratory. We shall have the capacity to manufacture the whole of Britain's needs at this site in two years. In the meantime, we are all over the place. We have our drawing office next to a distillery in Finsbury Street, we've got a laboratory in Birmingham, and the assembly work is being done in Leeds and Chatham.'

'We've come to see you about this,' Bragg said, laying the

pink despatch note on the desk.

'Ah, yes. I'm glad you've got round to that,' said Worseley. 'Our Chatham people have been hung up for weeks waiting for those castings.'

'We haven't recovered them, sir, if that's what you're thinking. It's the reason they went astray that interests us.'

'Yes, indeed.' A worried frown creased Worseley's forehead.

'Can you tell me,' asked Bragg, 'why the goods were being sent here, when you needed them in Chatham?'

'I would have thought that was obvious, Sergeant,' said Worseley, looking puzzled. 'But perhaps I assume greater knowledge on your part than you in fact possess. What do you know of our work here?'

'I imagine you are developing a new type of naval gun,' hazarded Bragg.

'Ah! I see we are at an impasse,' said Worseley, rubbing the bridge of his nose, so that his spectacles rode up and down on his forehead. 'We certainly need police assistance, and yet I am precluded from giving you the information that would make that assistance effective . . . Please excuse me for a moment.'

Worseley left the room, closing the door carefully behind him.

'Quick, lad,' Bragg hissed. 'They're going to put up the shutters. Can you see anything interesting on the desk? I'll take this table.'

After some moments they heard Worseley talking in a raised voice. 'He's ringing someone,' whispered Bragg. 'Have you found anything?'

'No,' said Morton. 'There's a letter here from some engineers in Birmingham, acknowledging an order, but it doesn't give any details – just a number and quantity.'

'I expect that's the number of the working drawing,' said Bragg. 'There's nothing here, either. Most of it's done up in bundles a mile thick. I daren't untie them.'

The telephone conversation next door ceased abruptly, and Bragg and Morton scrambled back to their chairs.

'We are to go to the Admiralty,' Worseley announced. 'Captain Jeffreys is in charge of this project, and he wishes to impart the necessary information to you personally.'

They trooped out of the ramshackle building, and took a cab to the station. Once in the train, Worseley avoided all conversation; sitting in the corner of the compartment, and covering the pages of a notebook with mathematical symbols. Indeed, this prudent silence prevailed even while they were sitting in the stone-flagged corridor of the Admiralty building itself. Then a black-coated clerk arrived, and showed them into a large and richly-panelled room, overlooking a small court-yard.

Captain Jeffreys was a tall, red-faced man in immaculate uniform. He rose from behind his desk, holding out his hand.

'Have a chair,' he directed, 'and a smoke if you wish – I shall.' He began to fill his pipe from a jar on the corner of his desk. Bragg tasted the dry craving for tobacco at the back of his tongue, but determined to resist it. This wasn't the kind of interview where you could afford to relax.

'I must warn you that you are fishing in perilous waters, gentlemen,' Jeffreys began breezily. 'We demand the highest degree of secrecy from everyone involved in this project, and we take great pains to ensure that no one outside Dr Worseley's team knows more than a small part of what we are about. I shall therefore require from you a most solemn undertaking that you will in no way divulge what I tell you.'

'There may be difficulties in that, sir,' said Bragg. 'I am bound to make a report to my superiors, and if criminal charges are pressed, some information may have to be given in court.'

Jeffreys lit his pipe, then watched the smoke spiralling from the dead match, his brow creased in thought. 'As to prosecuting people,' he said at length, 'I think my masters might prefer to deal with that in their own way. So far as any report is concerned, I would ask you to include only the barest factual information necessary, and to show me your draft before letting anyone else at all see it.'

'I could agree to that, certainly,' replied Bragg.

'Very well, Sergeant.' Jeffreys settled himself back in his chair, then shot a piercing look at Bragg.

'What do you know about torpedoes?' he asked.

'Well . . . nothing. I know they exist, and last summer I sat on the cliffs and watched them being tested on the range in

Portland Harbour. Apart from that, nothing.'

'Then I'd better fill in the background for you a little. The torpedo has been around for a long time; but for practical purposes there are only two designs that matter, the American Howell torpedo, and the one we use, which was invented by Robert Whitehead. Funny sort of chap,' he said reflectively. 'For all that he was born in Lancashire, he set up his works on the Adriatic sea. He's produced some brilliant designs, which the Germans duly pirated – and serve him right, in a way. Though I must say he's been even-handed, selling to all the navies of the world, so long as they could afford his price. And their appetite is so insatiable that he can sell every torpedo he can make. When the market approaches satiety, he brings out an improvement that starts the whole process again.' He looked down in irritation at his pipe, which had gone out.

'For some years, we have manufactured the Whitehead torpedo in England, under licence. It hasn't been wholly satisfactory; in part because the facilities of the Royal Laboratory have been inadequate. We've even, on occasion, had to buy some of the German Schwarzkopf version. Our present project is intended to put that right.' He probed the bowl of his pipe with a spike attached to his pocket-knife, then, pressing down the tobacco with his finger, lit it once more.

'We could, of course, buy all the torpedoes we need from Whitehead. I'm sure that's why he's built his new factory at Portland. But we want to break out of this merry-go-round of buying his latest design, only to find that the French, or whatever, have it also. Dr Worseley has put together a quite brilliant research team, and we think we can go one better than Whitehead. Isn't that so, Worseley?'

'Indeed,' Worseley replied, with no intimation of modesty.

'Before he gives you the technical side, I'll tell you a bit about the problem we hope to overcome,' went on Jeffreys. 'A torpedo is just a missile, which is launched from a boat, and propelled along – or preferably under – the surface by an engine. When it collides with the enemy vessel, it explodes. In theory, there isn't a ship afloat that couldn't be sunk by a torpedo in the right place. When you think of the cost of a modern steel battleship, and reflect that a torpedo costs a little

212

over four hundred pounds, you have to acknowledge that it is the weapon of the future. The trouble is, we've been saying that for twenty years. We have overcome one problem, only to highlight another. Now, with Whitehead's new eighteen-inch design, we are near to the perfect torpedo. It is safe to handle, it has a reliable engine which can be developed to give much greater range, it infallibly keeps to its pre-set depth below the surface, it has an enormous warhead . . . but it has one crucial defect – directional error.'

'What does that mean?' asked Bragg.

'Well, imagine you are on a torpedo boat, about to attack a hostile ship. The situation itself is beset with problems. For a start, you will be attacking the side of the enemy, since that provides the biggest target. That means it will be moving across the path of the torpedo at a speed you can only guess at. You know, within close limits, how far away your target is, and you know the theoretical speed of your weapon, but again you can only guess at the effect that tide and current will have on its course. Even if the weapon performed perfectly, it would be difficult enough to hit the enemy. But, of course, no torpedo runs to the theoretical specification; each one has its own peculiarities, and nowhere more marked than in directional deviations. To have anything like a chance of sinking an enemy ship with current torpedoes, you have to launch from about five hundred yards range. Facing modern quick-firing guns, that is nothing short of suicide. The Royal Navy extends the range a bit, by testing the torpedoes to determine their characteristics. Each weapon has a log book, in which is recorded the information relating to every test-launch, such as sea conditions, deflection angle, speed, tidal flow, and so on. But in my view, that's little better than useless. You are unlikely to meet the same combination of conditions in a real battle, so you'd still be left guessing. What's more, this damned constant testing wears out the machinery, so you can't be sure your earlier results are still valid. What you have to develop is a device which will ensure that, once released, the torpedo will follow its predicted course to its target . . . And that's what we think we can do.' He struck a match. 'Worseley, take over.'

'Captain Jeffreys has told you the lengths to which the Royal

Navy goes, in order to maximize the performance of the Whitehead torpedo,' began Worseley. 'But even this cannot reduce the margin of error below three degrees. If you release the weapon from an acceptable distance of, say, one thousand yards, you are just as likely to miss the target as to hit it.' His voice was soft and thoughtful, after the assertiveness of Jeffreys. 'The answer is to incorporate a device that will ensure any deviation from course is corrected. In a sense, the Americans showed us the way. The Howell torpedo is not driven by compressed air, but by a large fly wheel which is set in motion by a turbine, before launching. What is interesting is that this torpedo has considerably better directional stability than the Whitehead design. This can only come from the use of the fly wheel. What we are developing is an application of the fly wheel principle to allow corrections to be made to the attitude of the torpedo, should it deviate from its course.' He turned to Jeffreys. 'Is it in order to give them some details, sir?'

'Can't see how they'll understand anything, if you don't,' growled Jeffreys, scowling at his dead pipe.

'Recently,' said Worseley, 'a Russian called Petrovich produced an improved gyroscope. It's not a new invention. Astronomers have used it for centuries, to demonstrate the rotation of the earth. But the Petrovich design offered the first prospects of a practical application for it. Essentially, a gyroscope is a heavy rotating disc mounted by its spindle in a ring, which in its turn is held in gimbals. This means that the axis of the wheel can move in any direction. Or, to put it another way, the wheel will rotate in the same plane, even if the object to which it is fixed alters its attitude. It is possible to use this characteristic to correct directional deviations from a torpedo's course, by means of a rudder . . .' He looked at Jeffreys. 'I think that's about as far as I can go, sir.'

'Do you understand the problem?' asked Jeffreys.

'Enough for our purposes,' Bragg replied.

'The difficulty,' went on Worseley, 'is the manufacture of the gyroscope itself. Unless the materials used are made to the highest specification, so that there is no qualitative variation in them, and unless the engineering is carried out to the finest tolerances, the device will not be effective. Petrovich's is, frankly, useless for our purposes, and we are developing our own, following his principles.'

'Which is where people like Glengal Brass, Pontifex and Cutler's come in?' asked Bragg.

Worseley shot an uneasy glance at Jeffreys. 'Yes,' he said.

'Then will you let me have a list of all the firms involved in the project, with a note of what each one does for you?'

'Oh, I don't think I can do that,' Worseley exclaimed. 'No one knows that outside my office.'

'Somebody is able to make a damned good guess,' said Bragg drily. 'There's been labour trouble at the Pontifex and Glengal works, and we only prevented a strike at Cutler's by arresting the agitators. In addition, that consignment of castings from Cutler's was diverted to Glasgow, and vanished. How do we know that kind of thing hasn't happened before? Whoever's behind it could end up with your perfected gyroscope as soon as you do.'

'That's a point, Worseley. Let him have what he wants.'

'Have you any idea, Captain, who would wish to delay your work, or steal the results of it?' asked Bragg.

'Any damned country in the world, from Argentina to Zanzibar; but in practice it would be one of the industrial countries with the expertise to reproduce what they'd stolen.'

'It would be useful if you could narrow that down a bit,' said Bragg.

Jeffreys knocked out his pipe in the ash tray, and began to refill it. 'My guess would be the Americans,' he said thoughtfully. 'They are fine engineers; they are familiar with the fly wheel, and this is a natural development; above all, they realize that their own torpedo is hopelessly outclassed. We know that they secretly bought some Whiteheads last year. What more natural than to try to get to the top of the league at one bound? Yes . . . the Americans, I'd say.' He rose to his feet. 'We've done all we can to help you,' he said dismissively, 'now I hope you can help me.'

'Well,' said Bragg with a glance at the ashtray, 'I think if you changed to twist, you'd get on better. It has more body than shag.'

'Do you know what your name means, James?' Helga looked up with an affectionate smile.

'I haven't the remotest idea,' Morton replied, taking her hand as they crossed the road.

'It means "supplanter". I can show you, when we get back. I bought a book yesterday.'

'Supplanter?' Morton savoured the word. 'I'm not at all sure I like that.'

'Oh, it is a very English trait,' declared Helga with a toss of her head. 'I think it suits you very well.'

'What you are called doesn't remotely matter.'

'But it does, James. I believe that people's names affect the way they behave.'

'That's absurd, Helga.'

'No, no,' she insisted. 'Take Karl Siegfried Eugen von Friedeburg as an example. How could anyone who was named as a "victorious noble" be other than arrogant in his actions?'

'I wouldn't say Karl was arrogant,' said Morton, with a smile.

'You haven't forgotten the picnic at your home, when he sprang at you. That was not youthful high spirits only; he wished to assert his dominance.'

'Oh, come! Helga.'

'You knew it at the time. I was watching you. Almost you decided to fight back, and then you behaved like a James; you let him think he had conquered, because you knew you could supplant him if you wished.'

'This is all rather fanciful,' said Morton uncomfortably.

'I think I like "supplanter",' mused Helga. 'He is obviously the one who would win in the end.'

'I wish I could think I had won you,' said Morton, checking at the entrance of her apartment building.

'You have supplanted every other loyalty, desire, hope in my life, James.' She smiled enigmatically and turned up the stairs.

Morton hurried after her. 'Does that mean you will marry me?' he asked.

Helga did not reply till they were in her sitting-room, and when she turned to him her face was serious. 'I would like to, James. At the moment it appears like a fairy tale. But we must be practical. For a beginning, I do not think your family likes me very much.'

'That's nonsense,' Morton protested. 'My parents are enchanted with you. Emily might be a bit silly for a time, but it's only her age. Anyway, in a couple of years she will be married, and gone. And we wouldn't live at The Priory.'

'Oh, but I would want to, though the thought of someday being responsible for that enormous house is a little frightening. But it is part of you, and I know that you would never forsake it, not for any woman.'

'Then we'll compromise,' said Morton with a smile. 'For a few years we will have an apartment in London, and you can sit at home, waiting for your policeman husband to come back.'

Helga shivered theatrically. 'I am not sure I like the policeman part of you.'

'I must do something until The Priory is mine . . . But I suppose I need not continue in the police.'

'James, you are so considerate. I think you are the kindest man alive . . . But still I am frightened.'

'Whatever of?' asked Morton in amazement.

'I am three years older than you are, and, also, I have been married already.'

'That isn't of the slightest consequence to me.'

'Not at the moment, perhaps; but it may become so in time. Then what should I do?'

'I love you,' said Morton emphatically. 'That's the only thing that matters, and it won't change.' He made to put his arms round her, but she held him off.

'I am troubled also, because I was foolish enough to let my passion for you overwhelm my modesty. A man who has taken a woman to his bed may think afterwards that he was perhaps not the only one.'

'But I am, am I not?'

'You are the only one. And even if we continue only as friends, there will never be another.'

'Well, then, we will forget that it ever happened. It is totally expunged from my memory. Will you marry me?'

Helga put her head against his breast. 'Yes, James,' she murmured, 'I will marry you.'

Morton began to kiss her in fierce delight, but she wriggled free of him.

'James!' she admonished him breathlessly, 'we both know where this will lead us . . . To something that has never before been.' She propelled him protesting to the door. 'Go home, and respect my virtue . . . but come again tomorrow.'

19

Bragg was checking his watch with the church clock when Morton burst into his office.

'I've got some tremendous news!' he cried. 'I've been picked to tour Australia!'

'What are you on about, lad?'

'Lord Sheffield's cricket team . . . It means I'll be playing for England!'

'Stop bouncing about. I thought it was something that's important to grown-ups.'

'So it is, to most,' grinned Morton, refusing to be deflated. 'And that's not all . . . I'm getting married!'

'That will please your mother. Who's the future Lady Morton?'

'Helga Speidel. She accepted me last night.'

'That was quick,' Bragg observed sourly. 'How long have you known her?'

'A bit over a fortnight, on this occasion; but we first met years ago, at Cambridge.'

'I see. Getting married and going to play cricket in Australia seem a bit contradictory to me.'

'They needn't be,' replied Morton, with bubbling excitement. 'We don't sail till October the second. We could be married before that, and she could come with me.'

'Will you be leaving the force?' Bragg asked gruffly.

'Well, not immediately.' Some of Morton's exuberance faded. 'I intend to ask for special leave to cover the tour.'

'I see.' Bragg cocked his head. 'She doesn't fancy being wed to a copper, then? Well, if the Foster case is to be your swan song, we'd better give it a push.'

'Yes. Sorry, Sergeant.' Morton drew a chair up to the desk. 'Are they still saying nothing?' he asked.

'Cousins has admitted to transporting the body of a man to Great St Helens, but nothing more.'

'Was he on his own?'

'He says Ruddick was with him.'

'I suppose it's a start,' Morton remarked.

'Not in my book, it isn't. What can we charge him with? Indecent behaviour in a churchyard? He'd get two months maximum.'

'Ruddick ought to break. He knows two people have identified him as the driver of the cart.'

'That bugger won't even admit to what I saw with my own eyes. If I'd my way, I'd belt him till he couldn't stand up . . . but he'll keep.'

There was a knock at the door. 'Letter for you, sir,' said a young constable. 'Just delivered by hand.'

'Open it, lad,' said Bragg, feeling for his pipe.

Morton tore open the envelope. 'It's the list of subcontractors we asked Worseley for, headed "Hightly Confidential". It's not long.'

'Read it, then.'

'It's in two columns, the first giving the name of the firm, the second its function in the project. So . . . "Pontifex & Wood – gimbals; Glengal Brass Works – casting of housing; Greenwood & Batley – rudder linkage; Grovessen – machining gyro wheel; Ransome & May . . .".'

'Go on lad.' Bragg looked up, to find Morton staring in front of him, his face white. 'What's the matter?'

'Oh, my God,' Morton muttered. He gazed unspeaking for a time, and to Bragg he seemed to be shrinking in on himself. Then he looked up. 'I'm sorry,' he said bleakly. 'I'm afraid I brought all this trouble on you.'

'You what?' exclaimed Bragg in astonishment.

'The list that was being sent by pigeon; that last name wasn't Grove Ben, it was Grovessen. I should have seen it, if I hadn't been such a blind idiot.'

'What the devil are you talking about?'

'That list was written by someone whose native tongue is German. They use a special gothic sign for a double "s", which they call an "estset". It's like our small "f" joined at the top to an "s". In his haste the man used that sign in place of the double "s" in Grovessen, and wrote Groveßen. Because the letters were unevenly spaced, we read it as two words.'

'No wonder we couldn't trace them. But why the slough of despond?'

'I know who that German is,' said Morton bitterly. 'My friend Karl von Friedeburg.'

'What?'

'Looking back, I see that he wanted to avoid me right from the start, but I chased after him. Like a fool, I told him what I was doing – about Foster's murder, I mean. I boasted about how brilliant you are, and how you would catch the murderers in a week . . . A few days later, you were accused of rape, and out of the hunt.'

'But the girl had been living in Kennington for weeks,' Bragg protested. 'You're not saying they put her there just on the off-chance?'

'If it were merely that,' Morton went on doggedly, 'I could put it down to chance. But there's more. One weekend I asked Karl if he could make sense of the label from Foster's pocket. I thought it could be some East European language he was familiar with. It was he, apparently as an afterthought, who suggested it might be Welsh. They'd always intended to point us in the wrong direction, and when we didn't pick up the trail first time, Karl gave us a push.'

'It looks bad, certainly,' murmured Bragg.

'There's worse to come. Like the naïve fool I am, I agreed to take him to the Amalgamated Engineers' meeting. He pretended to be afraid of mob violence, and I showed him how to identify the Special Branch men who were there. No wonder the corpse on the tomb seemed familiar – I pointed him out to Karl myself.'

'Where is he?' Bragg demanded.

'He has rooms in number ten, St James's Square.'

'Come on, lad. Maybe you can make amends.'

They clattered down the stairs, and ran the length of Old

Jewry before they got a cab. Every time it was checked by the traffic, Bragg would hammer on the roof; but even so, it took a full half-hour before they turned into the square. Morton flew up the stairs, while Bragg was paying off the cab, and soon was tearing down again. 'It's locked,' he shouted. 'Porter! Porter!'

With some difficulty they found an old man in a green baize apron, and he wheezed upstairs to open the heavy mahogany door. The rooms were empty, the bed recently slept in. Bragg flung open the wardrobe. There was a neat row of coats and trousers. The chest of drawers was full of shirts and underwear, socks and ties. They went back into the sitting room, and Morton picked up a paper from the side table.

'Here's a *Saturday Review* that's only two days old. So he's still living here.'

'Let's sit down a bit, and see if he comes back.' Bragg took a chair by the wall, behind the door.

'You know,' cried Morton, pacing up and down, 'the more I think, the more I realize the man's effrontery. I've had something niggling away in my mind ever since our visit to Jeffreys. If you remember, he said that the gyroscopes were being assembled at Chatham, and the torpedoes were being tested on the Portland range. According to Emily, while Karl and Helga were staying at The Priory, Karl spent a day in Rochester – which is only a stone's throw from Chatham. Then later on, Helga told me in a letter that Karl had gone to Weymouth, to catch a boat to Jersey.'

'And Weymouth practically runs into Portland,' Bragg grunted. 'I wonder if your young lady would have any idea of where he is now.'

'It's worth a try.'

'Then let's go like Christians this time, shall we? Not like dancing dervishes.'

They went down to the street, and into the next building. Morton felt reassured by the familiar curve of the staircase, and the ponderous gaselier. He knocked on the door and waited. There was no answer. He turned the knob and to his surprise the door swung open.

'Helga!' he called, and rushing in, almost fell over a large leather portmanteau in the hall. He looked down in disbelief at the label, which was addressed to Frau H. Speidel at a house in Berlin.

'Helga! Helga!' He pushed into the sitting-room, but it was empty, impersonal, stripped of all the trinkets that had made it hers.

Bragg made a rapid survey of the apartment. 'She's gone, all right,' he said, emerging from the bedroom. 'There's an envelope here, with your name on it.'

With desperate hope, Morton tore open the letter. It was no more than a few words.

James,
  I retain the fondest memories. Goodbye.

He was suddenly flooded with anger. 'No wonder she wouldn't let me stay last night,' he said coldly. 'Even as she accepted my proposal of marriage, she was packing to leave . . . So Emily was right, after all. She is his mistress. Dear God! She's been pumping me for information all the time. Karl persuaded me she was his cousin, and that I'd met her at Cambridge. If I hadn't been so besotted with her, I'd have known all the time it wasn't true . . . I told her we didn't think the Dic Penderyn message was relevant to our enquiries, and three or four days later we find the second body, with a more explicit message. Only last Wednesday I told her that we knew Mary Jessop was a fraud. No wonder they were always a jump ahead. I must have been a gift from the gods to them.' He flung out of the apartment, and Bragg could hear his voice raised in the hallway. When he returned his face was suffused with fury.

'She left at half past seven last night, to catch the night ferry to Calais. I could hardly have been round the corner, before she was calling for a cab . . . The treacherous bitch!'

'Stop posturing like a ravished mother superior,' said Bragg harshly. 'Shut up, and let's do some thinking for a change.' He walked over to the window, and peered out.

'You may have unknowingly supplied them with information, but you also panicked them more than was justified by what we really knew. When we arrested Ruddick and his mob, they must have decided to pull out, with whatever they'd managed to secure . . . Here lad, pass me the poker. I wouldn't like to think of your ex-fiancée getting one of the Glengal castings out under our noses.'

He smashed savagely at the locks, and levered up the lid. On top was a jumble of silk petticoats and lace. Bragg tipped the portmanteau over, spreading out its contents with his foot. As he did so, a silver photograph frame went skidding over the polished floor towards Morton. He bent and picked it up.

'Look at this,' he said bitterly.

It was a photograph of a young man in naval uniform. Bragg tried to decipher the scribble on the bottom of it.

'It means "To my darling Helga, from Karl". That was never on display when I came here.' Morton flung it on to the pile of clothing. Bragg quietly retrieved it, and put it into his pocket.

'It may be a photo of your friend Karl,' he said, 'but it also happens to be a photo of the man Ruddick met at the King's Head. So he's the boss, eh? Let's think . . . The thugs he's used have been arrested, and he's sent home his accomplice, fellow agent, mistress, whatever you care to call her. Yet he's still here. Why? . . . What would you do, lad, if you were him? Let's suppose you've got some castings that have been machined by Cutler's, and perhaps you've got another component or two – but you haven't got them all. He can't have, can he? Otherwise he'd be on the run with his *frau*. What would you do, realizing you're not going to get any more of the bits? . . . If your mind wasn't besotted with bloody women, you'd go for the working drawings, wouldn't you? Where did they say the drawing office was?'

'Finsbury Street.'

'Good lad! Let's get there, and damned fast.'

This time their cabby took them by back streets, twisting and turning, yet with his horse always at the trot.

'There it is, the tall building by the distillery,' Morton called, and tossed a half-crown to the driver. He glanced at the board in the hallway. 'They're on the second floor.'

They hurled themselves up the stairs, and into an empty office. From a cupboard door came a shout and knocking. Morton unlocked the door and a frightened youth stumbled out.

'Did he get the plans?' cried Bragg.

'He had a gun . . . I tried to fob him off with some others, but he knew what he wanted.'

'When did it happen?'

'Just now. He'd no sooner gone than I heard your feet on the stairs.'

'He must have hidden on a landing, to let us pass,' said Morton, peering out of the window. 'There he is! Walking north, and hugging the wall.'

'Come on, lad, we'll have him yet.'

They were within three hundred yards of him, and gaining rapidly, when he glanced back, saw them, and started to run. He dashed across the main road, dodging and twisting through the traffic.

'He's going straight on, into the Artillery Ground,' Morton gasped.

'Look at those bloody balloons,' said Bragg. 'It's that sodding army display. He's aiming to lose us in the crowd.'

It was some moments before they could work their way through the stream of vehicles and, as they reached the fringe of the crowd, they could hear a disturbance ahead. Men were shouting, women screaming. Then came the sound of a shot. There was a sudden stillness, and Morton felt the crowd opening under his pressure. He pushed his way to the rope barrier, which kept the crowd at a distance from a huge balloon that was tethered to a post. At one side of the clear space lay a man, blood oozing from a wound in his arm. In the centre, a woman was climbing a rope ladder into the balloon's basket, and Karl was pressing close behind her brandishing a revolver. The woman tumbled over the edge, and Karl started shouting to the soldier by the post. Now he had his leg on the edge of the basket, and was levelling his revolver at the soldier. This galvanized him into casting off the tether, and the balloon began to rise. As it did so, the woman got to her feet, grasping the edge of the basket.

'Oh, God!' exclaimed Bragg, at his elbow. 'It's Catherine Marsden.'

As they stood dumbfounded, an army officer pushed his way through the crowd towards them.

'What the bloody hell is going on?' he barked.

'Police,' said Bragg, waving his warrant card at him. 'You've got a wounded man there.'

The officer ran across, shouting for a stretcher, and gently lifted the injured arm. 'Not much of an MO myself,' he remarked, 'but it seems a clean enough wound. Did you see what happened?'

'The balloon was seized by a fugitive criminal,' Bragg said. 'He's taken a young woman with him as a hostage.'

'That complicates things,' said the officer. 'Anyway, it's too late to bring it down now, it might explode in the streets.'

'What is it filled with?' asked Morton.

'Hydrogen. That's why at shows like this we have to keep the public and their matches well away; there's always a slight leakage of gas.' He looked up at the balloon, which was now drifting away towards the Tower. 'Looks as if they'll be all right, anyway.'

'What's that supposed to mean?' Bragg demanded.

'It seems to be settling at a height which will take them clear of the buildings. That's an observation balloon, and we use it tethered to a wagon. It's not meant for free flight, so it doesn't have refinements like ballast. It will have to find its own level.'

'How long will it stay up?' asked Morton.

'As long as its gas will hold it off the ground, assuming it hits nothing. Of course, to some extent it depends on the weight it's carrying.'

'How heavy would you say Catherine is, Sergeant?'

'With all those clothes it's hard to tell. I'd put her at nine stone.'

'And Karl might be fourteen; that makes twenty-three. Would it carry that weight all right?'

'Oh yes,' said the officer, with a touch of pride in his voice.

'Would it be able to reach France?'

'France?' He hesitated. 'Well, the wind's blowing a steady twelve to fifteen miles an hour; no sign of thunderstorms; it's a new balloon, so the leakage will be minimal. Yes, given time, they could get to France. They'll clear the North Downs at that height, there's nothing after that to worry them.'

'Blast it,' said Bragg. 'We must alert the police along the

route it's taking. Beyond that, we're stumped. Even if we knew where it was likely to come down in France, they'd have vanished before we could get the Home Office to act.'

'I hope he's not going to take Catherine with him,' Morton said with a smile. 'Life would be very dull without her.'

'Why the hell are you taking it so lightly?' demanded Bragg wrathfully.

'Because I have an idea. Captain, where is the wind blowing from?'

'The north-west.'

'And will it stay in that quarter?'

'Almost certainly. The weather chart in this morning's *Times* shows a very settled pattern.'

'Good. Now, you seemed to be suggesting that had you realized earlier what was happening, you might have brought the balloon down.'

'It wouldn't have been possible, actually, because it was over the buildings almost immediately. But if you have enough room, you can puncture the envelope with small-arms fire, so that enough gas escapes to cause it to sink back to the ground.'

'Is there no danger of igniting the gas?'

'Not so long as you shoot at the gas-bag itself. There's no metal up there to cause a spark, and the friction from a bullet going through goldbeater's skin is negligible.'

'Well then,' said Morton, pulling at Bragg's arm, 'we have no alternative. We must go on a balloon hunt.'

'For God's sake, lad,' exclaimed Bragg as they hurried away, 'what are you letting us in for now?'

'Don't you see? The balloon is following the same path as the pigeon flew. So if it is still in the air in three hours time, it should be somewhere around the Priory.'

'Do you think we could shoot it down?'

'We've got to have a damned good try.' Morton pulled out his gold hunter. 'One o'clock now. Let's take a cab to Old Jewry, so that you can give instructions to alert the Kent police, then we'll get a train.'

As they rattled along, Morton composed a telegram for his father. 'How will this do?' he asked, handing it to Bragg.

Urgent. Meet me Bragg Hollingbourne station half-three today. Bring guns for balloon shoot.

'You'll have to be more explicit,' Bragg commented, 'or he'll think you're talking about a kid's party.'
'You're right. I think this should do the trick.'

Karl abducting Catherine.

'Do they know Catherine?'
'I think I've mentioned her in passing,' Morton replied airily.
They lost ten minutes at Old Jewry, and a further five at the telegraph office. By the time they arrived at London Bridge station, the balloon was a small coloured bead in the sky above the circle of hills enclosing London to the south. It was no longer possible to distinguish the basket suspended beneath it. For a quarter of an hour they sat fuming till the train began to pull slowly out of the station.
'It's express to Orpington,' said Morton, 'so we should catch up quickly, now.'
For a time Morton seemed to be right. Bragg, his nose pressed against the window, saw the golden disc begin to grow in size against the clear blue backdrop. Then suddenly, emerging from a cutting, it was no longer there. He looked around frantically, and spotted it much further to the left than it had been before.
'Christ, lad, we're going away from it.'
'We have to. The railway swings to the south here, towards Sevenoaks. Then we shall go east for a while.' Nevertheless, Bragg's anxiety had communicated itself to Morton, and they sat, each glued to a window until long after the balloon had disappeared from sight.
Bragg took out his pipe, then thrust it irritably back into his pocket. 'Are you sure we're doing the right thing?' he asked. 'Suppose the girl gets hurt?'
'Don't think it hasn't occurred to me,' replied Morton. 'But we can't let those drawings leave the country.'
'For my part I don't give a tuppeny bugger for them. I think a lot of that lass, and I wouldn't want any harm to come to her,

just to salvage your self-esteem.'

The thrust struck home, and Morton felt the excitement draining out of him. They sat in wordless antagonism until long after the train had turned eastwards and taken up a more leisurely progress.

'All right,' said Morton, breaking the silence. 'We'll leave it to my father. He's expert in these matters, so let him decide – that's if we ever get within range of it.'

'Agreed,' said Bragg, mollified. 'How many more of these blasted little stations, lad?'

'One more, then Maidstone. After that we should be running parallel to the balloon's course, and we shall only have two more stations to go.'

As they turned south to run into Maidstone station, Bragg let out a shout. 'I can see it! Over there, beyond the town.'

'Damn!' Morton chewed his lip. 'It's a bit further to the east than I'd hoped. That means we shall have to go up on the Downs. It's going to be exceedingly tight.'

The very reason for their haste seemed to delay them now. The porters kept pausing in their task of loading mail bags to gaze at the balloon. At last they were moving again, but the balloon seemed to have drawn level with them. The stop at the next station was mercifully short, and as they coasted towards Hollingbourne, Morton was relieved to see not only his father, sitting at the wheel of the Daimler, but also Emily with a dog cart. They flung themselves out of the train.

'No time to go into details,' cried Morton. 'We've got to get up the scarp of the Downs, quickly. Have you brought the guns?'

'Two rifles,' replied his father.

'Good. Karl has stolen an army observation balloon, and we've got to shoot it down . . . What are you doing here, Emily?'

'I'm coming too! You don't think I'd miss this, do you?'

'Gives us more tactical mobility,' said Sir Henry. 'Crank the engine, will you?'

Bragg looked at the dog cart critically. 'You're not going to drive that, are you miss?' he asked.

'Of course,' Emily said spiritedly.

229

'Oh, no! That pony's too strong for this cart. A little lass like you will never hold him.'

'I couldn't bring Blossom. She'd be no good for racing down country roads.'

'Then give me the reins, and you just look pretty.'

Emily looked rebellious for a moment, then seeing the Daimler chugging out of the station yard, capitulated. Before long they came to a steep hill, and both got out to reduce the strain on the horse.

'You'll have to be easy on your brother for a while,' Bragg remarked, as they plodded upwards.

'Why?' enquired Emily breathlessly.

'His lady-love has gone away for ever.'

'Which one? He has so many.'

'Mrs Speidel.'

'Helga? Good!' she said emphatically. 'I knew there was something wrong about her . . . Daddy said there's a girl in the balloon; is it her?'

'No, she went to Calais last night. She'll be well on her way to Germany now.'

'I told you, didn't I? But none of you would listen. Then who is the girl in the balloon?'

'Catherine Marsden, a reporter with a London newspaper.'

'Oh, good! I've been wanting to meet her.'

'I only hope you get the chance, miss,' growled Bragg.

The Daimler reached the top long before the dog cart, and Morton could see the balloon sailing serenely along, like a great orange suspended in the sky. It was alarmingly close. His father took out a pair of binoculars, and studied it intently.

'Big enough target, anyway,' he remarked laconically.

'Is Catherine still there?' asked Morton anxiously.

'Yes, they're both there. I think Karl has seen us . . . yes, he's pointing this way.'

'We mustn't hurt Catherine, sir. I've promised Sergeant Bragg. Short of that, we've got to capture Karl. He has stolen the drawings of an invention to improve the torpedo. We've got to take them from him.'

'Don't worry, my boy. It should be possible.' Sir Henry began to study the terrain carefully. 'I take it,' he said, 'that when we've put enough holes in the thing it will come down. Somehow, we've got to contrive that it does so in the open. There are rather too many coverts around here, for my liking. Where are the others?'

As he spoke, they breasted the rise, and came towards the Daimler.

'The balloon's a lot nearer the ground now, than it was when they set off,' Bragg remarked.

'Look down the road ahead, Sergeant,' Sir Henry instructed. 'Can you see that road off to the right?'

'The one about three hundred yards down the hill?'

'Yes. We will take that road, and we should be running parallel with the target, and within easy range of it. The road winds a bit, then turns off to the right after a distance of a couple of miles. In that time we've got to inflict enough damage to the envelope to ensure that it comes down. If it doesn't ground before the road swings west, then James and the sergeant will have to pursue it on foot, till it does. Is that understood?'

There was a general murmur of assent.

'The sergeant will drive the dog cart, and Emily will take the Winchester. I will drive the Daimler, and James, I've brought you one of the new Mannlicher thirty-twos. I think you'll like it.' He flung the drive lever over, and the motor car began to move forward.

'You're not going to use that thing, are you miss?' Bragg asked in amazement, as Emily began to feed cartridges into the Winchester's magazine.

'You forget, Sergeant,' she laughed, 'that my grandmother used to defend the American frontier with one of these.'

Bragg shook the reins, and they clattered down the easy slope. The balloon seemed to be poised over the road for a moment, then began to slide away to the right. The motor car was at the turning now, and they heard the sharp crack of a rifle. Bragg was about to remark on it to Emily, when there was a tremendous explosion by his left ear, and he was fighting to control the pony. At least the Daimler didn't care about gunshots. It was motoring slowly along the lane, while Morton loosed a steady stream of shots into the gas-bag.

'Let me get round into the lane, miss,' Bragg shouted. 'Then you can have your share of the fun.'

She took him at his word, for no sooner had he straightened up than she shot off the rest of the magazine, making his ears ring.

'It doesn't seem to have any effect,' she complained as she reloaded.

'You are hitting it, I suppose?'

'Of course I am,' she said scornfully, raising the rifle again.

The fusillade of shots was echoing round the countryside, sending the rooks and seagulls wheeling for cover. But now the road was bearing to the left; soon it would intersect with the path of the balloon. Sir Henry accelerated to close the range, while Morton pushed back the canopy, and, resting his rifle on the frame, emptied his magazine into the envelope drifting above his head. As soon as the last shot was fired, Karl's head appeared above the rim of the basket, and he began to shoot back with his revolver. Bragg heard the whine of a ricochet and, jumping down, grabbed the pony's head.

'Steady boy . . . I think the balloon is lower now,' he called to Emily, 'and it seems slack under the net.'

In answer, she loosed off another fifteen rounds into the yellow globe. Now it was drifting out of range. Sir Henry accelerated till the engine drummed, and Bragg jumped into the dog cart to follow.

'The road loops left, to the village, here,' cried Emily. 'Daddy will be trying to get round, so as to meet the balloon head on again.'

Bragg flicked the reins, and the pony took off after the motor. A spurt like this would finish him in a mile, thought Bragg, but by then it wouldn't matter. They rattled through a farmyard, scattering ducks and chickens, ploughed through a shallow ford, and up a slight hill towards the village. The local policeman, digging shirt-sleeved in his garden, looked over the hedge in amazement at the sight of a four-poster bed trundling through his village pursued by a trap. He dashed into his cottage and, ramming his helmet on his head, set off in pursuit on his bicycle.

The pony was tiring now and his muzzle was flecked with

foam; but the road was swinging to the right, to intersect once again with the balloon's course. The Daimler was stationary and Morton was firing desperately at the flaccid bulk of the gas-bag. Sir Henry got down and walked across as Bragg brought the dog cart to a halt, and Emily joined in.

'The road goes west now,' Sir Henry said.' So we've got to down it here.'

There was a pause in the firing, while both James and Emily reloaded. The balloon was drifting over their heads, and they could hear Karl shouting, 'Stop shooting, or I will throw out the girl.'

'Cease fire,' Sir Henry ordered. 'It's not going to clear those trees anyway. Off you go, you men, and make your arrest.'

Bragg and Morton clambered over the field gate. Sir Henry was clearly right. There was a fair-sized wood at the other end of the field, with a group of large elms forming its core. As they jumped to the ground and began to run, the balloon collided with the branches of the biggest tree, and was held there. Morton could see the figure of Karl climbing out of the basket, and dropping down through the branches. The balloon seemed firmly held, so Catherine was safe for the moment.

'Watch the front,' Morton gasped. 'I'll work round the side.'

He slipped into a thicket of rhododendrons which had been planted to give shelter to pheasants. Would Karl try to get through the wood, he wondered, and escape across the fields at the other side? Morton ran crouching through the bushes, mindful of Karl's revolver, until he could see a barbed-wire fence, and open country beyond. He moved cautiously to the fence. There was no sign of Karl, no hedgerow he could be creeping along, no crops to give him cover. So he was still in the wood. No doubt he had seen the landscape from the balloon, and would know there were no roads in this direction. Probably he would decide to break back, and follow the lane to the main road with the idea of getting to the coast. No doubt he'd leave it till dark, and navigate by the stars. If so, he'd stay in the wood and try to avoid capture.

Morton began to work his way cautiously towards the centre of the wood. He could hear Bragg thrashing about near the stranded balloon. It was always possible that Karl might try to slip round him on the flank. But that would be risky. For all Karl knew, Sir Henry and Emily might be waiting for just that eventuality. His revolver would be no match for their rifles. The undergrowth was sparser here, under the big trees, and Morton had to dodge silently from trunk to trunk, scrutinizing the area minutely before each dash. Now, the ground began to fall away slightly; there was a break in the canopy of leaves, and grass and bracken covered the ground. He dropped on his belly, and began to wriggle forwards, between the green stalks. By the sound of it, Bragg was on a converging course. Morton pushed himself forward another foot, and found himself looking over the edge of a low cliff. Someone had quarried chalk here in the past, and he was looking down from the top of the face. The opposite side of the quarry sloped down gently, and was covered with bracken and bushes. Bragg must be quite near the top of that slope now. Morton lay still, listening, and trying to decide on his next move. Then, as Bragg flailed about in another tangle of rhododendrons, Morton heard the crack of a twig below him. It couldn't possibly be an animal, after all this racket. He eased himself forward, peering through the green fringe of grass, and saw Karl ten feet below him, crouching behind a jumble of rocks and scrub. He was listening intently in Bragg's direction, and looked as if he might shift cover any moment. Morton pushed himself back from the edge, alert for any movement below; then silently raising himself upright, he took a couple of quick steps forward, and launched himself feet first at the crouching figure below. He struck him squarely in the middle of the back, and though Morton went sprawling, Karl was left writhing on the ground.

'Sergeant!' Morton shouted, and limping over to Karl wrenched his arms behind his back, and secured them with the hand-cuffs.

'You've got the bastard, have you?' cried Bragg trundling down the slope. 'Well done! I hope you haven't damaged him too much.' He pulled Karl to his feet, and began to drag him, groaning, out of the quarry.

Morton ran up the slope towards the balloon. It had shifted as the gas-bag became progressively deflated, and now it seemed to be held only by a slender branch caught in the net. If that broke, the basket would drop like a stone. Emily, still cradling her rifle, and Sir Henry were looking up anxiously. As Morton ran up, Catherine shifted her position, and there was an ominous creaking from above.

'Stay still!' he shouted, and jumping for one of the lower boughs, swung himself into the tree. He climbed up slowly, hampered by the wide gaps between the branches. He managed to get hold of the tethering rope, and tied it to a substantial branch. Now, at least, the basket would not plunge to the ground, though it might still overturn and throw Catherine out. He began to edge along a branch towards the basket, conscious of her white face above it. Then he grabbed a branch above, and swinging on it, brought the tip within Catherine's reach.

'Get hold of that,' he called, 'and keep hold even if the basket goes.'

She had scarcely taken hold, when, with a scraping sigh the balloon broke free and collapsed to the ground, leaving Catherine dangling.

'Hold on!' Morton called, and shuffled along the branch till he could get an arm round her waist.

'Now let go, and take hold of me.'

They swayed for a moment, as Morton recovered his balance, then holding on to the branch above, he slowly edged back to the trunk. Once there, Morton lowered her to the bottom bough, and she slid down until she was sitting on it. Then with a squeak of apprehension, she pushed herself off. She landed in a heap, and was swooped on by Emily. Sir Henry brought the trap into the field and, helping the two girls into it, set off for The Priory.

Bragg and Morton half pulled, half carried Karl to the field gate, where a perspiring policeman regarded them stolidly.

'You the owner of this vehicle?' he asked, gesturing towards the Daimler.

'No,' said Bragg.

'Whose is it then?'

'It belongs to my father,' said Morton.

'And who might he be?'

'Lieutenant-General Sir Henry Morton, of Ashwell Priory.'

'Oh yes?' The policeman's face remained impassive, but they

could see his lips moving as he committed the information to memory. 'Was it you lot doin' the shootin'?' he asked.

'Yes, it was,' replied Morton.

'You some of they society folk, on the spree?'

'We're City of London police officers, making an arrest,' said Bragg, pushing his warrant card under the policeman's nose. He looked at it uninterestedly, and began to mount his bicycle, then looked back.

'You won't leave that contraption in Charlie Blackburn's field, will you?' and without waiting for an answer, cycled slowly away.

They propped Karl on the front seat, opposite Bragg, for the journey back. To Morton it was a bitter reminder of the drive to the river bank, a mere fortnight before. He looked angrily across at Karl, and saw that he was watching him.

'I'm sorry, James,' he said painfully, 'but one's country must come first.'

Catherine Marsden was lying languorously on a *chaise-longue* in her room at The Priory. Every time she moved, her bruised body protested, yet she felt surprisingly contented. Perhaps the fact of surviving such an ordeal at all was cause for satisfaction. She heard a rap at the door.

'Come in,' she called.

'And how is our charming Miss Management, this morning,' asked Morton with a mocking smile. 'You really ought to join a circus . . . "Beautiful woman in death-defying leap".'

'I'd have been perfectly all right, if I hadn't twisted my ankle when I landed.'

'Is it very bad?' asked Morton. 'May I see?'

'Indeed you may not!' exclaimed Catherine, flicking her skirt over her foot.

'I think if Mother had her way, you would be here for a month.'

'If I wasn't a working girl, I'd be glad to, after yesterday's excitement.'

'Poor Emily,' said Morton with a grin, 'her shoulder is all

236

black and blue from the recoil. Still, she seems to think it was worth it.'

'I suppose you saved my life again,' Catherine said glumly.

'Don't belittle us, we saved you from a fate far worse than death . . . You know, I think the only real casualty on our side is likely to be my father. The local constabulary have just presented him with a summons for exceeding the permitted speed of four miles an hour in a mechanically propelled vehicle. He won't be able to explain what it was all about. He'll just have to plead guilty, without extenuation. I daren't think what damage it will do to his reputation!'

'Are you going back to London now?'

'Very soon. Sergeant Bragg is taking a statement from Karl, then we shall all three be off.'

'James, I feel such an idiot,' Catherine burst out in mortification.

'Whatever for?'

'All this . . . this splendour.' She waved her hand in the direction of the window, where the Jacobean brick glowed warm in the sun. 'What an insult, to take you down to the kitchen for a cup of tea.'

'Are you still worrying about that?' Morton bent over, and planted a brotherly kiss on her forehead. 'As soon as you are back, I shall come for a repeat performance, and then I can tell you the whole story.'

'Ah, yes,' Catherine said, her eyes brightening. 'I'd almost forgotten.'

'Oh, and don't let Emily persuade you to turn her into a reporter. She hasn't got your stamina!'

20

The commissioner leafed through Bragg's report.

'So all this Welsh business was a blind?' he remarked.

'Yes, sir,' replied Bragg. 'They must have thought we were getting too close, when they caught Foster, and they left us those messages to lead us in the wrong direction.'

'The Home Office will be relieved about that, at least . . . And you say their strategy was to get a sample of the part, and then foment a strike to stop further production of it.'

'That's right. The only bits they hadn't succeeded in getting were the gyroscope wheel, and the rudder linkage.'

'Then the Germans pretty well have it all.'

'On the face of it, yes. But I gather from Dr Worseley that the rudder linkage is the really tricky bit. He doesn't seem particularly worried.'

'You know they're going to hush it up, I suppose,' Sir William remarked.

'What?' exclaimed Bragg angrily.

'There's been an almighty row between the Admiralty and the Foreign Office. It seems von Friedeburg was a naval attaché at the German embassy. The Foreign Office are saying he was entitled to try to steal the invention – a kind of licensed spy.'

'That's bloody stupid.'

'I know. According to them, all we can do is send him home, like a naughty schoolboy, for being found out.'

'But he had at least three men killed,' Bragg protested.

'I gather that as part of the bargain, von Friedeburg is to make an affidavit, implicating everyone else.'

'But that won't stand up in court.'

'The trials are to be held *in camera*, so we shall never know.'

'Well I'm buggered.'

'You did well, Bragg,' said Sir William tepidly. 'And so did young Morton. I wanted to promote him to sergeant, but he'd rather play cricket for England. Funny chap.' He closed the file, and clasped his hands on his stomach. 'There's only one bright spot in this whole affair,' he said with a self-satisfied smile. 'The Admiralty have informed me they have recommended that I should be made a Commander of the Most Honourable Order of the Bath, in recognition of our services. You should be proud, Bragg. You should be proud.'